THE *KOCHI MARU* AFFAIR

For Dick Horvath
With best Wishes.

Dan Held

10 . 23 . 2012

THE *KOCHI MARU* AFFAIR

A Novel

Daniel C. Helix

DEVIL MOUNTAIN BOOKS
P.O. BOX 4115
WALNUT CREEK, CALIFORNIA 94596

Daniel C. Helix

The *Kochi Maru* Affair

A Novel

Editorial Assistant: Barbara M. Sturges

Cover: David R. Johnson

Typesetter: Encore Design & Type, Martinez, California

Typestyle: Palatino

This book is a work of fiction. Names, characters, businesses,
organizations, places, events, and incidents are the product of the
author's imagination or are used fictitiously. Any resemblance to
actual persons, living or dead, events, or locales is entirely
coincidental.

Library of Congress Cataloging-in-Publication Data

Helix, Daniel C., 1929-
    The *Kochi Maru* Affair: A Novel /Daniel C. Helix.
      p. cm.
    ISBN 0-915685-14-0
    1. Intelligence officers—Fiction. 2. Military intelli-
gence—Fiction. 3. Americans—Japan—Fiction. 4. Japan—
Fiction. I. Title.
    PS3608.E446K63 2004
    813'.6—dc22
                                  2004041315

For Mary Lou

THANKS

I want to acknowledge and express my appreciation to those who helped along the way, technically and inspirationally. First and foremost thanks to Donald R. Gordon, a Canadian writer and teacher-guru, who patiently led me through the early rocks and shoals. Very little escapes Don's eagle eye.

During visits to Don's home in Waterloo, Ontario, his lovely wife, Dr. Helen Gordon, M.D., cooked mainly healthy food, except for some great Canadian breakfast sausage. Yummy!

At the deservedly famous Maui Writers Conference, Ridley Pearson's admonition, "Dan, stay in that chair," provided more encouragement than he may have known. Inspirational support also came from Bryce Courtenay, a truly wonderful man. And I'll never forget Elizabeth Engstrom Cratty's seminar as a perfect blend of tough love, professionalism and compassion.

In Contra Costa County some friends were kind enough to read the manuscript and offer constructive criticism. Thanks for this to Barbara Sturges, Lura Dymond, Elizabeth Schmidt, Howard Jenkins, Rear Admiral Russell Gorman, U.S. Navy—Ret., Colonel Vladimir Sobichevsky, U.S. Army—Ret., Dave McDonald, Marcia Dickerson, Carol Faust and, of course, my wife, Mary Lou Hiott Helix, who deciphered my handwritten first draft and put it on a computer disk.

A huge thank you to Clark Sturges, publisher of Devil Mountain Books. We met for lunch in Walnut Creek, California, and he said the six words a writer lusts to hear:

"I want to publish your book." My response: "I'm buying lunch." Thanks also to Clark for recommending David R. Johnson as cover illustrator and Carol Yacorzynski as designer and typesetter.

The final thanks is reserved for a very special person, no longer with us. John Toffoli, longtime General Manager of the Concord Pavilion, was the complete personification of everything that defines friendship. I treasured his wise counsel, great sense of humor, superb instincts, and total support. He taught me the meaning of "my best friend." I miss him very much and think of him often. ✦

THE *KOCHI MARU* AFFAIR
A Novel

PROLOGUE
Berkeley, California
MAY 12, 1940

His mother had described him as her boy with smiling eyes, but that was not the case today. Little Kenny Grainger sat on the couch, head bowed, looking down at his folded hands.

He held his back rigidly straight, as if afraid to move. The red wool sweater he wore had been patched at the elbows and his khaki pants were clean, but needed pressing. Dark hair flowed down over his forehead and his head arched forward as he alternated between biting his lower lip and pulling his mouth into a grimace.

"You know, Kenny," his Uncle Herman said, "some day you'll be a man and understand these things."

Kenny smiled sheepishly and tapped his feet on the floor.

"But why do I have to stay here?" he asked in a voice that was almost a whisper.

Uncle Herman let his breath escape in a sigh.

"Because your mother has to stay in the hospital, maybe for a long time. Your Aunt Martha and I can't take you back to Milwaukee with us, we ain't got room. We only got room for your two sisters. I'm really sorry, Kenny."

"But this is an orphanage," Kenny said. "This is for kids who don't have a mom or dad. I got both."

Kenny's father was a drunk and an abuser. He was also a steelworker from the age of 14, when he quit school. He had grown up working the toughest jobs in the mill. He was tall, broad-shouldered and strong enough to bully anyone, which he did.

It was obvious from Kenny's wide shoulders, strong arms, and husky appearance, that he had inherited some of his father's genes. It was equally obvious that he had acquired his mother's good looks. When a friend made mention of this in front of Kenny and his mother, she was quick to let him know how she felt.

"You know, Kenny," his mother said, "God has given you a handsome face, that's true, but He did it. You can't take any credit for how God made you look. It's what's here," she said, pointing to her heart, "and what you make of yourself that counts."

Uncle Herman cleared his throat and looked down at Kenny.

"I know you got folks," he said. "You got a mom, all right, but when the police catch your dad for what he did to your mom, he ain't gonna be around to take care of no one."

He hitched his trousers nervously and glanced up at Mother Klaxon, head of the orphanage, who was standing behind Kenny. He shook his head and gestured with his palms up.

"You have to believe me," he said, "we really didn't know about any of this stuff going on. I think we may have suspected it. Our mother tried to talk Alice out of marrying Ernie. She told her he was no damn good. But, she was in love. She was beautiful, like a movie star. Look at her now, with all her teeth knocked out."

"No," Kenny screamed, putting his hands to his ears.

"Damn, I'm sorry," Uncle Herman said. "I shouldn't of said nothin'."

He shook his head in frustration and anger.

"You know, Ma'am," he said, looking at Mother Klaxon, "all our family's back in Wisconsin and Illinois. We don't have no family out here, neither does Alice. Ernie worked for the American Forge Company and when they opened a plant out here in California, they asked him if he wanted to move out here. They promised him a raise and he took it."

He looked around the room, wondering if to continue, and again exhaled loudly.

"We're poor people," he said. "It's going to be really tight to even take Kenny's sisters. Alice ain't got no folks to speak of. Her father died when she was young. She worshipped that man. Her mother got tied up with a traveling salesman; he plays a harmonica. She doesn't deserve the daughter she has. She won't help."

Tears streamed down Kenny's cheeks. He tried to will them to stop, but it was no use. He ran his forearm across his eyes, wiping them on his sleeve. When his nose began running on his upper lip, he did the same thing.

"How long will I have to stay here?" Again, his voice was barely a whisper.

Uncle Herman shook his head.

"I have no idea," he said, "and that's the God's honest truth, Kenny. Maybe your mom will come out of it. The doctors just don't know."

He rubbed his hands together as if he were cleaning them.

"Look, Kenny," he said, refusing to make eye contact, "I know you're only 11 and this is hard to understand, but you've always been a smart kid. Your mom wrote and said you got top grades in school. Maybe you won't have to stay here too long. Right now, I really gotta go. Your sisters are with Aunt Martha back at the house. I'll tell 'em you said goodbye."

Kenny could hear and feel his heart racing.

I don't want to live without my mother, he thought. *I don't want to be here. I don't want to be anywhere. Why won't Uncle Herman listen to me? This is not fair.*

"Please take me with you, Uncle Herman," he begged. "I don't need a room. I can sleep in the hall, in the kitchen, anywhere. I'll work and make money. I won't eat much, I promise."

Mother Klaxon, tall and slender with premature graying hair, stepped forward, pursing her lips in a tight smile. She put her hands on Kenny's shoulders. He tried to shrug them off, but she gripped him tightly.

"This is a difficult time for everyone," she said. "Don't worry, Mr. Krueger, Kenny will be just fine. Chandler Home is the only charitable institution in the City of Berkeley, but we do everything we can to make the children feel as if this is just like their real home. I'm sure Kenny will fit in with the other children."

She looked down at the back of Kenny's head.

"Won't you, Kenny?"

She pushed on his shoulders, waiting for an answer that didn't come.

Uncle Herman slapped his thigh with his fedora.

"I'm sure you're right," he said.

He pulled a pocket watch out of his trousers, studying it briefly as it dangled from a brass chain.

"Oh, it's late," he said, "I gotta go."

He walked over to Kenny and extended his hand.

"Men don't kiss like women do," he smiled. "Men just shake hands."

He reached down and took Kenny's small hand, giving it a squeeze.

"Just do what Mother Klaxon tells you to do," he said. "You're a good boy. You don't make trouble. I'm sure if you do what she says, everything will be all right."

He glanced again at Mother Klaxon.

"Do you and your husband both run this place?" he asked.

"I'm not married," Mother Klaxon said with another tight smile. "I've never married. Actually, I've been too busy with my duties, and besides, I have all the children I could want."

Uncle Herman nodded and glanced down.

"Well," he said, "walk with me to the door, Kenny."

Kenny's mouth was drawn in a straight line as he followed his uncle to the door. He stood silently as the stoop-shouldered man walked slowly down the concrete steps to his car parked at the curb. Kenny's eyes were so flooded with tears he did not see Uncle Herman turn and wave. At the sound of the car engine pulling away, Kenny straightened his shoulders and turned back into the orphanage.

His mother died that night in the county hospital.

The following Christmas Kenny received a card from Uncle Herman and Aunt Martha. It was signed by his two sisters, Katherine and Louise, and contained a five-dollar bill.

If there had been an award for the Orphan of the Year, Kenny would not have qualified for consideration. It was not that he was loud or contentious, nor was he discourteous. He lived as if he wanted to disassociate himself from being a part of the Chandler Home family.

He never volunteered for anything and simply did as he was told. He responded to Mother Klaxon with a "yes, ma'am," or "no, ma'am," but could not bring himself to the point where he called her "Mother Klaxon." This bothered her a great deal, and she was forever prompting him to address her in this manner. He refused.

The clash of wills was subtle, but there was no backing down on either side. Initially, all the adverse impact landed on Kenny. Mother Klaxon made the rules. She was the sole arbiter. Those who failed to defer totally were denied weekend privileges. Primarily this meant being able to attend the double-feature matinee on Saturdays at the Rivoli Theater on San Pablo Avenue five blocks from the orphanage. Kenny's orphan siblings were quick to point out that he held the all-time record for denied privileges.

At first Kenny was required to sit in his room during the time the other children were at the movies. It was not until the start of his second year that he was allowed to go to the West Berkeley Y.M.C.A. on Saturdays. It was there he met Mr. Johnson.

Manley Johnson, an elderly black man, was the boxing coach. He had been a prize-fighter during his youth. His fighting nickname, "Scrap Iron," spoke volumes. More than one promising fighter had his dreams derailed after a few rounds with Manley.

He lost some of his early years owing to Army service during World War I. By the time he got out, he was not able to penetrate the barriers set up to deny indigent fighters a crack at the big time. Years later, after serving as sparring partner for those who were contenders, Manley accepted a job teaching boxing skills to young men at the various Y.M.C.A. branches in the city of Berkeley. Saturdays were spent in West Berkeley.

Manley liked Kenny from the first day they met. The boy was quiet, hard-working, and never complained. More than that, with the encouragement he received from Manley, Kenny was not afraid to get into the ring with anyone, regardless of size.

"That boy's had a tough life," Manley told his wife, Norma, one evening at dinner. "He's been whipped on plenty, but they couldn't break his spirit. He trains like he's on a mission. If you don't mind, I'd like to invite him to have Christmas dinner with us."

"I don't mind at all," she said.

The next day after the training session, Manley said to Kenny, "You know, it's getting close to Christmas. Norma and I wondered if you would like to have dinner with us."

"Yes, I would," Kenny said. "That would be great."

"I suppose I should call over to the home and get it okayed with the lady who's in charge. Is that Miss Klaxon?"

"Yes, sir," Kenny said, "but she wants to be called Mother Klaxon."

"Someone pointed her out to me at the store one day," Manley said. "Tall, spinster lady, gray hair, wears them dresses go all the way to the floor, looks like she's been suckin' on a lemon?"

Kenny ducked his head, eyes shining, his hand covering his smile, head bobbing up and down.

"Think I better have Norma call her," Manley said.

Kenny turned to go.

"Oh, yeah," Manley called after him, "got an old Army buddy comin' out from Detroit, haven't seen him for years. He'll be havin' dinner with us. He's a real character. Name's Wallace Washington, calls himself 'WW.' I just call him Wally."

Kenny was waiting for Manley in the hallway at 2:00 in the afternoon when the doorbell rang. Mother Klaxon opened the door and stepped back in surprise.

"You're Mr. Johnson?" she asked.

"Yes, ma'am," Manley said. He was wearing a sport coat and slacks. The collar of his shirt, open at the neck, was folded back over the jacket. He looked down at Kenny and smiled.

"That turkey's about ready to carve, Kenny. You ready?"

"Uh, Mr. Johnson," Mother Klaxon said, "will you excuse us just for a minute, please?"

Manley nodded.

Mother Klaxon put her hand on Kenny's shoulder and guided him back to her office. They entered and she closed the door.

"You didn't tell me Mr. Johnson was a Negro," she said.

"What do you mean?" Kenny asked.

"Well, where does he live? Does he live in an apartment? Do you feel safe going to his home?"

"Sure," Kenny said. "I feel safe. I feel safer with him than I ever did with my father. With my father I was always afraid. Mr. Johnson is showing me how to take care of myself. I'm not afraid any more."

Kenny listened during the dinner while Manley and Wally, "WW," kept up a steady patter of verbal jousting. The two old friends never seemed to tire of getting one up on the other.

Wally looked much older than Manley. He was bald-headed and had a huge stomach that flopped over the front of his trousers. He had a habit of reaching up and snapping his suspenders as if to punctuate his comments.

"You don't say too much, Kenny," Wally said. "Cat got your tongue?" He reached up, pulled the suspenders and let them snap.

"No, sir," Kenny said. "I just like to listen. I like to hear grown-ups talk about what they did when they were young."

Norma placed a piece of pumpkin pie, with a large dollop of whipped cream, in front of Kenny.

"After that dinner you ate," she said, "can you handle that?"

"Yes ma'am," Kenny said, his eyes shining brightly. "It looks just like the kind my mom used to make." He ran his fingers through his dark hair, pushing the locks off his forehead. He dipped his fork into the pie and took a bite.

"Uhmmm, good," he said.

"Did you know that Manley used to be a lieutenant in the U.S. Army?" Wally asked Kenny.

"No, sir," Kenny said.

"Sure was," Wally said. "We was in a Quartermaster Company during the great war. I was the First Sergeant. He was the only brother who got to be an officer. You know why they made him an officer?"

Kenny shook his head.

"Had to." Snap went the suspenders. "In those days, the First Sergeant had to be able to whip any man in the company. They did it to protect him from me."

"You could beat Mr. Johnson?" Kenny asked.

Manley laughed.

"You are some kinda fool," he said to Wally. "If I wasn't there backin' you up, you wouldn't a been the First Sergeant for a week."

Wally laughed and slapped Kenny on the shoulder.

"Just kiddin,'" he said. "We were all real proud of him gettin' those gold bars. Sometimes he got a little uppity, but we kept him humble."

"Like when?" Manley asked.

"Like when you gave that old mess sergeant, the one from Atlanta, Georgia, a bad time. He was nobody's fool."

"I remember," Manley said. He nodded and smiled.

"What happened?" Kenny asked.

"Well," Wally said with a snap, "the lieutenant decides to check up on the mess sergeant, see what he's doin.' He walks over to the stove and looks in this big pot full of soup. He calls the mess sergeant over and in a loud voice asks, 'How come the soup's bubblin' in the middle and not around the edges?'

"The mess sergeant fixes him with a look that would kill.

'Because, Lootenant,' he drawled, 'I'm keepin' the soup in the middle for the boys on guard duty, they're gonna be late.'

"Everybody laugh their ass off," Wally said. "The lieutenant just said, 'good idea,' and got outta there fast. Didn't nobody mess with that sergeant."

Snap went the suspenders.

Kenny let his eyes wander over to the Christmas tree with its many lights and ornaments. His eyes misted over and he swallowed hard.

Norma was the first one to notice he wasn't paying attention.

"You know, Kenny," she said, "your mother is watching you from heaven. I know she's real proud of you."

Tears flooded Kenny's eyes. He sat there with his shoulders shaking.

"Hey," Wally said, "I got an idea. Manley, you said young Kenny here was a true warrior. We got to get him a tattoo. Make him a member of our special club."

"You're right, Wally," Manley said. "I been thinkin' about that and I got an idea."

Later, on the way back to the orphanage, Kenny said to Manley, "Mr. Johnson, if you liked the Army so much why did you get out?"

"I did like the Army," Manley said. "It would have been a good career, but Norma wanted to settle down and have a home. I wanted to be with her."

By the time Kenny was 14, he was developing the thick neck and sloping shoulders of a powerful athlete. He grew steadily. When he was supposed to be fighting in the welterweight class, he was beating middleweights who outweighed him by 15 pounds.

"I'm worried about that boy," Manley told his wife. "He doesn't know how hard he hits with that left hook. I just hope he doesn't kill someone. Dy-no-mite."

Manley's concerns were not without merit. In the spacious backyard of the orphanage three of the older boys were taunting one of the teenage girls, saying she was "a tub of lard," and "a fat slob." The girl was crying.

Kenny was in the yard and saw what was happening. He walked over to the boys and said, "Hey, why don't you guys leave her alone."

They looked at him in surprise.

"Keep your nose out of our business," the largest boy said, "or I might have to bust it for you."

The other two boys laughed and nodded in agreement.

"I'm just asking you," Kenny said in a quiet and deep voice, "leave her alone, she's not hurting you."

"You don't hear too good," the larger and older boy said. "I think you need a lesson in manners."

He turned and faced Kenny directly, flanked by the other two teenagers.

"Yeah, you're a punk," the older boy declared. "You need a lesson."

"Let's kick his ass," one of the other boys said.

Kenny looked at them and shook his head.

When they rushed him, the girl, fearing for his safety, ran screaming for Mother Klaxon.

By the time she got to the yard, all three boys were sprawled in the dirt, bleeding and moaning in agony. One hugged his ribs while another groaned loudly, clutching his groin.

The medic who assisted the boys into an ambulance to have them checked out at the hospital reported his findings to Mother Klaxon: The biggest boy had a broken nose and severely damaged ribs; another had two broken teeth and multiple bruises. One boy would be singing falsetto for a couple of weeks.

"One kid did all this?" he asked.

Mother Klaxon nodded and called the Berkeley Police Department, asking for an officer to counsel Kenny against the future use of his fists.

Officer Vierra met with Kenny in Mother Klaxon's office.

"You want to tell me how all this started?" he asked.

"Yes, sir," Kenny said. "I don't like it when boys bully girls. I just asked them to leave her alone. They came after me, they started it, the three of them. I just finished it."

Officer Vierra cleared his throat.

"Yes, uh, well," he said. He wiped his nose with his hand. "You know you're not supposed to solve your problems with your fists."

"Sir," Kenny said, "my father beat my mother to death. That's why I'm here. If I see a boy abusing a girl, I'm not going to just stand there, I'm gonna step in. Is that against the law?"

"Uh, well not technically, I guess," Officer Vierra said. "You can help defend someone who can't defend themselves. But I understand they were only talking to the girl."

"Yes, sir," Kenny said. "And I was just talking to them. They came after me."

Officer Vierra stood.

"Look, kid," he said. "You're okay, I like you. Just don't get too frisky."

He scratched his neck and grinned.

"By the way, when you graduate from high school, if you want a job, come see me at the department. I think you'd make a damn good cop."

At Berkeley High School Kenny became an all-league fullback on the football team and an all-league catcher in baseball. He continued boxing with the Y.M.C.A. and became the Golden Gloves light heavyweight champion in northern California.

One week later, his world collapsed.

Mother Klaxon asked him to join her in her office. "Ken," she said, "I have some very bad news. That nice Mr. Johnson, the one whose home you go to for dinner, the one with the Y.M.C.A."

Ken nodded.

"He was killed today," she said. "Up on Shattuck Avenue. A car went through a red light and hit him. He died. His wife called and wanted you to know."

Ken bowed his head. The tears that had been shut off in the orphanage the day he saw his Uncle Herman walk down the front stairs, the tears he swore would never flow

12

again in front of Mother Klaxon, welled up like an erupting volcano and flowed through his fingers in front of his face.

His eyes were red and swollen when he nodded to her and said, "Mother Klaxon, I want to go over and see Mrs. Johnson."

Tears filled Mother Klaxon's eyes. After a moment she spoke, her voice throaty with emotion.

"That will be just fine," she said.

A few weeks after the funeral, Ken graduated from Berkeley High School. He took a bus to downtown Oakland and walked aimlessly around the town, looking in store windows. He came to one with a sign saying it was an Army Recruiting Office. He looked up at the sky, walked in and enlisted. ✦

ONE

Ch'orwon Valley, Korea
JUNE, 1952

U.S. Army Captain Ken Grainger stood at one of the battle stations notched into the forward slope of the communication trench on Hill 327, in Ch'orwon Valley. From his position he could see the surrounding low-lying hills, lined with bunkers. They had been bombarded by thousands of artillery and mortar rounds, and seared by hundreds of canisters of napalm until the terrain around the topographical crests and down the slopes was devoid of trees and vegetation, wearing only a bald spot of monotonous brown.

Grainger commanded an Infantry rifle company in the 45th Infantry Division. Men of the 45th were "The Thunderbirds." They occupied the main line of resistance in Ch'orwon Valley, facing elements of the well-trained and battle-tested 38th Chinese Army who intervened in the war in November of 1950, when it was apparent that the North Korean Army was about to be crushed.

War fighting had changed for Grainger since the early days of the Korean War. As a member of the 1st Cavalry Division he was engaged in large-scale operations, and earned a Battlefield Commission. He was one of the few who agreed to extend his tour of duty in Korea. This guaranteed his promotion to captain, well ahead of his peers.

When the fighting slowed down, because of the truce talks, Grainger was the only one who volunteered to stay and complete his tour with the National Guard 45th Division, which relieved the 1st Cavalry Division when it returned to Japan for a well-earned rest.

During the stalemate, fighting was limited to local attacks, counterattacks, and combat patrols. Soldiers adjusted to living in bunkers scattered along the forward slope of their hill. Communication trenches, five to six feet deep, cut into these hills and followed the contour of the military crest. They served a dual purpose. Infantrymen used them during daylight as protection from sniper fire. They also provided security for bundles of telephone wires lying along the edges of the bottom, safe from anything except a direct hit. Constant shelling caused the walls of the trenches to fracture and striate like giant spider webs.

Grainger turned and watched Staff Sergeant Lee Winters lurch toward him when his left foot caught in the bundle of wires. Winters bumped into the wall of the trench and a clump of dirt fell away, exploding in a small cloud of dust as it hit the ground. The dust, like powdered snow, billowed up and enveloped their boots.

Grainger towered over Winters as he stood next to him in the trench. The sergeant weighed a scant 140 pounds, but despite his small stature had the distinction of being a statewide wrestling champion during his high school days in Salina, Kansas. He helped Grainger keep the company in fighting trim when they were not on the line fighting. The two of them led the others in physical training exercises. It was seldom that anyone beat them in push-ups, pull-ups, or the mile run.

Winters glanced at Grainger's right hand as he took a drink from his canteen. He noticed once again the presence of a small purple triangle tattooed in the fleshy webbing between his thumb and forefinger. He wondered about it, but didn't ask.

As Grainger surveyed the area in front of his company's position, a movement caught his eye and he quickly looked back to confirm his sighting. There was activity at the company outpost at the base of their hill, a sandbagged semicircle the company used as a nighttime listening post.

What the hell? Grainger thought. His eyes widened.

"Winters," Grainger asked, "do we have anyone down at the listening post?"

Winters wrinkled his forehead and rubbed his chin.

"I believe so, sir," Winters replied. "Sergeant Taft and Arkie were going to replace the wire for the sound power telephone in the LP. It got hit last night by artillery." He glanced at his wristwatch. "They're supposed to leave about now and stay in the shadows because of the snipers."

He hesitated, then leaned forward looking to his left, in the direction of Sergeant Taft's bunker.

"Wait a minute, there's no way they could be down there already."

"I don't think it's them," Grainger said. "The guy I saw wasn't wearing a steel pot. He had some kind of soft cap. I thought I saw a drum on the weapon. Does Taft still have that Thompson?"

"No, sir," Winters said, "he sold it to a Marine down in Seoul."

Grainger nodded.

"Damn," Winters said, "if someone's down there, and the line's out, we can't reach 'em to tell 'em."

Grainger nodded. A shaft of late afternoon sunlight reflected off a face. He clenched his fist, his mouth set in a straight line.

Sonofabitch.

"We've got a problem," Grainger said. "I can see two bad guys have definitely checked into our LP."

Winters followed Grainger's eyes down to the outpost.

"Holy shit," Winters said, "Gooks."

"Yeah," Grainger said. "Taft and Arkie are going to walk right into an ambush. I don't know where they are so I can't use mortars. It's starting to get dark; I better get down there. Maybe I can surprise 'em. Quick, round up some help and follow me."

He slapped the bottom of a banana-shaped magazine in his M-2 carbine with the heel of his palm to make sure it was firmly seated. Slinging his carbine over his shoulder, he put both hands on the top of the commo trench and vaulted out. He paused, reaching back to get his carbine, released the safety and checked to make sure the weapon's setting was on full automatic. As he did this, the purple tattoo on his right hand seemed to take on a darker hue. He looked down for a moment, then pushed off toward the outpost.

His sprint down the precipitous dirt trail was marked by a small rooster's tail of dust. His eyes locked on the small group clustered below.

Whoa? Oh, no, there's four of them, not two.

He held the stock of his carbine against his hip and opened fire on full automatic. The clatter of the gunfire echoed in the valley. The Chinese soldiers crouched, wide-eyed in bewilderment. Their mouths were agape as they watched the figure hurtling toward them like an avenging angel or avatar of warriors past.

The swiftness of his descent caused two soldiers to bump into one another in the open as they scrambled in confusion for cover. Grainger fired two short bursts and the men were cut down as if a giant hand batted them violently to the ground.

Another Chinese soldier, armed with a Russian submachine "burp" gun, raised his weapon and fired. The weapon had one dominant failing. Its rate of fire was so rapid that it was practically impossible to deliver accurate fire while on full automatic. This now happened. The muzzle lifted sharply into the air, spraying bullets over Grainger's head. They popped and cracked like multiple snaps of a bullwhip. Grainger fired a burst and heard the dull click that told him he was out of ammunition. Without breaking stride, he pressed the release catch, dropped the empty 30-round magazine and inserted a loaded one into his carbine. He fired two short bursts into the soldier with the "burp" gun who went down with his finger still frozen on the trigger, firing harmlessly into the air.

The remaining Chinese soldier stood and aimed his rifle at Grainger. He fired and a bullet tore into the bicep of Grainger's upper left arm causing him to momentarily lose his grip on the upper stock of his carbine. He felt the warmth of the bullet, but no pain as he staggered a couple of steps, then righted himself, and placed his left hand back on the weapon. He got closer and unleashed a long burst into the rifleman's midsection.

Grainger jolted to a stop a few feet from the outpost and surveyed the carnage. There was no movement from the bodies lying at the listening post. He noticed that blood was dripping from his left sleeve. He took out his first aid packet and wrapped the gauze bandage around the wound at his elbow. Holding one tie-down strand with his right hand, he cinched the knot with his teeth.

I can still bend my elbow. I was lucky, he didn't hit bone.

"You okay, sir?"

Grainger looked up to see Sergeant Taft perspiring heavily, and holding a large reel of communication wire.

"Hey, sir, guess you took care of these Gooks," Taft said. "Where the hell did they come from?"

"I don't know," Grainger said. "Someone must be sleeping or playing cards up on the line. They should have picked them up before they got this far. By the way, where's Arkie?"

"Shit, sir," Taft said. "When I heard the firing, I sent him back to get our weapons. We just had our .45s and I can't hit anything with mine. I can't believe we came down here without our weapons. We were just goin' to lay wire, those spools are really heavy. When the firing started I saw you and came down to help. They never get this close in the daylight."

"I know," Grainger said. "I'll deal with that later."

He started at the distinctive chatter of a Russian machine gun.

"A Tokarev," Grainger said. "Taft, check these bodies. See what they've got. When Arkie gets here with your weapon, follow me so you can give me cover."

"Yes, sir, will do," Taft said.

The ripping sound of the Tokarev sounded again. The fire was coming from the draw between a series of small hilly knobs above and to Grainger's right. Further east another series of small hills, with a line of similar knobs, formed what the Americans called the Alligator Jaws.

Grainger checked and realized his carbine was empty and he had no additional magazines. He bent over and pulled the "burp" gun from under the soldier's body. He ejected the drum and picked up two that had spilled out of a cloth bag still slung over the soldier's shoulder. He loaded one and shoved the other into his fatigue jacket.

"They're firing at our guys coming down the hill to help me," Grainger said to Taft. "Our guys are sitting ducks. They're out in the open, no cover. I think I can outflank that Tokarev."

He turned and sprinted left along the contour line that paralleled the sound of the firing. The conformation of the hill masked his movements. As he ran, a more ominous sound came from a point further left, and behind where the Tokarev was firing. It was an American .30 caliber Browning light machine gun.

Not another one. That's a light .30. We don't have any people with Brownings there. Those are Chinese firing one of our weapons. If I can get behind them....

19

He sprinted to a point where he was sure he was behind the .30 caliber, and cut sharply to his right, like a halfback running to daylight.

As Grainger reached the crest of the small hill, he saw that he was less than 30 yards behind the Chinese machine gun crew set up in a slight depression. They had no real cover. He dropped to a kneeling position and canted the "burp" gun on its side to use the tendency of the muzzle to elevate to his advantage. He pulled back on the trigger, and made a series of tight, rapid "ess" movements, raking the crew with bullets that scythed from left to right and back again. In a matter of seconds, three more Chinese lay dead.

A metallic thud sounded as the bolt went forward and stopped. He reached into his jacket, took out the other drum and loaded it.

He watched for any sign of movement as he warily approached the gun position and surveyed the small depression. Bodies were splayed with arms and legs bent crookedly. He checked them quickly. They were no factor. He was now about 50 yards above and behind the crew manning the Tokarev, crouched behind a small earth berm. They were focused on Winters and the men coming down the trail. He put down the "burp" gun and stripped off his fatigue jacket, wrapping it around the barrel of the .30 caliber machine gun.

That's better.

He bent down and picked up the weapon trailing a four-foot belt of ammunition.

Looks like about 100 rounds, that oughta be enough.

Cradling the barrel in the crook of his left arm, he sprayed the enemy machine gun position like a fireman hosing down a fire. He could feel the heat of the barrel through his jacket as he pulled back on the trigger, firing a series of short bursts into the gun crew until he could see there was nothing more to fear from those manning the Tokarev. Holding on to the pistol grip, he lowered the muzzle of the machine gun to the ground. The bandage on his left arm had worked loose. Sweat and blood dripped to the ground.

An eerie silence fell over the valley. Dusk crept towards nightfall as smoke and dust drifted over the scene of the battle. The ringing in Grainger's ears muted the sounds from the platoon members that veered off the path to join him.

I'll never get used to how quiet it is after a firefight.

He wavered unsteadily, using the barrel of the machine gun as a crutch.

What am I doing out here? There had to be a better way to handle this. I could have called artillery on these two guns. They were out in the open. I don't think there was time.

The soldiers surrounded him. Sergeant Waterhouse, company medic, reached him first and checked his bleeding left arm. He wrapped a fresh combat dressing around it and studied Grainger's eyes.

"How's your pain, sir? Do you want a shot of morphine?"

"I think I'm okay," Grainger said, waving him off.

"Are you sure, sir?" the medic persisted.

"I'm okay," Grainger said. "It's only a flesh wound; he didn't hit the bone."

The medic nodded.

"You know, sir," he said, "if you're going to be crazy, it helps to live a charmed life."

Grainger smiled and said nothing.

"Sir, I'm the medic," he said. "In a very short time you're going to need this."

He held Grainger's arm while he gave him a shot of morphine.

"You're lucky, sir," he said, "there is no bone involvement, but you're going to need some surgery and stitches. We'll get you back to the battalion aid station where they can clean you up and get you a tetanus shot before you go back to the MASH."

Grainger looked down at his arm. He bent it at the elbow as if to confirm again that the bone was not hit.

"You're right, Doc," he said. "All of a sudden, I'm really beat. Maybe I could use some help getting back to the line."

"That's your adrenaline wearing off," the medic said. "You must have used up a week's supply."

"Right now," Grainger said, "we better get out of here. If they don't send someone out, they sure as hell will open up with their mortars."

One of the sergeants reached out to get the .30 caliber machine gun.

"Yeah," Grainger said. "Check to see if it's the one that King Company lost on patrol last week. Check the pockets of these guys as fast as you can. They may have something of Intelligence value. You never know."

They counted a total of 10 dead Chinese soldiers.

Colonel Matthew Moran, Grainger's regimental commander, strode into the battalion aid station and walked over to Grainger as the doctor bandaged his wound. He shook his head.

"Would you mind telling me," Moran said, ignoring the doctor, "just what in God's name was that all about? Dammit, you should know we're short of officers and you go charging around the hills like you're bullet proof."

"Yes, sir," Grainger said. "First, sir, I had two of my men about to walk into an ambush. There was no way to contact them without putting them at risk. They were too close for me to use mortars. And I didn't want any Chinese in my LP. What happened after that was just me reacting to what I felt was needed. I had no radio and my guys were wide open and getting shot at. I thought I could take out the guns."

"And you did," Colonel Moran said. "You're also lucky the artillery forward observer saw you run up the draw. He was about to call in artillery on those guns."

Grainger looked down at the ground and nodded.

"About those Chinese in your LP," the colonel said. "At first I was upset because I thought we had easy pickings on some prisoners, especially when we found that one of them was an officer. We would have liked to talk to him. I didn't know you had two men working their way down to the LP to lay wire. Did you think about taking prisoners?"

"Frankly, sir," Grainger said, "I didn't think about it."

"Colonel," the doctor protested, "I really ..."

"I know, I know," said the colonel. "Looks like you got him ready to go. I've found out what I wanted to know. I wanted to see how bad he was hit."

Colonel Moran walked to the opening of the tent and started out. Then he stopped, turned his head toward Grainger. He was not able to completely suppress a smile.

"I'm putting you in for a DSC, Grainger," he said. "That was a helluva job, and I'm proud of you."

Three weeks later Grainger was back on the line with his company. That night they were hit hard with an all-out attack. The Chinese who made it to the top of their hill had to be repulsed with bayonets. Grainger earned his third Silver Star, but his company sustained high casualties and was pulled off the line.

A week later, Colonel Moran had a Regimental Dinner for his company commanders and Grainger was given the seat of honor at the colonel's right hand.

"I understand you're scheduled to rotate to Japan before your unit goes back on line," the colonel said.

"Yes, sir," Grainger said.

"I'm giving First Lieutenant Woodberry the company," the colonel said.

"That's what I heard," Grainger said. "He's a good man, Airborne. He'll do a great job."

"What about you?" the colonel asked. "Do you have any idea about your next assignment?"

"No, sir," Grainger said. "When I get home, I'd like to attend the Advanced Infantry Course at Fort Benning."

"They could use you as an instructor," Colonel Moran said.

"I haven't had a chance to apply for the school, so I expect to wait for the next class. I'll do that when I get to my new assignment."

"You have a damn fine record, Grainger," the colonel said. "From this point on you need to think more about your career. I've seen a lot of talented people get dead-end assignments and wind up going nowhere."

"I didn't think I had a whole lot of choice," Grainger said.

"Well, you're wrong," the colonel said. "Your record will help you get the kind of assignments that will move you up into command positions. Your next goal should be to get educationally qualified so you can command a battalion."

"I appreciate your guidance, sir," Grainger said.

"Remember," the colonel said, "watch out for the jobs that take you away from regular troop units. Once you start down that track it's easy for your career to get derailed."

"How do I avoid the wrong kind of assignments, sir?" Grainger asked.

"A lot of it's unofficial. Believe me, if you don't call and try to get some of the plum assignments, someone else will. You contact someone who knows you, a colonel or a general," Moran said.

Grainger smiled. "Sir, I don't know any generals," he said.

"Well, General Ruffner certainly knows you. He's pinned three important medals on your chest, and that's not counting the Purple Hearts and Silver Star you earned with the 1st Cav. When you call, just remind him how pleased you were to serve under his command in Korea. Those calls are made all the time."

Grainger nodded.

"And get your education," Moran said. "After you complete the advanced course, you'll need command and general staff, then the War College."

Grainger nodded again, not sure how to respond.

"When you get to Camp Drake," Moran said, "go to the assignments branch and put in your papers for school."

Three days later, Grainger leaned on the railing of the *USNS Barrett,* anchored in Pusan, and headed for Japan. He watched the men board the troopship that would take them away from Korea. He smiled to himself when he saw the sign that had greeted him a year earlier and would be there tomorrow to greet the new arrivals. It always elicited nervous chuckles from the young infantry officers.

"Welcome 1542s," it said.

The number 1542 was the Military Occupational Specialty (MOS) designation for infantry platoon leaders. Their average time of survival in combat was 28 seconds. The odds were not a well-kept secret. Grainger knew he had defied the odds and in the process, lessened someone else's chances.

That'll ruin someone's breakfast tomorrow, he thought.

Grainger walked to the railing above the fantail and watched the water eddying below. A misty rain made the decks too slippery for easy movement and most of the men elected to stay below playing poker, shooting craps, or munching on sandwiches from box lunches. He was mesmerized by the sound of the waters lapping against the side of the ship.

So many great guys didn't make it, Pappy, Jensen, Boozer, others. Funny, I always thought I'd make it, but....

He looked up as a passing tug, steaming out of the harbor, created a wake that caused the *USNS Barrett* to shift slightly away from its mooring. The heavy lines groaned and

25

creaked as they strained against their moorings. He was deep in thought as darkness descended on the hills surrounding Pusan. An occasional light glowed dimly in the void.

Grainger turned at the sound of the ship's lead lines being slipped. The huge bow edged away from the pier. The stern lines were released moments later and the ship eased through a curtain of mist into the Korean Strait, destination Tokyo/Yokohama.

He shook his shoulders, sending drops of water scattering to the deck. The olive-green rain gear, one-size-fits-all, barely reached his knees. From a distance it distorted his outline, giving him the appearance of a large solid object.

Soft rain drifted on to the ship as it pressed forward. Grainger sensed movement behind him and shifted his weight to look over his left shoulder. The bulkhead light revealed a man in a dark, three-quarter-length coat and visored hat. He guessed it was one of the ship's officers.

The man nodded as he approached Grainger. He was heavy-set, of medium height. His raised coat collar covered his ears. He reached into his right coat pocket and extracted a pipe, leather tobacco pouch, and a box of wooden matches. Grainger looked down and nodded as the man smiled.

"Y'know," the man said, "it's a different breed that comes back than goes over."

He tamped tobacco into the encrusted bowl of the pipe, took out a match and ignited the tip with his thumbnail. The light revealed a pockmarked face with deep-set eyes. His rubber-soled shoes made little noise on the steel plating as he shifted his feet.

"Yep," he continued, "comin' over you find everything. I've found helmets, rifles, duffel bags, field jackets, parkas, you name it. Once I even found a wallet full of cash."

The man paused, puffed on his pipe, and exhaled a cloud of smoke. Then he coughed and cleared his throat.

"Comin' back, she's clean as a whistle. Nuthin'. Nobody leaves nuthin'. It's spooky, almost like we come back empty."

Grainger grunted.

"You learn," he said, "your equipment can keep you alive. Those who get careless and lose things don't make it. Sometimes you don't even have to be careless."

"Did you fight North Koreans or Chinese?" the man asked.

"Both," Grainger said, "mostly Chinese."

The man sighed.

"I met a Chinese gal in Shanghai once," he said. "She was so beautiful, I ached just lookin' at her. I gave her a month's pay for one night and got the better of the bargain. She had shiny black hair down to the small of her back, skin like a porcelain goddess."

He paused and puffed on his pipe.

"I ain't been satisfied with a woman since."

Grainger nodded.

"In combat, you don't think of your enemy as having a face," he mused. "Probably just as well. It's hard enough to kill, without thinking of them having a life and a family. You just think of them as the enemy. They wear padded clothes and tennis shoes and make a little packet of dried fish and a ball of rice last all week. Our job was to kill them before they killed you. The Chinese were good soldiers, tough, well disciplined. I respected them."

Grainger flashed back to the day his First Sergeant, Pappy Gonzales, was killed. Without a word he turned toward the open sea and lowered his head. He didn't notice as the mate nodded, murmured a "g'nite," clamped down on his pipe, and padded back to his post.

Grainger remembered his early days as a platoon leader. Even though he was promoted because of his leadership on the battlefield, he had a lot to learn about leading a platoon. Pappy was his platoon sergeant and mentored him. They became close friends, and when Grainger became the company commander, he selected Pappy as his First Sergeant.

Pappy was wiry and muscular with a large bushy black mustache. When he laughed, which was often, his white teeth seemed gigantic.

"With those teeth," Grainger told him, "you must have some Teddy Roosevelt in your background somewhere."

"No chance," Pappy responded. "If my ancestors had fought in the Spanish-American War we would have kicked his ass."

Grainger remembered Pappy being killed by a mortar round outside their company command post. He took a deep breath, sighed, and felt a chill when the ship surged forward as if it shifted into a higher gear. He moved to the railing near the center of the ship and out of the wind and looked into the blackness toward Korea. ✦

Two

Atsugi Naval Air Station
50 MILES SOUTH OF TOKYO

As the USNS *Barrett* steamed toward Tokyo, an unscheduled planning meeting for covert operations was under way at the CIA's Office of Policy Coordination (OPC) at Atsugi NAS.

Joe Fellinger, head of OPC, Far East Division, settled his huge frame into a leather chair and ran his hand through the few wispy strands of graying hair still atop his head. His cherubic face, in stark contrast to his bulk, was far from angelic. He gripped the leather arms and shifted uncomfortably at the conference table.

"I hope you've got a good reason for this special planning meeting, Art," Fellinger complained.

"I do, Joe," Arthur Church, the CIA's Tokyo Station Chief replied, a deep Southern accent echoing in the conference room. He smiled and Fellinger noticed once again that no laugh lines appeared around Church's eyes when he smiled.

Church tugged at his necktie as if it were gripping his starched white shirt collar too tightly. He glanced quickly around the conference table, cleared his throat, then coughed into a white handkerchief.

"We have an opportunity to do something that's been on my agenda for a long time," Church began. "Everybody knows we've been trying to get agents into China. So far, we've had no real success. Right now, I have four Chinese-American agents in training and ready for infiltration. We also have a vehicle, thanks to Major Templeton Perkins of Army Intelligence, and Colonel Sukow Kim of the Korean CIA."

At the mention of Kim's name, Fellinger's mouth clamped shut to the point where it appeared he had no lips. He studied the .45 pistol in Kim's shoulder holster.

"Excuse me, Colonel Kim," Fellinger said, pointing at the weapon. "Is that goddamned thing loaded? Didn't anyone tell you that I specifically said we do not need guns in our conference room?"

Kim's cheeks reddened.

"A member of your staff did say something," Kim replied. "I told him I carry it everywhere I go, even in the KCIA conference room in Seoul. And yes, it is loaded."

"Said something?" Fellinger said, his nostrils flaring. "I was told my deputy made it crystal clear that you were not to bring a weapon in here. At first I thought your English was faulty, but now I can hear that's not the case. Colonel, we're not in Seoul and this is not your conference room. It's my headquarters and my conference room. Either park that damn thing outside or this friggin' meeting's over."

"I'm sorry," Church said. "I should have said something."

Fellinger stared at Kim who squirmed, but sat with his chin thrust forward.

"Well, Colonel Kim," Fellinger rasped, "what's it gonna be?"

Kim grimaced, his face a deep scarlet. He held his chin high and slowly pushed back from the table. He removed the pistol from his shoulder holster and left the room.

"Thank you," Fellinger said when Kim returned. "Now," he added, looking at Church, "let's hear your great idea for getting agents into China."

Fellinger glanced at Kim who sat staring straight ahead, a sneer frozen in place.

This guy's dangerous, he thought. *Underneath those overly starched fatigues and pomaded hairdo is one vicious SOB. Church better keep a tight rein on this bastard.*

Church cleared his throat.

"As I was saying," he said, "we now have a vehicle for putting our agents into China, but we need money for the cargo. Our plan is to load a freighter with scrap metal, have the agents on board as crewmembers. We sell the scrap in Shanghai. While they're in port our guys jump ship. They then set up operations somewhere around the docks."

"Where'd you get the ship?" Fellinger asked.

"Actually," Church said, "Colonel Kim got it."

"We liberated it from the Japanese in '45." Kim's monotone was forced. He continued scowling when he finished.

"Maybe I can help with this one," Perkins said.

Fellinger's eyebrows raised.

"Tell me again, Major Perkins, who you are representing?"

"The Far East Command Liaison Group," Perkins said.

"That's the group that has partisans on the outer islands on both coasts of North Korea?" Fellinger asked.

"Yes sir," Perkins said. "We rescue downed pilots and do behind-the-line operations."

"You work for Tom Beane," Fellinger said, a tight smile appearing briefly. "How the hell did you folks get mixed up with Art Church?"

"We've been working with the CIA in Korea," Perkins said. "Colonel Beane has made it clear that he wants our

Liaison Group at FECOM to cooperate wherever possible. It has never been stated that this cooperation is limited to the Korean peninsula."

Fellinger looked at Perkins, a skinny six-footer who constantly fidgeted and straightened his papers. His dark hair was pushed up in a three-inch pompadour. It was his high-pitched, Midwestern twang that made Fellinger wince, as if hearing the sound of fingernails scraping on a chalk board.

Fellinger shook his head.

"I heard you were good at building empires, Art," Fellinger said, "but this one has got 'em all topped. You got the Korean CIA and Army Intelligence working for you and you don't even have to pay them. Congratulations."

"There are times when we can work together," Church said, his head nodding. "This is one of them. All we really need is money to buy the cargo. Your office has the only budget for covert operations, Joe. I need your approval and authorization to buy the cargo that will give us our entrée to Shanghai."

"So what's the name of this ship?" Fellinger asked.

"It's the *Kochi Maru*," Church said. "The ship has been to Shanghai a dozen times. The Korean ship captain has contacts there who are eager to get scrap metal."

"I can imagine," Fellinger said. "How do you know this captain won't get cold feet? What if he spills the beans about your four guys jumping ship?"

Colonel Kim straightened from his slouch and cleared his throat.

"He knows me. He knows I will hunt him down and that he will die very slowly."

Fellinger nodded without smiling.

"I believe you," he said. He turned to Perkins. "You sure the Army wants its signature on an operation sending scrap metal to China? It's going there to be turned into bullets and shells. That could raise a few eyebrows."

"This is Art's operation, not ours," Perkins said. "Besides, it'll take them a long time to process the stuff."

Fellinger snorted.

"Don't bet on it," he said. "They can be firing that stuff back at you in 30 to 60 days tops. The one thing they're never short of is laborers."

"Even so," Church said, "getting four agents into China can get us needed Intel and that can save a lot more lives by ending this war early and planting assets for the future."

"I don't know about it helping to end the war early," Fellinger said. "It'll take those guys a long time to get set up. I know it's been tough planting agents. You really believe you can guarantee a payback to justify the price tag?"

"There's never a guarantee that anything is going to work," Church said. "You know that, Joe. But I've got to try something. We've lost 212 agents, killed or captured, trying to get into mainland China. I've already spent a small fortune with damn little to show for it."

"I have to agree with you, Art," Fellinger said. "So far you do have a lousy batting average. "Now, with this *Kochi Maru*, you think you finally broke the code, got a sure-fire plan?"

"Yes," Church said, "and Shanghai is perfect. New faces are common. We got four agents, safety in numbers. They stick around the port, make friends, and start establishing contacts. If they survive for six months, the cost of the operation will be negligible."

"That's not what's worrying me," Fellinger said. "It's just that too damn many things can go wrong. There's no way you'll be able to get them out in a hurry."

"That's my problem," Church said. "The bottom line is that nothing else has worked. We need some eyes and ears over there. We're flying practically blind. As you know, I've got someone in place who can get out whatever these guys can develop."

"Any of these guys get picked up," Fellinger said, "you know they're gonna talk. You've got absolutely no plausible deniability. I'm not sure, Art, but my gut tells me that no one outside of this room knows what the hell you're planning."

He glanced quickly at Perkins, then back to Church. His instincts told him that it took all of Church's willpower to continue eye contact as he pressed his lips together. He nodded to himself when Church finally looked down at his papers.

"Okay," Fellinger said, "I'll give you the money for the operation. I'm justifying it on the basis of your position, Art. I just hope it doesn't come back to bite me."

"This plan will work," Perkins said, slapping his palm on the table.

Fellinger flared and glared at Perkins.

"Fine, Major," Fellinger said, staring directly at Perkins, "I'll remember your enthusiasm. If it works, we'll all drink to your promotion. If it winds up on the front pages of the world's press, well ... you're gonna be outside looking for work." ✦

THREE
Yokohama, Japan

The *USNS Barrett* docked at Yokohama in the early evening. Grainger and the other Army passengers boarded a chartered bus to the Camp Drake Replacement Depot on the south side of Tokyo. The Japanese bus driver, barely able to see over the steering wheel, kept one hand sounding the horn. The bus lurched and bounced in measured time surrounded by a continuous, deafening cacophony of automobile and truck horns. Nothing at home prepared the soldiers to deal with this bizarre custom. They gaped dumbly, subdued by culture shock.

Gradually, the riders were engaged by the more compelling sights of a dynamic civilization, one that contrasted sharply with the varying grays of Korea. Huge neon lights shouted their commercial messages in enormous Japanese characters. Though they remained a mystery of undecipherable graphics to the American passengers, the lights of Broadway were never as insistent.

The sea of bobbing heads became full-bodied figures. Kimonos were everywhere. Older men and women were dressed in blacks and browns. Younger men wore suits. Young women in finely textured kimonos of pastel colors, sporting upswept hairdos and stocking feet encased in padded wooden platforms, minced their way along the walkway. The appreciative young men on the bus startled the pedestrians with their whoops of joy and impromptu propositions.

"Oh, honey, don't move, I'll be right back," was one of the salutations barked from the cigar-shaped metal container filled with hot-blooded men. One target of this overt expression of lust caused the young lady to walk faster, and then break into a run, constrained only by the tight folds of her garment. She stopped in frozen relief as the bus hurtled past her.

A number of girls on the promenade sashayed in bright-printed Western dresses, some escorted by smiling GIs in uniform, others walking in pairs. They elicited cheers when they greeted the lusty comments with smiles and the waving of arms. One young soldier begged in vain for the bus driver to stop and allow him to get off.

The excitement stopped abruptly when they reached Camp Drake. It was more like a fenced prison compound than a military installation. Perimeter light towers surrounded clusters of drab buildings. Each two-story building had red fire lights next to wooden fire escapes. Landscaping was nonexistent. The lack of interest on the part of the Military Police, as the bus lurched through the main gate, communicated the message that their presence was more to keep the inmates in than to stop anyone from entering.

Camp Drake, like all replacement centers, was a hive of activity. Everyone, with the exception of a few permanent administrative personnel, was either on the way to or coming from the war zone in Korea. Those destined for the Land of the Morning Calm were not smiling or animated; the others were. In either case, it was rare for transient personnel to stay for more than a few days. This was just as well, since the austere facilities offered little in the way of comfort or recreation.

Grainger and the other officers, married or single, were billeted in the Bachelor Officers' Quarters. Each BOQ building accommodated 50 men. The entrance, through a screened door in the middle of the building, opened on a small day-room equipped with vending machines for soft drinks and cigarettes.

The entire wall at one end of the building served as a bulletin board where orders and phone messages were posted. In other places, the Army's idea of interior decorating was much in evidence: Four-by-six colored posters extolled the virtues of water conservation, the joys of re-enlisting, the dangers of loose lips and the woes of venereal disease.

Grainger and the other officers were told it was their responsibility to personally check the bulletin board twice daily for news of their next assignment.

Grainger was also aware that for his career branch of Infantry, the prospects for an interesting job were limited. In the Infantry one is usually in combat, receiving training, or serving as an instructor.

The day after Grainger's arrival, four sheaves of papers, stapled together at the top, were posted on the board in the day-room. The first and largest packet identified those slated for units in Korea. A second group would return to the continental United States (CONUS). The third had assignments at various installations in the Tokyo area. Members of the fourth group, also arranged in alphabetical order, were being assigned to the 1st Cavalry Division in Hokkaido. A notice appended to the fourth group's roster indicated that volunteers were being solicited because a year in combat had depleted the division's strength and it was in a rebuilding mode. Combat-experienced officers would be given a special five-day delay-en-route leave before reporting to their new assignments.

First Lieutenant Tim Foley, Grainger's roommate and friend from their days as enlisted men, barged into the room laughing. Foley was short of stature and wiry. He played baseball at Fort Riley with Grainger and had the reputation of being a real bantam rooster who would fight anyone, anytime, any place.

"They love you, old buddy," Foley said.

Grainger sat up and shook himself awake.

"Don't tell me, I'm going to the First Cav."

"Give that man a ceegar," Foley drawled. "Right on target and guess what, they're gonna give you a five-day delay-en-route, just like you be a volunteer."

Grainger smiled and settled himself back against the wall. He accepted and took a long pull from the bottle of Kirin beer handed him by Foley.

"Thanks," Grainger said. "Damn, you would think with all the assignments open here in Tokyo I could get something other than the 1st Cav Division in Hokkaido?"

"You got something against the 1st Cav?" Foley asked.

"No," Grainger said. "That was the division I fought with when I first got to Korea. It's just that training in an Infantry division is dull and boring. Right now I don't care to be training in a place where the snow is ass deep and the roads are icy.

"I haven't been away from Korea long enough to forget how cold it got in the mountains. Sometimes I felt like the marrow in my bones was frozen, they just ached. I used to wonder if I would ever get warm again."

Foley nodded in agreement.

"Well," he said, "as far as the 1st Cav is concerned, old buddy, it's Queen of Battle. They checked out your decorations and made you their first draft choice."

Grainger 's eyes narrowed.

"I think I'll check out the Tokyo-area military telephone directory," he said. "There must be somebody I've served with who can help with a better assignment than frozen Hokkaido."

"Didn't you tell me Colonel Moran talked about staying in main line units?" Foley asked.

Grainger flipped his empty beer bottle into the cardboard box in the corner. He stood up and tucked his shirt in his trousers.

"Yeah," he said, "but I'll worry about that after I finish the advanced course."

Grainger's survey of a Tokyo area Army phone directory turned up a likely contact. Colonel Ned Williams had been Grainger's regimental commander when he served with the 87th Infantry Regiment of the 10th Mountain Division, back at Fort Riley, Kansas. Grainger, then a staff sergeant, had helped his regiment win trophies in football and baseball. The listing showed that Colonel Williams was now assigned to the Plans and Operations Directorate of the Armed Forces Far East Command, AFFE-G-3.

Foley looked up from writing a letter and saw Grainger making notes on the border of the *Stars and Stripes*.

"Do you remember Colonel Williams from Fort Riley?" Grainger asked.

"How could I forget him?" Foley said.

Jumping up from his chair Foley pointed at the wall and shouted in a hoarse voice, "Give that man a three-day pass."

Grainger laughed.

"He never missed a game, baseball or football," Foley said. "Remember his little adjutant, Major Bankston? The colonel would drag him to the games and every time one of us got a big hit or recovered a fumble, he would holler that about a three-day pass. Bankston spent most of his time at the games scribbling in his notebook."

Grainger walked over to the telephone exchange and dialed Colonel Williams' office. He gave his rank and name, and asked if the colonel had a minute to talk to him. Williams came on the line almost at once.

"Is Captain Grainger the Sergeant Grainger I knew at Fort Riley, Kansas?" the voice boomed.

"Yes, sir," Grainger replied. "Thanks for taking my call."

"Not at all, Captain. You've come up in the world. It's really good to hear from you. Where are you and what are you doing these days?"

"Right now I'm at Camp Drake, sir. Just got back from Korea. I'm calling you about the second part of your question, what I'm doing. Sir, I'm not sure if you can do anything, but I could use some help with an assignment. I'm kinda new at asking for a job, and I could use some advice."

"Do you have any plans for dinner tonight?" Williams asked.

"No, sir," Grainger replied.

"Fine," Williams said. "Come to our house for dinner. You can tell me all about it. Millie and I will be waiting for you at 1900. She'll be so pleased to see you. More than once she's asked me what happened to that nice sergeant who came to our daugher's wedding at Fort Riley. Tonight you can tell her yourself. I'm at 19 Bradley Terrace over at Washington Heights. Any taxi driver knows the main entrance and the guard at the gate will give you the directions from there."

Colonel's Row, referred to as Camp Geritol by the younger officers, was a four-block line of large two-story houses. They looked like they were all built from the same set of antebellum plans for a manor house in Alabama or South Carolina. They were all painted white and had four large wooden columns in front, two on each side of the double-door entryway. Crab grass extended from the porch to the sidewalk and a large weeping willow tree shaded the front of each house.

Grainger arrived promptly at 1900.

Colonel Williams greeted him and glanced at the ribbons on the left side of Grainger's new tropical worsted shirt.

"Well, Captain," he said, "some pretty impressive decorations. Did you get a Battlefield Commission?"

"Yes, sir," Grainger said as Williams stepped aside and ushered him into the house.

"Millie is just finishing up in the kitchen. She'll join us in a minute. Can I fix you a drink?"

"A beer would be fine, sir."

Millie came in to the living room and greeted Grainger with a warm hug. She stepped back and surveyed him.

"We wondered what became of you, Ken," she said. "Now, our handsome young sergeant is a captain and has older eyes."

"Sit down, please," she said.

She sat next to Williams and smoothed her apron.

"I remember when Ned came back from Europe after World War II. He looked like he had aged 10 years."

"It's good to be back," Grainger said.

"By the way," Williams said, "I made some calls after you contacted me. There's one job in particular that I think you'd like and one for which you are obviously qualified. I got a call from a friend of mine who's looking for a company grade officer with combat experience."

He reached over and patted Millie's knee.

"He's an old friend of ours."

"A very dear friend," Millie said.

"Call my office in the morning," Williams said. "Give them a phone number where you can be reached." ✦

FOUR
Atsugi AFB

Colonel Sukow Kim left the meeting in a controlled rage. The confrontation with Joe Fellinger continued to fester in his mind. By the time Kim and Major Perkins reached the parking lot, Kim's anger was beyond reason or logic.

Perkins had no idea how volatile his companion could be, but he sensed he was still smarting from the rebuke he received in the conference room. He tried to break through the wall of silence by changing the subject.

Looking into the west he saw the hulking presence of Mt. Fuji, Japan's highest mountain. In June its perfect volcanic cone was barely capped with snow and the summer haze shrouded its peak with a thin veil of clouds. Yet, it remained a magnificent sight.

"They tell me," he said, "this is the best view of Mt. Fuji in all of Japan."

"There is nothing beautiful in this country for me," Kim snapped. "These people occupied my country and treated us worse than slaves. They stole our language and forced us to adopt theirs. They took our women and made them whores. They cut off the balls of our men. I despise them and their damn country."

Perkins' mouth fell open. He swallowed hard and stared wide-eyed at Kim, who was looking straight ahead. This was the first time he had ever heard such a storm of pure bitterness and hatred. And Kim was not finished.

"After the war revenge was sweet for us. Many of the whores who took Japanese lovers, including my mother, died exquisitely. My personal trademark was to pour acid on the women's private parts. Traitors' screams are music to my ears. We took the samurai swords from the Japanese soldiers and did to them literally what they had done to us. We let them suffer before we hacked them to pieces. It was the greatest time of my life."

Perkins took another deep breath and swallowed.

Kim continued to look straight ahead as they walked. His eyes blazed and his mouth was set in a tight line as he thrust his chin forward.

Perkins, in a mild state of shock, felt he had to say something.

"I didn't know how bad it was," he said in a weak voice as he got behind the wheel of the Plymouth sedan they had requisitioned from the motor pool in Tokyo.

"We should be back in Tokyo in about an hour," he said. "Traffic gets a little heavy this time of day."

Kim sat back and closed his eyes. He needed to meditate, to work on a plan to retaliate for Joe Fellinger's insult. He mentally scrolled down his list of personal guidelines: Trust no one; keep your own counsel; kill all the bastards who needed killing.

He stopped. That was it. He felt the handle of his .45 pistol, once more in his holster and pressing hard against the inside of his left arm. He pictured a bullet hole, neat and round, the diameter of his thumb, appearing in the center of

Fellinger's forehead. The exit wound, large and jagged, splattered brain tissue across the back of Fellinger's leather chair, and above the conference room wall, as he was catapulted backwards. Fellinger's mouth gaped in dismay. The light in his eyes dimmed. His massive head slumped forward and the blood ran down the back of his head and neck.

Kim smiled to himself. Wide-awake daydreams were the best. Fellinger would pay. *I am a sleeping volcano*, Kim thought. *I am dormant until someone wounds me, then I erupt. Every fiber in my body comes alive to help me to dominate my enemies. They have no idea how powerful I am. They will only know when they die.*

When he was a boy, his father whipped him with his belt until he screamed and begged for mercy. No infraction was too small for his father to reach down, unbuckle his belt and withdraw it with a flourish, as if pulling a sword out of its scabbard. He would grab young Kim by the arm, swing him around and whip him relentlessly.

Kim hated his mother because she never made any effort to intervene. One word from her, because her family had money, would have stopped the beating. But she always remained silent.

He made an important discovery when he was 13. As his father was whipping him, Kim thought about killing him. He experienced a wonderful calm and the strokes no longer hurt as much as before. He stopped trying to move away from his father and stood there in silence as the whipping was administered. At first this seemed to infuriate his father and he tried to hit even harder, but Kim remained quiet, thinking of when his moment would come. From that point on he knew that his love of self was well deserved, and he dedicated himself to the belief that he was destined for greatness.

He turned and glared at his father, focusing all the hatred he could summon. His father faltered. Blood seeped from Kim's buttocks and legs and through the thin cloth now stuck to his skin. His father, perspiring heavily, began to tire and his flailing slowed.

That was the last beating he gave Kim. The boy never shrank from what he knew was now his destiny. He waited and watched and plotted until his time came. He began sneaking home so the neighbors would not know when he arrived. He observed the time they went to the marketplace and when they returned. He closed the windows on the sides of the house that were left slightly ajar for ventilation and made sure the curtains were drawn.

When he was 14, the opportunity arose and he was ready. He came home through the vacant back lot and found his father in a drunken stupor. He knew his mother was at the market and would not return for at least an hour. His father was lying face down on a sleeping mat. Kim picked up a piece of firewood and brought it crashing down on the back of his father's head. Blood poured through his matted hair. Kim reached down and pulled the hated belt loose. He made a loop and grasping his father's hair with one hand, he raised his father's head and slipped the loop around his neck.

Snarling savagely, he yanked the belt tight. He put his foot against the back of his father's neck and pulled on the loose end. After an eternity with the belt taut, his father stopped thrashing and his bowels released. The odor caused Kim to retch. He let go of the belt to cover his mouth as he stumbled into the kitchen and grabbed a towel to catch his vomit.

Kim's heart raced and he sweated profusely. He felt a surge of panic and an urge to run. He stopped and struggled to compose himself. He went back into the bedroom with deliberate steps. The smell was now overpowering and he again retched into the towel. He could not look directly at his father, but forced himself to find the piece of wood he used and pulled the belt loose.

Kim went to the back door and eased out. No one was around as he bent low and moved quickly to the rear of the lot. He crossed a small stream where he dumped the piece of firewood, rinsed the towel and knotted it into a ball. He threw the cloth and the belt into a garbage container shortly before he reached his school.

He went to the room that served as the library at his school. He checked out a book without bothering to note the title or subject and walked home. He saw neighbors standing in front, their hands to their mouths as he neared the front door. They looked at him sadly and shook their heads.

All he could see were uniforms when he entered the house. It seemed as if all the Japanese policemen in town were in his living room. They all turned toward him.

"What happened?" he asked.

"Where were you?" one of the policemen asked.

"I was at school," he answered, "in the library."

He held up the book.

The policeman took the book and checked the date stamp.

"Where's my mother?" Kim asked.

"She's here," the policeman said. "Something has happened to your father."

"What?" Kim asked, his voice rising in apparent concern. "Is he all right?"

"No," the policeman said.

Kim started to cry and moved toward his father's room. The policeman reached out and grabbed his arms. Kim allowed himself to be held by the policeman and sobbed.

"I want to see my father," he cried.

"You're going to have to be strong," the policeman said. "You will be the man of the house now."

"I want my father," Kim said.

He allowed himself to be led to a chair in the living room where he covered his head with his hands and sobbed uncontrollably.

The death was ruled a homicide. The police concluded that some itinerant trying to rob the house killed Kim's father and fled out through the back door.

Kim's reverie was broken by the twang of Perkins' voice.

"That Fellinger is tough," he said. "I couldn't believe he made you take out your pistol."

"It's not important," Kim said.

"Maybe we can have dinner tonight," Perkins said. "I have to get some files together for an interview to pick the next liaison officer for the Sasebo Detachment. We'll go through the motions, but I've already decided who our man will be." ✦

FIVE
Tokyo, Japan

Colonel Williams called Grainger early the following morning.

"Can you get to the Mainichi Building in downtown Tokyo by 1400?" he asked.

"Yes, sir," Grainger said.

"Good. You have an appointment with Colonel Beane of the Far East Command Liaison Group, AFFE G-2. Tom Beane is the dear friend I mentioned last night. He's an old OSS hand. I'm not sure exactly what he has in mind, but it should be interesting."

The Mainichi Building was a new, six-story, steel-reinforced office building in the center of Tokyo. Mitsubishi Industries leased it to the Armed Forces Far East (AFFE) shortly after the beginning of the Korean War. It housed elements of the headquarters staff auxiliary to the primary sections. If your job did not require you to be immediately available to the Commanding General, AFFE, but was important enough for you to be called on short notice, you were allocated space at the Mainichi Building.

Grainger arrived promptly at 1345, signed in, and was directed to Colonel Beane's office on the fourth floor.

Colonel Beane's secretary, Edna Rasmussen, a senior career Department of the Army civilian, had him wait until 1400. She then announced his presence on the intercom and ushered him into Colonel Beane's spacious inner office. He stood as Grainger entered, then moved out from behind his desk and greeted him.

Grainger smiled appreciatively. He had been in the Army long enough to know it was not standard procedure for a colonel to greet a captain in this manner.

Beane's office was decorated in the fashion of old-time senior colonels. To the right of his desk was a large American flag on a lacquered wooden pole topped by a brass eagle with flared wings.

The walls contained a number of framed 8 x 10 photographs evoking memories of an earlier era. A picture of Beane when he was a major showed him shaking hands with the legendary Major General "Wild Bill" Donovan, head of the Wartime Office of Strategic Services (OSS), precursor to the CIA. The color photograph was inscribed with the words "valued comrade" and "unparalleled leadership." On Donovan's tunic was an unmistakable pale blue ribbon with five small white stars. "Wild Bill" was a recipient of the Congressional Medal of Honor, an award that caused very senior officers to initiate the salute for individuals many grades below.

Grainger stood facing an aging Colonel Beane whose most prominent facial feature was a large, pockmarked nose colored like a fading strawberry in stark contrast with the pallid skin surrounding it. He was tall and still rugged-looking with a midsection just beginning to show the effects of a sedentary life with a bit too much fine food and wine. The colonel was still an imposing presence. He wore no ribbons, but a shadow box displaying his medals, both U.S. and foreign, was affixed to the wall. At the top was the Distinguished Service Cross, suspended from a blue ribbon with white and red edging, for extraordinary courage in direct combat with the enemy.

Beane's handshake was firm and friendly.

"Welcome, Captain," Beane said, "I'm glad you could make it."

Grainger started to salute and report according to military protocol, but Beane had already turned and was heading for the leather chair behind his desk.

"Have a seat," he said, gesturing to a chair in front of his desk. "Would you like some coffee?"

"No thank you, sir," Grainger said.

Beane sipped some coffee from his mug, and then took a moment to glance at Grainger's decorations. He looked up.

"I see you were wounded," he said. "Any serious injuries?"

"No, sir," Grainger replied. "I was lucky, all flesh wounds."

"Good," Beane said. "Glad to hear it. Did Ned tell you what we do over here?"

"No, sir," Grainger replied. "He just indicated it was in the field of Intelligence."

"Do you have any experience in Intelligence work?" Beane asked.

"No, sir, I don't. All of my service, enlisted and commissioned, has been in the Infantry."

Beane looked thoughtful for a moment.

"Tell me about fighting the Chinese, their tactics, what kind of soldiers are they? If you faced North Koreans, I'd like to hear about them, too."

"Yes, sir," Grainger replied. "We faced both. During my last assignment my unit primarily faced the Chinese. We were up against some North Koreans briefly in Ch'orwon Valley, but the Chinese replaced them shortly after we arrived.

"The Chinese were more deliberate and calculating in their tactics. They would probe our line, attempting to get us to respond with crew-served weapons, to locate our heaviest firepower before an attack. They would make brief contact, get a reaction, and withdraw. It was important that we maintain fire discipline, responding only with M-1s, grenades or automatic carbines.

"When they did attack, it was usually in a skirmish line, like we do. We'd concentrate on creating gaps in their lines. We usually blasted away at their middle because that's where their officers were positioned. They would take some casualties, then withdraw and hit us at another point. Sometimes they would wait as long as a half-hour before hitting us again. Only one in three carried a weapon, usually a Russian "burp" gun. The ones we picked up had a hammer and sickle stamped on the trigger housing along with the initials CCCP.

"When you took out the gunner, one of the other two members of the fire team who carried ammo and grenades would retrieve the weapon and, according to our Intel folks, he was the one who would get promoted on the spot to gunner. The grenades they carried were concussion-type. They'd have 15 to 20 in a cloth bag. They were round, smaller than a baseball. They would throw these two or three at a time. As long as they landed 20 feet or so away, they were more like giant firecrackers than grenades. They did have some fragmentation grenades, but fortunately the ratio to the concussion-type was pretty low.

"I would say the Chinese soldier is basically well-disciplined but lacks experience in using his initiative. If there was enough light, we always went for the ones with the shiny boots. They were the officers. If you could take them out, there was a chance the rest would withdraw. Then we'd walk them back home with an artillery escort.

51

"The North Koreans were completely different. They must have learned their tactics from the Japanese. Every attack was like a banzai charge. They would come at you like a mob, firing everything they had, trying to break through your perimeter. Once we got a heading on their line of attack, we would concentrate our firepower. They would keep coming. You had to kill 'em, to stop 'em. I thought they were brave, but stupid. Our firepower was just too much. There was no guesswork involved in knowing whether you were facing Koreans or Chinese. You knew immediately from the difference in tactics."

Colonel Beane listened intently during Grainger's recital.

"Every war has its own unique kind of hell," Beane said. "How would you feel about fighting with Koreans?"

"Sir?" Grainger asked.

"Fighting with Koreans," Beane said, "both North and South. We hire mercenaries to engage in partisan or guerrilla operations, behind the lines."

"I'm a little surprised to learn that some of them have changed sides," Grainger said. "I thought they were too *gung ho* for that."

"Not all North Koreans are committed to Nam II," Beane said. "We use them in task forces on both the east and west coasts." He pointed to a map of the Korean peninsula. "One of our most important missions is keeping people on the small islands off both coasts to help downed pilots escape and return them to flying status or at least keep them out of POW camps. It's a great source of morale and comfort to the pilots flying those missions.

"Your job will be to support these task forces, primarily with logistical needs. You will also be assigned other duties according to operations we are supporting.

"We operate under the umbrella of CCRAFE, Combined Command Reconnaissance Activities in the Far East. In Korea we have worked with other agencies like the Central Intelligence Agency, but that's not our main focus or mission.

"The job I'm filling is Detachment Commander in Sasebo. You'll coordinate primarily with our people in Korea. It's possible, but not probable, that you will work on occasional projects that arise as targets of opportunity. But that really isn't your mission.

"You'll have very little contact with Army personnel assigned to Camp Sasebo, but you will requisition support items from them. Just check in, your orders will let them know you're affiliated with AFFE G-2. Our current liaison officer is Captain Jerry Doutter. He's a Reserve officer and is going home. He's done a good job.

"By the way, do you know anything about boats?"

"What kind of boats, sir?"

"PT boats or fishing boats, the ones the Japanese use."

"No, sir, I don't know a thing about boats. I was never around them growing up."

"Well," Beane said, smiling, "that's why we've got the Navy. This will be an occasional, but important part of what you'll be doing. We've got some good people who can be called upon when the need arises."

He paused.

"I don't have any doubts about your being able to do the job down there in Sasebo. Are you interested?"

"Yes, sir. It sounds interesting. I would like the job."

"Good," Beane said. "I'm sure you'll do a fine job for us. Those were good comments about Chinese and Korean tactics. I think the clear thinking and good judgment you communicated is exactly what we need from you in that position."

He reached down and took a long drink from his cup.

"We need officers of your caliber, Grainger. You handled yourself well under fire. That's a good quality. I'd like to congratulate you on joining our team."

Colonel Beane studied him for a moment, then stood up and extended his hand.

"Your point of contact and the person you'll be working directly with is Major Templeton Perkins. He's an experienced and well-trained Intelligence officer. He can help you in many ways. I think you'll like him. He'll be assigning you tasks and providing guidance. Any time you have a question or need help in Sasebo, just call him."

Grainger followed Colonel Beane out of his office. They turned toward a little alcove across from the secretary's desk. It had been empty when Grainger first arrived. Now, there were four officers, all captains, seated there. They rose in unison as Colonel Beane approached.

Grainger noticed that two of the officers wore the branch insignia of the Intelligence Corps and the other two had brass insignia indicating the Transportation Corps branch.

He asked me about Intelligence training and boats, Grainger thought. *Those guys are probably well qualified for the job, but I got it. I'm glad the Colonel is a good friend of the Williams family. I better get some field manuals on Intelligence and Transportation....*

"Thanks for coming over, fellows," Beane said, "but I've selected the man I need for the job, so I won't waste any more of your time."

He turned and re-entered his office.

All four officers eyed Grainger. One of them, a tall, blond, athletic type, built like a college fullback, with Intelligence Corps brass, bit his lower lip and shook his head from side to side.

"Congratulations, Captain Grainger," said Mrs. Rasmussen. "I'll call down and tell Major Perkins you've been selected. We can get started on the in-processing today. I'll also call AFFE G-1 and get you off the 1st Cavalry list. We'll cut orders assigning you here."

Mrs. Rasmussen's eyes widened in amazement when she heard Major Perkins' reaction to the news of Grainger's selection as the new liaison officer.

"He did what?" Perkins' Midwestern twang was now at high pitch as he shouted into the telephone. He stood so quickly that his thighs hit the bottom of his center drawer and propelled his desk forward.

"Damn," he said as he winced in pain and bent over to massage his thighs.

"You must be joking, Edna," Perkins said, barely able to contain his anger. "Why did he do that? The guy hasn't even been vetted. Good God, we send him four fully qualified candidates, one superbly qualified, and he picks who? Some Infantry captain, fresh off the boat from Korea. Is this fellow qualified for the job? I just don't believe it."

Perkins' Adam's apple bobbed like a yo-yo. His twang became shrill.

"I'm the one who's responsible for supervising that detachment. I would hope my recommendation was worth something."

"I'm really surprised at your reaction, Major," Mrs. Rasmussen said. "I'll let the colonel know of your concern with his selection."

Perkins slammed the telephone into its cradle.

Lieutenant Grippa, Perkins' assistant, looked up. He was short and pudgy. He received his commission from the Reserve Officers' Training Corps (ROTC) at a small college in North Georgia. Although he completed the basic Intelligence course for officers, once assigned to the FEC/LG, Perkins quickly identified him as the perfect resident gofer.

"Did he pick the Infantry guy?" Grippa asked. "The guy we just heard about this morning?"

"Yeah," Perkins said, "not only did he pick him, he didn't even interview Jawinsky, the best running back in Iowa's history and the top graduate of the Intelligence School at Fort Holabird. Do you have his file?"

"Jawinsky's?" Grippa asked.

"Dammit, Grippa," Perkins snapped, "where the hell is your brain? No, not Jawinsky's, the Infantry captain, what's his name, Grainger. Get me Grainger's file. Now."

"I took it up to Colonel Beane's office," Grippa said. "I'll go get it from Mrs. Rasmussen."

"I don't believe this," Perkins said.

He sat down and cradled his forehead in his hands. His telephone rang.

"Major Perkins," he growled into the telephone.

"Major, this is Edna. Colonel Beane says he doesn't have time to talk to you today. He said he will see you first thing in the morning."

"Do you know where this guy came from?" Perkins asked.

"I believe Colonel Beane said that Colonel Williams knew him from the States and gave him a very high recommendation," she replied.

"Has he been vetted? Has he been to Atsugi and gone on the box, the lie detector?" Perkins asked.

Edna laughed.

"That's not my department, Major," Edna said, "but it's interesting that Colonel Beane thought you might ask that question. He said if you did, I was to inform you that the captain's loyalty is beyond question, he's honest to a fault, and that ..." she paused, having difficulty to keep from laughing,. "Well, he said, 'If that captain's not straight, I'll resign my commission!'"

"That's not the only thing we're trying to find out," Perkins stormed. "What's his security clearance?"

"It's 'secret,'" she said.

"Great," Perkins moaned. "I've got a new Detachment Commander that I can't talk to since he's not cleared for top secret. This is incredible."

"Major," Edna said, "you know that General Rogers can approve an interim top secret clearance for him based on his secret clearance."

"I know," Perkins said, "I suppose that's what we'll have to do."

Perkins hung up the phone and slammed his fist on the desk as Grippa returned with Grainger's file and handed it to him.

"I doubt if there's anything negative in that guy's file," Grippa said.

Perkins shook his head.

"Rule One is that if there's nothing negative in a file, it's just because it hasn't been posted yet. Rule Two is that everyone is suspect. Is that clear?"

Grippa looked at the floor.

There was a knock at Perkins' door.

"Come in," he shouted.

Ken Grainger entered.

"Major," he said, "my name's Ken Grainger. I was sent down here to start in-processing. Colonel Beane just hired me to take over the Sasebo Detachment."

Perkins scowled.

"That's what I hear," he said. "You're in the right place. I'm Major Perkins and I'll be your supervisor and commanding officer as long as you have that detachment. By the way, this is my assistant, Lieutenant Grippa. In my absence, you can tell him whatever you need me to know. He'll get it to me. He's cleared up to and including top secret."

"I'm not," Grainger said. "My clearance is for secret, I'm ..."

"I'm aware of that," Perkins said, interrupting Grainger, "That's going to be one of the first in-processing problems I have to solve. Evidently Colonel Beane thinks you walk on water. Do you?"

"Not if it's more than an inch deep," Grainger responded.

"Oh," Perkins said, "are you a comedian, too?"

Grainger stiffened and stood straight, his eyes narrowed.

"Never mind," Perkins said. "That little detachment in Sasebo is involved in some highly classified operations. A background and some training in Intelligence would certainly be helpful. It's not the best time to work in on-the-job-training, or use the 'good old boy' network for that matter."

Perkins glared at Grainger.

"I disagree with your selection because you lack the skills that I know are needed for the job. If you can learn fast and follow orders without asking a lot of stupid questions, we'll get along just fine."

Grainger did not respond.

Perkins swung around and grabbed Grainger's file from Grippa. He flipped the cover, scanned the file, and shook his head.

"No Intelligence training whatsoever," Perkins grumbled. "No schooling in small-boat operations. You're going to be a real challenge for me, Grainger. The people you'll be working with are coming to you for support, not to train you. What they are doing is the reason you're being posted on liaison duty."

"I'd like to get started as soon as possible," Grainger said.

"Not until I get you cleared for top secret, at least on an interim basis," Perkins said. "I want you to go down to Atsugi tomorrow and take some tests."

"What kind of tests?" Grainger asked.

"A personality profile that everyone in the Group has to take, and a lie detector test."

"Lie detector test?" Grainger asked.

"Absolutely," Perkins said. "No one works here without going on the box. There are no exceptions. Does that cause you a problem, Captain?"

"No, sir," Grainger said.

"Fine," Perkins said. "Report back here at 0700 tomorrow. I'll have transportation take you down to Atsugi." ✦

Six
Sasebo, Japan

Grainger's train arrived at the Sasebo station late on a Thursday night. He looked out of the window and saw Jerry Doutter standing on the platform. Edna's description was so accurate Grainger knew who it was even though they had never met. He was a large, lumbering hulk of a man with a tanned face that looked like polished leather. He wore an old Army garrison hat with the grommet removed.

The grommet is what gives the hat its halo effect. Without it, the sides slop over to what is called a "50-mission crush." Old time Air Force pilots removed the grommets to accommodate their headsets and then did not replace them. Military purists frowned on grommet-less hats.

Doutter's hat was also cocked to the right in the traditional "I don't give a damn" position. His "Ike" jacket was unbuttoned, in need of pressing, and devoid of any ribbons or badges save his silver Captain's bars and brass "U.S." insignias. The cross rifles on his jacket lapels were dull and lusterless. His sweat-stained shirt collar was open at the throat, and the knot of his tan tie hung inches below its proper setting. When he made eye contact with Grainger his face brightened in a lopsided grin. Grainger smiled and nodded.

The door of the passenger car slid back in its recessed position and Grainger stepped down.

"You're the closest thing to Audie Murphy to get off that train," Doutter said in a deep bass voice, "so you must be Ken Grainger."

"Jerry Doutter?" Grainger asked.

"There is only one, thank God for small favors," Doutter said. "Edna called and said you'd be on this train. I was surprised because Perkins called the other day and said you'd be up there for a month. He screamed bloody murder when the colonel hired you. I don't suppose you know what it's all about?"

"No," Grainger said. "I just know that for some reason I'm at the top of his 'S' list."

"C'mon," Doutter said, "my jeep's parked out front. Maybe I can remove some of the mystery."

Grainger hoisted his duffel bag up on his shoulder and followed Doutter along the tiled walkway leading to the street.

"Perkins has been telling me for months that my replacement was a hand-picked water-walker," Doutter began. "It's his wife's brother, some big football jock back in the States. He joined up because he wants to go into politics. Figured it'll help him get elected, the veteran's vote and all that crap. He did it because Perkins told him he'd get him a cushy job in Japan, no combat. He had that interview rigged tighter than a virgin's pussy. Then, in you waltz with your big DSC and a shit-pot full of medals, recommended, according to Edna, by Beane's best friend from OSS days, Ned Williams. Joe College never had a chance."

Grainger nodded.

"I wondered if it was something like that. One of the four guys waiting to be interviewed looked like an All-American football player. I never figured it was a family matter."

"Bingo," Doutter said. "On both sides. It goes deeper. Beane and Williams served together in the OSS in Europe. That's where I first met Beane. He's a good man. Beane and Williams go back even further. They both loved the same gal. Beane stayed in Europe and Williams came home to work in the operations directorate at the Pentagon. Guess who won the pretty gal? Beane never got married because he still loves her. Hell, he woulda picked you over anybody."

They reached the jeep parked in a "No Parking" area. Grainger tossed his duffel bag on the back seat. Doutter squeezed his body behind the wheel of the jeep and slouched forward. He flipped the ignition switch and pushed the starter button. The engine roared to life. Doutter looked back to check for cars and eased slowly into traffic.

"Oh, yeah," Doutter said, "I've got you booked with me at the Sasebo Hotel. The Army leases the whole thing. It's a great hotel. It used to be the place where all the kamikaze pilots stayed just before they took off on their one-way trips to join their ancestors."

Grainger noted that Doutter stayed in the right lane of the thoroughfare. All of the traffic went by at a much faster clip.

Doutter saw him watching the traffic.

"I drive slow," Doutter said. "It goes back to my days in the Sheriff's Department in Fresno, California. There are too many things you don't see when you are going fast."

A taxi swerved in front of the jeep, passed two cars and again changed lanes.

"Let's see," Doutter said, "where was I? Oh yeah, the hotel. It's supposed to be for field grade, majors and above, plus high-ranking civilians. Down here, AFFE G-2 carries some weight. Technically, company grade officers stay down in a BOQ at the bottom of the hill. It's called the Bull Pen. You don't want to be there. Besides, this job calls for us to take care of our senior big shots from Korea who come over for meetings and conferences."

Doutter pointed to a large building set on a small hill and surrounded with trees.

"There it is," he said, "the historic Sasebo Hotel." He glanced quickly at Grainger. "You have to be careful about Perkins. He's a sore loser, and he seems to enjoy emasculating people. That's kinda his specialty. Some guys relish being an asshole."

Grainger shrugged.

"Why can't he get his brother-in-law another job?"

"Oh, he will," Doutter said. "But not like this one. For an ambitious guy with political aspirations it's perfect. Perkins could assign him here, send him over on TDY (temporary duty) to Pusan, far from the fighting, get him some theater-of-war ribbons, maybe a Combat Infantryman Badge for sending guys out to the islands for partisan operations. All that stuff helps if you want to be a politician-war hero."

"I don't care much for politics," Grainger said.

"Hey," Doutter said. "Join the crowd. I'll drink to that. Of course, I'll drink to anything. Now, for me, I'm goin' back to Fresno, kiss my beautiful wife a thousand times, and get back in the Sheriff's Department. On the weekends you'll find my fat ass out beside the pool. I've had enough of the Army."

"What's on tap for tonight?" Grainger asked.

"You hungry?"

"A little."

"We'll go to the club," said Doutter. "It's on the first floor of the hotel. You can get a sandwich and a beer. When you live there you can sign chits for everything. They give you a bill at the end of the month. Really adds up. There are twin beds in my room, so you'll bunk with me till I leave, then it's all yours. Tomorrow morning, you're supposed to go over and check in at Headquarters. It's a courtesy thing; you're expected to do it.

"I guess they told you, you don't belong to Camp Sasebo, you just eat and sleep here. Edna will send your 201 file to the local Counter-Intelligence Corps (CIC) office, not the Camp Sasebo Headquarters. That's very important because it keeps you off the Camp Sasebo duty roster. Newcomers and TDY people get all the weekend duty assignments."

Doutter pulled into a parking place at the hotel that had a sign reading, "Military Vehicles Only."

"I love that sign," he said. "It was put there so staff cars would have a place to park during the day. At night, all the military vehicles except the colonel's sedan are back in the motor pool. I get to keep my jeep with me all the time, so I always get a great parking spot. Sometimes I see field grade officers' wives leaving the club after dinner. They have to walk down the hill to the parking lot. They always give me a dirty look because a lowly, company grade captain parks three steps from the front door."

Doutter led Grainger through the lobby, past an unmanned front desk and up a flight of heavily carpeted stairs to the second-floor room. He opened the door and handed Grainger a key.

"This one is yours," he said. "By the way, I mentioned that your records would be at the CIC office. The CO over there is a damn good guy. He's Major Roberto Salencio. The best thing about Roberto is that you can trust him. Around here, that's saying a lot."

Doutter walked over to the dresser and picked up a half-empty bottle of Jim Beam whiskey.

"Boy, this stuff doesn't last long," he said. "Care for a snort?"

Grainger shook his head and watched while Doutter poured half a water glass full of the amber liquid. He downed it and let off a small shiver.

"Whew," he said, exhaling. "I hate that stuff."

He poured a few more ounces into the glass and sat on the edge of the bed.

"The Camp Sasebo folks are a small, tight-knit Army family," Doutter said. "Word about you will get out fast. You and I are just spooks in the woodpile to these folks. Damn, I haven't talked this much since I courted my wife."

He drained the rest of the liquid in the glass.

"After you check in tomorrow, I'll take you around and show you the layout, introduce you to some people you'll need to know."

Grainger had breakfast in the lower-level dining room and set out for his interview. He dodged traffic as he crossed the main thoroughfare diagonally from the hotel. His objective was an old four-story wood and stucco office building that housed the Camp Sasebo Post Headquarters. He remembered Doutter's warning,

"Don't take the elevator to the third floor."

"Why not?" he had asked.

"It's haunted by those kamikaze pilots," Doutter told him.

"Sure," Grainger had replied, smiling.

"All right," Doutter cautioned. "You'll find out. Only the Japanese can use it. The building used to be the only bank in town. Every time an American got on the elevator it stopped between floors. A Japanese maintenance guy had to come to their rescue."

Grainger nodded to the Japanese security guard on duty when he entered the building. He glanced at the elevator to the left of his desk but turned toward the stairs. A large gold tooth gleamed in the center of the guard's mouth as he smiled broadly. Grainger nodded and followed the signs to the third floor office of the Post Headquarters.

The secretary outside the Commanding Officer's office nodded to Grainger. "Colonel Beardsley is not in today, so Lieutenant Colonel Murphy, the Executive Officer, will give you the official welcome to Camp Sasebo, Captain."

Grainger wondered why she started to smile when she said "official welcome."

She pointed to a door marked "Executive Officer."

Grainger knocked and entered the small office.

Sitting behind a regulation walnut-stained Army desk was a bald, portly, florid-faced officer dressed in Army khaki. Large half-circles of perspiration extended from his armpits almost to his waist. His branch insignia was for the Transportation Corps. Faded campaign ribbons of the "been there" variety denoted areas in the world where he had served. There was no indication of time served in combat. He was an aging career officer. Grainger guessed he was on his last assignment before retirement.

He advanced to a point three steps in front of the lieutenant colonel's desk, halted at attention, and saluted.

"Sir," he said, "Captain Grainger reporting as directed."

He handed the officer a copy of his orders placing him on TDY at Camp Sasebo.

The Executive Officer took the orders and tossed them into his in-basket without a glance.

Grainger maintained his position of attention and began to feel uneasy about his welcome. He thought back to Doutter's comments about not belonging to this little Army family.

Colonel Murphy did not invite Grainger to take a seat or direct him to stand at ease.

"This is a small Army post," he began, "but it is an important Army post." He paused, swallowed, and seemed to be having a little trouble getting his breath. Sweat rolled down his cheeks. "As such," he continued, "we will not tolerate any misconduct." He paused again. "There will be no fraternization with indigenous personnel. We will not allow public drunkenness or any other immoral conduct. Do I make myself clear?"

"Yes, sir," Grainger said.

"And don't you forget it," Colonel Murphy shouted. "I know all about you young bucks. You get here and take advantage of these young and innocent Japanese girls, screw your brains out, and can't get your job done during the day." He paused to catch his breath. "We won't have it, you understand?"

"Yes, sir," Grainger said.

"Good," Murphy said, "that's all. Dismissed."

"Yes, sir," Grainger said.

He saluted, did a smart about-face, and was exiting the office as Murphy was slowly raising his hand in a loose return of the salute. Grainger smiled at the secretary, who had her hand over her mouth to suppress a laugh.

"The court-martial's at 1100 and the hanging's at 1200," Grainger said, smiling.

She nodded her head and burst out laughing.

Grainger walked back to the hotel. When he entered his BOQ room, Doutter was sitting on the bed with his back propped against the headboard.

"How'd it go?" he asked, pursing his lips.

"Oh, not bad," Grainger said, smiling. "Is that guy, Murphy, for real?"

"Oh, yeah," Doutter said and laughed, "he's real, okay." He hesitated.

"It's Friday, so later tonight, about 2130, we'll take a short walk."

Later, at lunch at the hotel, Doutter began telling Grainger about the work to be done.

"For the most part, this is a liaison job, supporting our folks in Korea with supplies and now and then buying Japanese fishing boats that we use for guerrilla operations on both coasts. Every now and then Perkins gets a wild hair up his ass and we're tangled up into some stupid covert operation. I really wonder if Colonel Beane is in the loop on some of these little adventures. I've rarely done any liaison stuff this past year, and that's supposed to be my job.

The waitress brought their respective lunch tags and smiled at Grainger. "Not now," Doutter said, smiling, "we've got to get our tour of the Post in before dark."

"That big one out there," Doutter said, pointing, "is the battleship *USS Missouri, number 63.* Those 16-inch guns are huge. Every time one of those babies is fired, the cost of a Cadillac goes out the muzzle. Over there, to the right, is the *Dixie.* It's one of three repair ships in the fleet. More importantly, it's where you'll be going to attend Intelligence conferences or briefings."

They drove past a sentry gate manned by a Japanese guard in a black uniform.

"All the guards and security people are Japanese," Doutter said, "but if there's ever a problem, the MPs show up right away and take charge."

Doutter turned into an area with block after block of warehouses. He went past another small guardhouse and turned left.

"We're in the middle of this block," Doutter said. Driving slowly, he pointed to a small stenciled sign reading "Port Officer."

"That's me, soon to be you," he said, smiling. "We use that as a front. We won't go in right now. I want to show you around a bit." Driving to the end of the street, Doutter pointed to a large pier. "That's where they berth the troop ships that stop here. You went right up to Yokohama, but sometimes the ships from Korea stop here. When you have to pick up boat crews from Korea, you'll meet them right there."

"How often does that happen?" Grainger asked.

"Not too often," Doutter said, "maybe once a month. It depends on partisan operations. I'll fill you in on that stuff later."

Doutter stopped at a U.S. Navy gas pump and filled up the jeep. Grainger saw him flash a piece of paper at the attendant who nodded. Doutter drove slowly away from the port.

"Let's go up in the hills and check out our radio station," Doutter said. "We use it to send propaganda messages to Korea and China. We can only use it a few hours in the wee hours of the morning. It's got 50,000 watts and when it's on, it blows the smaller stations right off the air."

"What else does the detachment have?" Grainger asked.

"Well, let's see," Doutter said. "Without checking the property book, we've got two PT boats, a 126-foot cargo ship, and a warehouse full of rice, five-in-one rations, nautical maps, charts, and a bunch of other stuff. It's a lot bigger operation than it looks like from the size of the office. I'm the only one who spends any time there."

After an hour's drive up into the hills to view the track-22 antenna and the small camouflaged building housing the radio station, Doutter decided to call it a day and headed back to the hotel.

"By the way," he said, as they drove down the steep mountainous road, "I mentioned Roberto Salencio. He really is an important guy for you to get to know, an absolute straight shooter. You can tell him what you're doing, even though Perkins will tell you not to talk to anyone.

"There's another guy," Doutter said. "He's a Reserve colonel on extended active duty, a two-year tour. He's a lawyer, works in the JAG shop over at the post headquarters. His name is Dave Levy. He's helped me a couple of times and is also a good guy. The important thing is that if you need to talk to a lawyer, you can talk to Dave. If he says it will be kept confidential, you can put it in the bank."

"Beyond that?" Grainger asked.

Doutter laughed.

"Beyond that? You're on your own."

They were in the hotel bar later that evening. Grainger looked at his watch and asked, "Did you say something about going for a walk at 2130? That's 10 minutes from now."

Doutter stood up and stretched.

"Yep," he said. "Just about time for the unveiling. Robert Ulysses Murphy, Lieutenant Colonel RUM," Doutter said. "It's Friday night, his one night out, and he has to be home by 2200."

"The Executive Officer?" Grainger asked. "Is this some kind of joke?"

"Unfortunately, you might say that," Doutter said. "C'mon, let's go."

"Where?" Grainger asked.

"Where, indeed," Doutter said. "Why, to visit a den of iniquity, the fount of libidinous living, one of the better sin palaces of Sasebo, the officer's recreational lounge, AKA the Field Grade Annex. It's right next door. Just west of where we sit at this very moment, you'll find the Izumi Hotel, where all your dreams come true."

"What are you drinking?" Grainger asked.

"Jim Beam," Doutter said, raising his glass. "The best sippin' liquor west of the Pecos. When I go home and have to pay full price, I may find I'm not a true alcoholic. You don't seem to have acquired a taste for whiskey, so, how about a beer?"

"Sure," Grainger said.

They walked down the driveway in front of the hotel, turned right and walked up a narrow street to a three-story wooden structure. There were two bright red neon signs. Beside the one in Japanese was one in English that said, "Izumi Hotel." When they reached the entrance, Doutter slid the wooden, grid-framed, papyrus door to the right, into its recessed compartment. They entered the reception area and stood waiting.

There was a small door with a sign saying "office" in English to the left. The entrance to the hotel bar was to their right, down a narrow hallway. The jukebox was playing American music. Grainger recognized the mellow tones of Eddy Howard crooning his theme song, "Careless." It echoed in the corridor and brought back memories to Grainger of his last Stateside posting and weekends in Kansas City, Missouri.

The threaded glass beads suspended from the lintel rustled gently as a young, kimono-clad woman advanced to greet them. She bowed and said, *"Komban wa"* (good evening).

"Komban wa," Doutter replied.

He looked at his watch and smiled.

"Chotto matte" (just a minute), he said to the young woman.

"It's 2130," Doutter said, "time for our boy to be heading home."

His timing was perfect. As if on cue, a loud noise, like someone falling, directed Grainger's attention to the stairway. He could not see the source of the racket, because after four steps there was a small landing and the stairs doubled back to his right and spiraled up to the floor above.

The noise grew louder with shouts of intermittent glee and apprehension.

"Oh no, ha, oops, wow, watch it, oh boy."

It was not difficult to discern that someone well into his cups was in a semi-controlled free-fall down the stairs.

He came around the corner and on to the small landing, propped up on both sides by kimono-clad girls, giggling and cooing. Old Colonel Murphy was feeling no pain and trying unsuccessfully to pinch the tightly kimonoed rear ends of his female escorts. The mama-san madam shadowed this intrepid trio as the good colonel lurched from side to side and seemed to be in danger of losing his balance. Mama-san seemed to be the only one not enjoying the maneuvering.

"Oh, hi there, Captain Stranger," Murphy shouted in a friendly greeting. "What brings you out tonight?"

Grainger glanced at Doutter who was smiling broadly. The incongruity of his morning welcome and this evening revelation caught Grainger at a loss for words.

"Hope you left something for us, Colonel," Doutter said, winking at Grainger.

"S'nuff for everybody," Murphy said, suddenly preoccupied with his trouser zipper.

He leaned far forward, supported by his companions, and suddenly sat down on the bottom step. He stared dumbly at his feet. The mama-san tried to keep him in an upright position while the two smiling young ladies attempted to reinsert his unyielding feet into his low-quarter shoes.

Finally, Murphy was assisted to his feet, weaving unsteadily. Sweating profusely from the exertion, he punctuated his progress to the front door with an unmistakable, window-rattling fart. His female attendants covered their mouths in a vain attempt to suppress their laughter.

Grainger shook his head and smiled.

"Two welcomes in one day," he said.

"Now you know the worst-kept secret in Camp Sasebo and why, with our military affection for acronyms, we refer to the dear, harmless lieutenant colonel as Colonel RUM."

Doutter paused, disappointment tinged with sadness reflected in his eyes.

"By the way," he said, "you saw that old wrinkled mama-san following them down the stairs?"

"Yeah," Grainger said.

"Salencio told me she is one tough cookie. Some of the local hoods tried to muscle her. She pretended to give in and invited them to spend some time with her girls before she paid their protection money. She spaced them in different parts of the house. While they were in the saddle, she sneaked into each room and slit their throats with a razor.

71

"She dumped the bodies in front of her place and then called the MPs. She said that some soldiers got into a fight with those guys right in front of her place and left the bodies out on the street.

"Salencio found out what really happened from some of his informants and suggested that the MPs drop the investigation and say the alleged perpetrators were apparently on their way to Korea.

"What was even funnier, the local police talked to the same informants and when they thought the Army was covering up the murders, they figured mama-san had some high-placed big-shot protecting her. The word got out in both official and criminal circles that she was not to be bothered. She's got the only house not affiliated with the local gangster element."

Grainger nodded.

"Let's get that beer," Doutter said.

"Lead on," Grainger said, and followed Doutter through the beaded strands that curtained off the bar area.

"Kirin," Doutter said to the young, but hard-looking bartender. He held up two fingers.

"Hai," she responded. "Two Kirin."

Another woman behind the bar, many years senior in age, looked directly at Grainger.

"I no see you before. You wanna catchee girl?"

"No thanks," Grainger said. "Not right now."

The older woman smiled at Grainger and turned. She called to a beautiful, young slim girl, standing by the jukebox. The girl walked slowly, accentuating the swing of her hips as she crossed over to Grainger.

"Hey, good-looking Captain, my name Julie."

She stood close to Grainger, the faint smell of jasmine filling his nostrils. There was no question of her appeal. She looked up at him and smiled. The invitation was clear and professional.

She's beautiful, Grainger thought.

"How long you stay?" she asked.

"This is Ken's second night in Sasebo," Doutter said, looking at the young woman. "He will stay long time, maybe one year."

She gave Grainger an up-and-down appraising look.

"Yes, you good-looking man," she said. "I want to be close with you tonight. You want to be close with me?"

Grainger smiled at her.

"That would be nice," he said, "but I don't have any money for a woman."

She pursed her lips and looked away.

She turned back toward him and moved in between his legs as he sat on the barstool. She placed her hands on his waist and then on his arms.

"Oh, you strong," she said.

What a time to be flat broke, he thought. *There's no way I'm going to ask Doutter for a loan.*

"Why you no dance with me?" she asked.

"Sure, I'll dance," Grainger said as he eased off the bar stool and stood up.

She put her hands on his waist again with her thumbs pressing his stomach.

"Very hard stomach, good," she said.

Doutter, seated at the bar, turned to watch Grainger.

"Hey, Ken," Doutter said aloud, "that's gotta be as good as it gets."

Grainger placed his hands on her small waist.

"Look," he said, "you're beautiful. I'd like to be close with you, but not tonight. The first day of the month, but not tonight. I just don't have any money. That's it. I'm really sorry, but 'no.'"

"Too bad," Julie said. "You not know what you miss."

"I'm sure you're right," Grainger said.

As they danced to the strains of Johnny Ray singing about "The Little White Cloud That Cried," Julie continued to move her hands on his stomach and then to his rear.

When the song ended, she did not release her hold. The jukebox played the next selection, "The Tennessee Waltz" by the "singin' rage," Miss Patti Page. Julie's body swayed against his in time to the music. This time she held her body even closer. Her right hand moved slowly down the front of his trousers.

"*Ana ma! Ana koto! Ana,*" Julie stammered.

"Oh, oh," the older woman at the bar announced to everyone, "she find something."

Everyone at the bar laughed.

"What did she say?" Doutter asked the old woman.

"Look at pants," the old woman said, laughing.

Doutter looked. It was true; the front of Grainger's trousers bulged alarmingly.

"Oh my," Doutter said.

Grainger shook his head and shrugged, and then he smiled.

Julie's cheeks flushed red, and she averted her eyes from Grainger's face, glancing down at her hand as she continued to hold him. Then she pressed her body against his. After a moment she looked up at him.

"Okay, I pay, I pay," she said. "You wait here. I go pay mama-san for room."

The other bar girls looked at him, nodding and smiling. One rocked her hips back and forth suggestively and crooked her finger at him in a beckoning gesture.

"Did you hear that?" Doutter cried. "She's gonna pay the mama-san. Man, that's historic."

"Historic, hell," someone chimed in, "it's a friggin' miracle."

The bar area erupted in laughter.

"All I got is a cute way of gettin' on and off," another volunteered.

There was more laughter.

Grainger walked over to the bar and sat down, sipping his beer.

The mama-san who helped Colonel Murphy down the stairs entered the bar area with Julie. She stopped in front of Grainger and looked him up and down.

"You muss be numba one," she said, a gold tooth gleaming in the light of a neon Kirin beer bottle rotating on the bar.

"First time any my girl pay. I no believe. She want marry with you. She love you."

Mama-san's pronouncement brought hoots and hollers from the entire assemblage.

Grainger looked at Julie, whose face was still flushed. She reached out, almost defiantly, and took his hand.

"Okay. You no pay, I pay. We go. We go now."

She led him out of the bar, pushing the beaded strings aside as though anxious to get away from the crowd in the bar.

Grainger glanced over his shoulder and saw that everyone at the bar was staring at them in amazement.

Julie put her right arm around his waist and rested her head against his arm as they went up the stairs.

She led him down the dimly lit hallway to the last room on the right, slid open the door, and pulled him into the room. The matted flooring was soft and pliable.

"I am very happy now," she said, as she turned to face him.

They stood facing each other. The dim light from the hallway filtered through the door's translucent rice paper, bathing them in shadows. She reached up and softly brushed his face with her fingertips.

"I see this face before," she said. "Maybe in my dream."

Grainger embraced her, holding her close as his lips moved from her neck to her eyes to join with her lips. Her mouth opened wide and her tongue darted in and out of his mouth. His hands wrapped around her waist, then moved to massage her back. He bent slightly and moved his hands down her body.

"Big, strong hands," she said with a husky voice. "You know, I see you before."

"I don't think so," Grainger said, "but it's okay."

"Oh yes," she said, "when I was younger. Maybe your brother, but he look just like you."

Grainger laughed as he tugged at her tight kimono.

"You're gonna have to help me, Julie," he said, "I don't know how to get this thing off."

She smiled and removed her obi.

Grainger started to unbutton his shirt.

She placed her hands on his.

"No," she said. "I want to do, for me."

She first removed her clothing. He stood watching her, marveling at how quickly everything came off. She removed a comb from her hair. With a light toss of her head, her raven hair floated down around her neck, bare shoulders, and uptilted young breasts.

"God, you're beautiful," he said. "Unbelievable."

She knelt to remove his slippers and socks. Standing, she unbuttoned his shirt. Her hands caressed his chest and arms.

"You are very strong," she said, "and beautiful."

She bent over and undid his belt, then kneeled to unbutton his trousers. She tugged them down, pulling his boxer shorts down as well.

"Oh, no," she said, laughing, "I don't know."

He reached down, put his hands under her armpits and lifted her up so her head was even with his. He gave her a long, slow kiss as once again her tongue raged inside his mouth.

Her breathing was rapid and irregular as she tried to swallow.

"I want you too much," she said, "but please go slow, take some time for me."

She was trembling as he slowly lowered her gently on the futon spread on the floor.

Her eyes were closed and her mouth opened in a sigh, then a moan deep in her throat as his rigid length slid into her. As he looked down he felt he was seeing the most wonderful smile he had ever seen. All of his senses concentrated on her face as their movements blended in perfect harmony. Then there was an urgent fury on both sides. She moaned again, this time a little louder, as he spurted into her. There seemed to be a timeless interval as she held him. He breathed heavily and collapsed, rolling onto his back and pulling her close, cradling her head on his arm. Julie, still trembling, moaned low and hugged him.

They held each other, legs entwined. She started to raise up, then curled into a fetal position and smiled.

It was much later that Grainger whispered, "Wonderful."

Julie, her head now resting on his chest, nodded.

"In Japan," Julie said, "we have another word: *suteki na*. It also means wonderful and splendid and beautiful."

"Where did you learn those words?" Grainger asked.

"From my father," she said. "My mother lived with an American for a long time before the Big War. She was famous Kabuki dancer. It is classical dance and drama. He taught me English and would get American films for us to see. That is where I first saw you."

Grainger laughed.

"Now I know you've got the wrong guy."

"No," she said. "He look exactly like you. Good man. He was nice to business lady and shoot many bad men. His name was, uh ... Ringo, yes, Ringo Kid."

"I'll be damned," Grainger said. "I know that movie. It was, uh, *Stagecoach*, with John Wayne, yeah, *Stagecoach*."

"Yes, yes," Julie said, sitting up. "John Wayne, you look like John Wayne."

"Thanks," Grainger said, "but I don't see the resemblance. By the way, what happened to your father?"

Julie fell silent.

"All Americans go home before the war," she said. "He write to my mother and tell her he will marry with American woman. She cried for two weeks. Then, one night she did not come home. Police come and say there was accident at Tokyo railroad station. She was killed. But I know, no accident.

"I come here, to Sasebo, to live with my mother's sister. I stay there for years. Go all through school, then my aunt say, 'Your mother's money all gone.' They cannot keep me. My aunt's husband bring me here, almost one year now. I was very afraid. A long time they let me be maid. Then I must earn money. Now I think it is my life."

Grainger held her close and kissed her.

They continued in the embrace for many minutes.

"Can I get you a biiru?" she said.

"No," he said. "But I do like those hot baths."

Julie laughed.

"I want to give you a long massage," she said. "Then we can make love again, but slowly. Don't make me too crazy."

Grainger opened the door to his BOQ room a little before 0600. Doutter sat straight up in bed as if wakened from a trance.

He scratched his head with both hands and yawned.

"Ooush," he murmured, thrusting his arms in the air and arching his back. He yawned again and struggled to a sitting position against the headboard. He reached across his body with his right hand and gripped the nearly empty bottle of Jim Beam. As always, it was the bottle he purchased the afternoon before. He picked up the empty water glass, poured in the remaining amber liquid, and downed it with one gulp, giving a quick shudder.

"I gotta stop startin' my day like this," he said. "I just can't seem to drown them damn demons."

He looked at Grainger and smiled.

"Man, you are really something," he said, raising a now empty glass. "One day in town and you're already a legend."

That story will be all over town by sundown."

He laughed and then started coughing. When the spasm passed, he laughed again.

"You're gonna be spoiled for that gal back home," Doutter said.

"No danger of that," Grainger said. "There was one I thought was special. We went together for about six months. She wanted me to get out of the Army. Sent the first letter I got in Korea. It was a 'Dear John,' mailed the day I left."

Grainger turned and took a fresh khaki shirt out of the dresser drawer.

"I felt more closeness and caring with Julie last night than I ever knew with Suzanne. Funny, even with the language problem we were able to communicate."

"I'll bet," Doutter said, smiling.

Grainger glanced at Doutter, smiled, and shook his head as he tucked the shirt into his uniform trousers.

"There's no family at home to worry about either," he added. "By the way, what's on the schedule this morning?"

"This morning we'll go down and check out your new office. I have to get you registered and signed in as the new Port of Sasebo Liaison Officer. The only place you'll officially be known as a Detachment Commander is in Tokyo, and on your records, of course." ✦

Seven

The Far East Command Liaison Detachment commanded by Doutter was housed in a small office tucked in the corner of a huge warehouse at the Port of Sasebo. Its appearance was not deceiving. It was strictly a one-man operation. Furnishings were Spartan in the extreme: A six-foot, walnut-stained desk; two folding chairs; a telephone; a field radio; and a squat, 500-pound, cast-iron field safe sitting on the floor next to the desk.

Other than the inside door that opened into the warehouse, the only outside access was a small opaque window covered with heavy-duty chicken mesh and vertical steel bars. A wooden sign wired to the chicken mesh, and set in the upper left quadrant of the window, had black stenciled lettering identifying the premises as the office of the "Port Liaison Officer." No one seemed particularly interested in what the Port Liaison Officer did except to note that he was seldom there.

Captain Peter Shelvoski, U.S. Army Transportation Corps, had his office on the second floor of the same building, where he and his staff conducted the legitimate military business of receiving and then sending the stored supply items housed below to their final destinations in Korea. Most of Shelvoski's clerks were Japanese civilians. They processed the myriad requests and related shipping forms involved in the moving of cargo.

Shelvoski and the Port Commander, Colonel Edward Kelly, were the only two individuals associated with port operations who knew for certain that the occupant of the liaison office had nothing whatsoever to do with normal port business.

Doutter and Grainger drove through the large double doors at the center of the warehouse, looped around two forklifts and parked directly in front of the small liaison office. The front of the jeep faced out toward the entrance; its windshield reflected the sunlight like a mirror.

Doutter dialed the combination and unlocked the padlock. When he pushed the door open he was greeted by a musty smell of stale air.

"Phew," Doutter said, "it's been a while. Leave the door open. We need some fresh air in here."

He walked over to the desk and motioned Grainger to one of the folding chairs set against the wall. Doutter sat behind the desk, reached down and spun the wheel of the combination dial on the safe, opened the door, extracted a large buff-colored envelope heavily sealed with plastic tape, and held it up.

"First things first," he said. "This one, I'm pretty damned sure, is going to be dropped or it will be trouble."

He tossed it on the desk.

"I can feel it in my bones. If it wasn't for what I've heard about this little operation," he placed his hand on the envelope, "I'd say this job is a breeze and well below your level of competency."

81

"What is it?" Grainger asked.

"Ken," Doutter said, "I'm really in a tough spot right now. I've been directed not to discuss this operation with anyone, but that doesn't mean I can't give you some idea about what you need to know to protect yourself in case the shit hits the fan. Perkins told me he'll want the file back, but he hasn't asked for it yet. It's classified top secret. Those words are stamped on every page. I could be sent to Leavenworth if I even tried to get it copied. Hell, it's not even supposed to be in this kind of safe."

"Well," Grainger said, "if it's something connected with what I'm supposed to be doing, what can you tell me about it?"

Doutter eyed Grainger closely and picked up the envelope in his right palm as if weighing it.

"This is not really Army Intelligence business," he said. "This is CIA crap. The problem is Perkins, the piss-ant we work for, spends too much time with Art Church, the CIA station chief in Tokyo, and gets us involved in their shit that's miles from our mission."

The sound of a forklift motor operating in the warehouse reverberated through the small office. Doutter got up and closed the door.

"I was all set to dump this crap on Perkins' brother-in-law and forget it," Doutter said. "Then along comes 'Jack Armstrong, the All-American Boy,' and I can see far enough ahead to know that if anything goes wrong, and my gut tells me it will, you're going to be left holding the bag. That bothers me."

"Does Colonel Beane know about this?" Grainger asked.

"He might, but frankly I would be surprised if he did," Doutter said. "He's an old OSS warrior and would know this isn't what we're getting paid to do."

"I don't understand," Grainger said. "If this is a CIA operation, why can't they just hire their own people and do whatever the hell they do without involving the Liaison Group?"

"Bingo," Doutter said. "Because the Group is just one of a whole blizzard of organizations here in the Far East that's involved with special operations. Ours is just one of them. The lines of command and coordination are blurred and Perkins uses that to get us involved with the CIA stuff not only in Korea, but also here in Japan and even China.

"China?" Grainger asked. "Don't they have their own people to do stuff in China?"

"Not really," Doutter said. "They've got tons of money, but they need the worker bees. Here, in the Far East, you've got the greatest recruiting source in the world. A bunch of military types who've been trained to respond, 'Yes, sir. No, sir. Difficult but not impossible.' When they're no longer needed, they sign an oath that they were deaf, dumb, and blind during their temporary duty and go back to the real Army."

Grainger tapped his fingers on his lips and looked thoughtful.

"So when will I find out if I get to read the file?"

"I don't know," Doutter said. "What I do know is that you better not break the seal on the envelope unless you find yourself in deep kimchee. Just don't underestimate Perkins. That smooth sonofabitch will always cover his tracks and make it look like you're the dummy who misunderstood orders because you have no Intelligence background. He'll blame Beane for hiring you and you for being stupid."

"I'm not feeling too good," Grainger said. "Right now I feel like I'm wandering around in the middle of a mine field. I'm not sure where to step, and frankly, I don't think that's right."

"It's not right," Doutter said, "but welcome to the world the way it is. There is one thing, and you need to keep it in mind — Perkins hates written reports. Something in writing has to be filed. Secretaries read things that have to be filed. There's a paper trail.

"You usually get instructions via the courier plane. It's a PBY that lands out in the bay about three each afternoon. It also serves other military operations, so you'll get a call if there is something on the plane for you. Take one of your PT boats out to meet it. The port launch goes out daily, but it's usually crowded, and it makes other unscheduled stops before it gets back to Port Headquarters. You could wind up spending one or two hours on what should be a 15-minute trip."

"When do we go visit the PT boats?" Grainger asked.

"We'll go this afternoon," Doutter said. "You've got two, an 85-footer and one new 90-footer."

"What are the PT boats for?" Grainger asked.

"If you like fishing, they're great for trolling," Doutter said with a chuckle. "Actually, they're tied into the CIA net. They use them most of the time. I don't ask why and they don't tell, but, as Detachment Commander, they're on your property book."

Grainger shook his head.

"When Colonel Beane asked me if I knew anything about boats, I thought he was referring to something locally available."

"He was," Doutter said. "We'll get into that when we go out to Smuggler's Gulch; that's our staging area."

Doutter picked up the heavily sealed envelope from the desk, tossed it back into the safe, shut the door, and spun the dial.

"Oh yeah, before I forget it, the combination to the safe is my wife's birthdate: 2.21.23. It's written on the back of this blotter." He lifted up the edge and showed the number. "Start to the right and on the last number pass it once. It clicks the second time."

He stood up and yawned.

"Right now, I'm hungry. You like sushi?"

Grainger nodded.

Doutter drove the jeep past the Port Headquarters and pointed to a large passenger ship anchored at a pier about 300 yards ahead.

"Once in a while," he said, raising his voice over the sound of the jeep engine, "you'll get a visitor from Korea.

That's where you meet them. He's usually a high-ranking officer—colonel or brigadier general. That's why you're at the field grade hotel. You help them with what they need. Mostly, they're over here for conferences on the *Dixie;* that's the big Navy repair ship I pointed out yesterday.

"As the FEC/LEG Detachment Commander, you're welcome to sit in on these meetings if you want. They're gloomy as hell; everything is a 'worst case' situation. Gives you the willies and a crappy outlook. Perkins will come down for some of these meetings. If he's here, he won't want you to attend. He never lets you know about them till the last minute.

"That brings us back to the file I showed you. If something is going to happen, it should probably happen soon, hopefully, before I leave.

"The name of the ship they're gonna use in that operation is *Kochi Maru.* I'm sure you saw the name on the envelope. Don't forget it. I'll leave the file in the safe. If it happens that you need it, read it and hide it. You should probably take it over to Salencio's shop. It may be the only thing that proves you weren't involved in this thing at the beginning."

Doutter leaned back in the jeep and arched his shoulders.

"I didn't want to dump all of this on you at one time," Doutter said, "but I'm a natural born pessimist and Perkins has a way of playing games. He'll call down and say I'm needed up there for an emergency meeting, and there'll be no more time for talking."

Their arrival back at the BOQ later that day coincided with the opening of the small package store located in the basement. The young Japanese clerk glanced at Doutter and smiled as he reversed the "Closed" sign to "Open."

He walked over to the bourbon section of the store without a word, removed a fifth of Jim Beam from the shelf, and placed it in a brown paper bag.

Doutter nodded at the smiling clerk, placed $3.25 in military scrip on the counter, picked up the bag and left the little store without comment.

A message was taped next to Doutter's nameplate on the door of their BOQ room. It said simply, "Call Major Perkins."

"If he can't reach you on your office phone," Doutter said, "he'll usually leave a message at the front desk and they tape it to the door. I'll have to run across the street to the Headquarters building. If the message is exactly three words, like this one, he wants me to call him on the secure telephone. Anything more than that I can call him from any telephone."

Thirty minutes later he was back. He opened the Jim Beam and filled half a water glass. He raised the glass in his right hand as if in a salute, his left hand curled into a loose fist and he tapped himself over his heart saying, "First one since breakfast." In one long gulp he finished off about half of the contents.

Grainger watched him expectantly.

"Bad news," Doutter began. "What I was saying earlier? I had a hunch this might happen. I'm supposed to meet the PBY tomorrow and go back with it to Tokyo. Perkins says he needs me up there for some meetings. I personally think that's bullshit. He's never needed me for a meeting up there the whole time I've been here.

"My guess is that he'll keep me there until it's time to come back and pack my gear. The same thing happened to the guy I replaced. I was going to have a week to get filled in on the job before I took over and he was gone the next day. That's why I spent so much time giving you all that background stuff. I just had a hunch this was going to happen."

He drained the remainder of the glass and refilled it. He propped himself against the headboard and stared into space.

✧ ✧ ✧

Grainger watched as the Consolidated PBY-5A Catalina circled over the choppy waters of the bay at Sasebo. It was the flying boat used to transport VIP passengers, deliver small quantities of high-priority equipment, and ferry top-secret couriers from one place to another on the three main islands of Japan and over to Korea.

The last stop on its daily run from Yokohama to Sasebo was, generally, around 1500. The U.S. Navy crew of four, under contract to Headquarters Far East Command, felt they had the best assignment in the Far East, except on those days when high winds and rough seas would barely allow flying operations. This was one of those days.

Because of the high winds and choppy seas, the bulky, slow-moving, passenger launch from the Port of Sasebo elected to forgo the trip out to the rendezvous point. The PT boat that carried Grainger and Doutter did not have the same option. When Doutter called Perkins earlier in the day to advise him of the heavy seas, he got no sympathy.

"I said I need you here, dammit," Perkins shouted. "If they can land, you can get on board. Grippa talked to the pilot and he said he could set it down and pick up a passenger. I don't want any more discussion. What's the matter, Doutter, afraid of getting a little wet?"

"No, SIR," Doutter shouted.

Perkins hung up without responding.

Now, Grainger was sprayed with salt water as he held onto the railing of the PT boat and watched Doutter kneeling on the edge of the boat as he reached out to the perforated metal ladder suspended from the open doorway of the PBY. The PT boat rocked and lurched in the turbulent waters of the bay and suddenly wheeled away sharply from alongside the flying boat leaving Doutter hanging precariously from the ladder. A young crewman struggled mightily and finally helped pull him into the bouncing PBY. Doutter turned to Grainger shaking his head in disgust. It was evident that he was thoroughly drenched.

The desk clerk woke Grainger the next morning at 0600 to tell him that a Major Perkins in Tokyo wanted him to call his office immediately. Grainger dressed and drove down to his office at the port.

Perkins picked up the telephone on the first ring.

"Grainger?" The high-pitched twang could not be mistaken. "The Red Ball Express will be docking at your place tomorrow at 1400. I don't know which of the ships it will be, but Doutter said you know where the Red Ball docks. I want you to meet it. Colonel Cunningham will be on the ship. Get him whatever he needs during his two-day visit, you understand?"

"Yes, sir," Grainger replied.

Perkins hung up.

Grainger arrived at the main port docking area shortly before 1400. The *USNS Sergeant Muller,* one of a trio of ships used to haul troops between Pusan and Sasebo, arrived a little earlier than scheduled and was in the process of being tied down. He glanced up as the gangplank was being rolled into place and watched an Army sergeant lead four muzzled German shepherds off the ship. The sergeant had a tab sewn to his olive drab shirt that indicated he was with the K-9 Corps. Once clear of the ship, the sergeant muttered some indistinct word and all four dogs immediately sat.

Grainger looked up at the ship's railing and did not see any senior officers debarking. He turned back to the sergeant.

"Where are you going with the dogs, Sergeant?" Grainger asked.

"I'm taking 'em to a Japanese vet here in Sasebo, sir. He'll put them to sleep. Since 1949, regulations say that after so many combat patrols it's not safe to bring them back home. The Army classifies them as equipment and now they're non-serviceable. That's just plain crap. Hell, police dogs at home live with the family of their handlers. I bring 'em over here because I don't trust Koreans with a live dog. They think dog meat's a delicacy. I won't allow that to happen to these fine animals that have served our country."

"Suppose someone here in Japan wants them?" Grainger asked.

"I don't know about that, sir," the sergeant answered. "I deliver them to this Japanese vet. He gives them a quick shot, and then I take 'em out to the boonies, bury 'em and hold a little ceremony. I'll go back tomorrow."

"Boy, that seems rough," Grainger said.

"Yes, sir," he said. "It breaks my heart. These dogs are not old. Butch, here," he pointed to a large black and tan shepherd, "was on 22 patrols. He sniffed out ambushes and saved our ass more than once, these other dogs, too. I want to be there when they need a friend the most."

"Sergeant," Grainger said, "I'm here to meet a colonel and help him get situated. It's my job. You see the Port Headquarters with the flag over it?"

"Yes, sir, I see it."

"Okay, go see the vet, but don't leave Butch, keep him with you. When you get back go two blocks past the front of the Headquarters." He pointed to a two-story white clapboard office building with a brass flag pole displaying an American flag. "Turn left, and go to Warehouse 27, you'll see the numbers in black near the roof. As you go in, look to your left, you'll see some stairs leading to a second floor office."

Grainger drew a diagram on a slip of paper.

"Go upstairs, ask for Captain Shelvoski, and tell him I asked you to wait for me. I'll be back as soon as I can. I can use a dog. I'll see that Butch gets a good home. We can talk about doing something for the other dogs on your next trip.

I'll try to find some homes for them with military families here in Sasebo. It's a lot better than the alternative."

"Yes, sir. Thank you, sir," the sergeant said, his voice husky with emotion.

He turned and walked away with his shoulders squared and head held high.

"Saddle up," he choked in a barely audible voice.

The four dogs rose as one and he led them away.

Grainger turned and found himself face to face with a short, wiry-looking colonel.

"Colonel Cunningham?" Grainger asked.

"Yes. You're Grainger, right?"

"Yes, sir. Hope you didn't have to wait long."

"No, it's okay. I waited until the troops got off. I heard part of what you said to the sergeant. I think that's a decent thing you're doing, Captain. I'm over here for a meeting on the *Dixie* tomorrow. Once I get on board I'll just stay there so I won't need quarters at the BOQ. I wanted to meet you and was hoping to see Doutter. I understand he's already in Tokyo."

He paused and looked around the port.

"As you know I command the Korean Detachment of the 8240th. You need to come over and visit."

That night Grainger went to see Julie as he had every night since they met. Her eyes filled with tears when he told her of his plans to find homes for the other dogs, and that he had a dog named Butch who was in a wire enclosure at the warehouse.

"He's got food and water," Grainger said. "Tomorrow we can spend some time together and start getting acquainted."

"That is so wonderful, Ken," she said. "You are a good man. You have a kind heart. I wish I could keep the dog here, but it is too big a problem."

"Don't worry about it," Grainger said. "I can't keep him in the BOQ either, but I can bring him here once in a while. It'll be better if he stays in the warehouse. He gets a lot more exercise that way." ✦

EIGHT

A tall, tanned and muscular man wearing a dark-blue sweatshirt, dungarees and light-blue canvas shoes was waiting for Grainger late the following afternoon when he arrived back at the BOQ. He had regular features with close-cropped, tightly curled auburn hair. A jagged four-inch scar ran between his left eye and nose.

"Grainger?" he asked.

Grainger nodded.

"Who are you?" he asked.

"My name's, uh, Forrest. You can call me 'AJ.'" He smiled faintly as he spoke. "Perkins sent me. I'm from the Navy. We need to buy some boats."

Grainger looked around the lobby of the hotel. A group of officers was huddled in conversation near the front door and a person at the front desk was discussing his bill.

"It's too crowded here," Grainger said. "Follow me."

The hotel had a small library and reading room adjacent to the cocktail lounge. When Grainger opened the door, he looked in and saw it was vacant, and he motioned to his visitor.

Once inside he moved to a small table by a window looking out on the hotel's landscaped grounds. His visitor followed.

"Okay," Grainger said. "Do you have an ID?"

Forrest pulled a well-worn wallet from his pocket and removed a plastic card. He flashed it so that Grainger could see the CIA insignia and the man's picture. His fingers covered his name.

"I want to see it," Grainger demanded, extending his arm.

The husky man frowned, but did not challenge Grainger as he took the card from his hand.

Grainger glanced at it quickly.

"So, William Dye, or whatever your name is, you said you're from the Navy, but apparently you're now working with the CIA. How do we get these boats?"

The muscles in Dye's cheeks rippled as he gritted his teeth and retrieved his card.

"I go out, find a fishing boat or two, and come back. You go look it over and pay the man. We then move the boats over to Smuggler's Gulch. After that, we go to the traditional 'we just closed a deal' party, drink his booze and screw his women.

"Then, you call Perkins. He radios the detachment in Korea to send over crews. When they show up, we outfit the boats and they sail back to Pusan. Simple. I've done it 20 times."

"You usually shop alone?" Grainger asked.

"Well, Doutter used to go along, but he knew something about boats."

"I want to go," Grainger said. "I need to learn something about boats."

"Okay," Dye said, clearing his throat, "suit yourself."

Grainger didn't respond.

"You know," Dye said, "there really isn't any need for you to come along. I don't bargain with these people. I find a good boat and agree to pay what they want. There's no quibbling over price."

"Where I grew up," Grainger said, "we always thought it was smart to bargain for the best price."

Dye's upper lip curled.

"Perkins told me you don't know jack shit about Intelligence. He didn't say you were a crusader, too."

"Just a little old-fashioned," Grainger said, turning to face Dye directly. "I'm trying to learn this job. If you don't like my going along, Dye, go get your boat money from someone else."

Dye's cheeks reddened as his jaw tightened again.

"No, that's okay," he said, staring at Grainger. "We'll do it your way ... this time."

"When do we go?" Grainger asked.

"I'll meet you here Monday, 0800. Oh yeah, no jeep and no uniform. We're supposed to be civilian businessmen. We're buying boats to transport to Korea so we can sell 'em for a big profit."

"Yeah, sure," Grainger laughed, "we're such hotshot businessmen we don't even bargain. One other thing, if your cover is supposed to be nonmilitary, I don't think it's a good idea for you to show up at a military hotel. Call and leave a message that the boatman needs to see me. Leave a 'best time' for me to call. I'll meet you at the warehouse at the port the following day, four hours before the time you mention in your message."

An hour later Grainger went out to the kennel he was able to get placed at the rear of the hotel near the maintenance shed. Butch wagged his tail as he saw Grainger approach. Butch nuzzled him when he was free of the kennel, clearly happy to move out of the confined space. They got in Grainger's jeep and drove down to his office at the port.

Grainger went upstairs to see Shelvoski. Butch followed at his heels.

Shelvoski jumped when he saw the large black and tan German shepherd.

"Whoa," he said. "Where'd you get Rin Tin Tin?"

"Hi, Pete," Grainger said. "His name is Butch."

He told Shelvoski about the sergeant and his plans for the K-9 dogs.

"If it's okay," Grainger said, "I'd like to make arrangements for Butch to stay in the warehouse at night. They don't allow pets at the BOQ. The cage downstairs and the kennel at the BOQ are kind of small. Butch isn't used to being locked up. The sergeant told me he'll wander around at night and scare the hell out of anyone who comes snooping around."

"Great," Shelvoski said. "We don't work as much at night since the war slowed down. I'd love to have him on patrol. Some of the other warehouses have had break-ins, nothing big, but you never know. The guards at the gate can't keep everyone out."

"What about placing some of the other dogs?" Grainger asked. "They're well-trained and if Butch is an example, they make good pets."

"Sure," Shelvoski said. "I'll mention it to the people at the housing project and put up a notice on the bulletin board. I'll let you know. I'm sure you'll get some takers."

"Oh, one other thing," Grainger said. "You know I've been seeing a Japanese girl. I've brought her to the club for dinner a few times. She already has a pretty good understanding of English. I've got her a basic reading course and she's doing well. Maybe you could keep her in mind if you expect to hire any more file clerks. I can bring her over for an interview if you'd like."

"My wife and I saw her with you the other night at the club," Shelvoski said. "She's quite a looker. Some of the wives aren't too thrilled about seeing her. Frankly, I congratulate you on your good taste. Not getting serious, are you?"

"Maybe a little," Grainger said. "Right now, we're spending as much time together as we can. I think I've got a place to rent so we can set up housekeeping in the near future. Right now there are some logistical problems I have to deal with."

"Sounds more than 'maybe a little,'" Shelvoski said, smiling. "Isn't she in a house right now?"

"Yeah," Grainger said. "I made an arrangement with the mama-san, but I want to get her a decent job. If something happens to me or if it doesn't work out, I'd like to at least take care of that much. I know about cultural taboos, but frankly I don't care what other people think. This is the first time in my life I've even thought about marriage."

"Okay," Shelvoski said. "When you get your 'logistical' problems worked out, and you're living together, come see me. Even though we've slowed down a bit, I can always use a person who speaks some English. When I first started here, I had to hire girls who spoke no English at all. I've got a guy who trains them. He's pretty good. If she can read at all, she's way ahead of my normal hire. Frankly," he said smiling, "she's pretty enough to start right away."

Granger laughed.

"Thanks, Pete," he said. "I really appreciate it. By the way, when she does move in, I'll want Butch to stay with her, but I'll get you another dog."

The boat-buying mission went smoothly the next Monday until it was time to settle the bill. The boat seller smiled at Grainger as he was counting the yen and asked in perfect English, "What rank are you?"

"How did you know?" Grainger asked.

"Easy," the broker said laughing, "haircut, all cash, new yen. American military have all new yen and pay cash."

"Just that, huh?" Grainger said, smiling.

"Yes," the man said. "New yen, pay cash, and haircut." Dye stood beside Grainger. His eyes were narrow slits and the muscles in his cheeks were working overtime.

"What about you?" the broker said, turning to look at Dye.

"I'm a civilian businessman," Dye responded.

"Ah so," the broker said, still smiling. "I understand."

"I need to talk to you," Dye said, snarling as he gripped Grainger's arm, pulling him aside.

"If you don't let go of my arm right now," Grainger said, "he'll also find out we're not good friends."

Dye released his hold and stood, feet apart, with his hands on his hips.

"Look," he said, "these guys aren't supposed to get it from us that we're military or with the government. They can believe anything they want, but we're not supposed to confirm it. If one of these boats shows up in North Korea and the engine numbers are traced here, it will prove that the government bought them for spying purposes."

"That's bullshit," Grainger said. "It won't prove that at all. They already know we're military. Even if they didn't, you told me your cover story is that we're buying the boats to re-sell them in Korea. You also told me the boats would be repainted. If you're really concerned about the engine numbers, file the goddamn things off. You know, Dye, these guys aren't stupid. Why would they ever say anything about markings or numbers? They're not going to get involved in someone else's mess and they're certainly not going to ruin a sweetheart deal. We're probably paying twice what they could sell these boats for here in Sasebo, and we're paying in cash."

Dye, still red-faced, turned away and approached the Japanese broker. In a matter of minutes he had agreed to buy another boat and signaled to Grainger who, once again, paid in cash with new yen.

"We always have a celebration party," the Japanese businessman said to Grainger. "Your other partner, the heavy man, always came and drank, but would not stay with a girl. I hope you will be able to attend. We will meet later at the Matsu Lodge."

Grainger was about to decline when Dye stepped in front of him.

"My partner will be happy to attend," Dye volunteered. "He knows it would be an insult not to accept such a gracious invitation."

Dye turned once again to Grainger and spoke in a low voice. "These guys got the best whores in town. It's not polite to turn down their invitation."

"Thank you," Grainger said to the Japanese businessman. "I will stop by for a while, but I can't stay long because I have another meeting to go to."

Turning to Dye he said, "In the future don't volunteer for me. If it's such an important obligation, which I don't believe it is, then you can go and uphold the honor of the partners."

"You've got a lot to learn," Dye said. "Right now, we gotta get these boats over to Smuggler's Gulch."

Smuggler's Gulch got its name because it was tucked into an almost inaccessible corner of the harbor, about three miles from the port headquarters.

Grainger drove to the site and was there when Dye brought the first fishing boat to the rickety dock.

"Did you call Perkins?" Dye asked.

"Yeah," Grainger said. "I'm supposed to pick up the crews tomorrow morning. We'll collect some gear from one of my sheds at the radio station and be here about 0900."

"Well, my job is almost done," Dye said. "Drop me in town. I'll get a taxi and bring the other boat over later, so it's here when the crew members show up."

Grainger scanned the area. Near the gravel road leading into the cove was a barn-like structure with a rusting, corrugated metal roof and sidings. The roof had a number of small holes as if someone had fired a weapon into the ceiling. There was no glass in the window frames. Bolts protruding from the concrete flooring made walking hazardous.

A cast iron water spigot on the outside of the building dripped continuously and had created a deep, circular hole that exposed the piping. A broken door that was pried open revealed a shattered commode.

The boat-buying celebration party was in full swing when Grainger sauntered into the private dining room at the Matsu Lodge. A long, rectangular table sat in the center of the room, covered with tempura, sashimi, norimaki, and all manner of sushi. Empty sake bottles rested on their sides in keeping with the custom of not removing empties. Geisha girls kneeling beside the diners kept little porcelain cups filled with hot rice wine. Half a dozen open bottles of Johnny Walker Black Label scotch were clustered at one end. The boat-seller businessman had invited a number of his friends to join in the celebration, many of whom were already showing the effects of the alcohol. Some were yelling at the top of their lungs, drinks were being spilled on the table and their clothes and they were groping the female servers who protested that they were not party girls.

The businessman who had questioned Grainger at the boat sale seemed to have lost most of his reserve. He had removed his coat and his shirttail was draped outside his trousers. A giggling geisha kept mussing his hair as he tried to unfasten the obi on her tightly wrapped kimono.

"Ah, General," he shouted when he saw Grainger. "*Komban wa.*"

He spilled his drink as his foot caught in one of the pillows on the floor.

"*Gomen kudasai*" (excuse me), he said. "I'm a little stinko, maybe a lot stinko."

He slumped backwards to the floor, holding his glass aloft.

Grainger spotted Dye on the floor in a corner of the room, wrestling with one of the geisha girls.

Suddenly Dye pushed her aside and got to his feet.

"Goddamn you," he shouted at the girl, "you bit me."

The girl stood slowly. Her eyes filled with tears.

"I am dancing girl," she said. "I not for sleeping, not for making love. I dancing girl."

"Bullshit," he shouted. "You're all for fucking."

Dye put his hand to his mouth and looked at the blood on his fingers.

"You did bite me, you bitch," he said.

He slapped her across the face, knocking her to the floor.

All motion in the room stopped.

One Japanese businessman made a slurred remark, causing his friends to burst out laughing.

The geisha girl bowed her head as she tried to stand.

"Bitch," Dye hollered, slapping her again. She collapsed on the floor.

"That's enough, Dye," Grainger said, advancing on the red-faced Dye.

"Fuck you, Grainger," Dye said. "Stay out of my way or you'll get something you won't like."

Grainger moved rapidly through the tangle of bodies on the floor, toward the stricken girl.

Dye turned toward Grainger, reached into his pocket and snarled, "I'll cut your balls off."

He pulled out a switchblade knife and pushed a button; a six-inch blade sprang out.

Grainger headed directly for Dye. When he got close, Dye slashed at his midsection.

Grainger leapt to his left, away from the knife, and smashed a roundhouse right into Dye's nose. Blood spurted on Grainger's shirt as he stepped back to his right and pounded a left hand into Dye's ribs. Dye's knees buckled. He staggered, but he did not fall.

Grainger reached out, put his left arm under Dye's right armpit, his hand on Dye's shoulder, and forced it down. At the same time his right knee came up, hitting Dye's face. The force of the blow drove Dye upright and he dropped the knife. Grainger quickly moved in front of Dye and landed a crushing right cross on his chin that snapped his head to the right. Dye staggered and a powerful left hook drove his head back to the left. He was barely conscious. He teetered in front of Grainger, arms hanging limply at his side.

"I don't like bullies who hit women," Grainger said in a low voice. "I saw enough of that when I was a kid."

Like a large, lithe cat, Grainger angled his body to the left and delivered another crunching left hook high on Dye's cheek, splitting the eyelid and skin below it.

Dye's knees gave way and he started to fall.

Grainger bent low and let loose with a vicious right uppercut that sent Dye flying backward, into a screen and then the wall. When Dye's back hit the wall he lurched forward, falling face first. He was unconscious before he hit the floor.

Grainger took a couple of deep breaths and turned around. He looked into a sea of wide eyes and open mouths.

"Where I come from," he said, "men do not hit women. I am sorry for spoiling your party. Please excuse me."

He bowed low and strode toward the door.

A short time later, Grainger returned to the Izumi Hotel for his date with Julie.

Mama-san eyed Grainger when he entered the bar.

"Ah, Ken-san," she said. "Good you are here. If you no come, Julie get sick, will not work. We know why. She will soon leave with you, yes?"

"Yes, Mama-san, but I will talk to you about that tomorrow," Grainger said. "Tonight we go out for dinner again, but I pay. We will come back later."

"Wakarimasu" (I understand), she said, as she nodded.

Julie came down the stairs smiling at Grainger.

God, she's beautiful, he thought, *I didn't know I could feel this way about anyone.*

He kissed her, gently cupping her cheeks in his hands. As she reached up to embrace him, she noticed that his knuckles were bruised and cut.

"What?" she said, loudly. "What happened?" Her face contorted with wrinkles and a pained look. "Are you all right?"

"I'm fine," he said. "I had an argument with someone. It's okay, it's all over. I'm not hurt, it's really nothing."

"Please don't get hurt," she said. "Let me get something for your hands."

She ignored his protests and got some ointment that she spread on Grainger's bruised knuckles.

She shook her head and held onto his right arm as they left.

The White Cloud restaurant was on a hillside overlooking Sasebo Harbor. Its distance from town and secluded location discouraged visits by transient military personnel. It had a number of private dining rooms. Most of them were small and intimate, giving the diners a degree of privacy not normally available.

Julie held Grainger's arm tightly as the hostess escorted them to a private room.

"I love to have a special time with my man," she said.

They were interrupted by the waitress who bowed, then kneeled and placed a pot of green tea and two cups on the low table.

"Would you like to order something to drink now?" she asked.

"We'll order in a few minutes," Grainger said, and turned to Julie.

"I think about you all the time."

"Me too," she said softly, covering his hand with hers.

"Today I rented the small house we talked about," Grainger said. "Did you talk to mama-san? Will there be any problems with your moving?"

"I talked to her," Julie said. "I find out for the first time she does not have papers for me as she does for other girls. Mama-san pays fathers of some girls who work at house. They must stay for five years or there is a lot of trouble. Girls at the house told me if mama-san has no paper there will be no trouble if I go.

"My uncle was very angry at my aunt when she sent me to the house. When my mother died, my aunt said she would take care of me, but I already tell you she said she had no more money for me. She wanted money from mama-san, but my uncle got very angry and said 'No.' He said if she do this he would find new wife. He said I must be free to go whenever I want. He is a good man I think, but my aunt, ugh, number 10."

"That means you can leave right now?" Grainger asked.

"Yes," Julie said.

"That's wonderful," Grainger said.

Julie nodded.

"Mama-san say American soldiers do not marry up with working girls. She say when you go home, I can come back to her house. But I don't want to. If you go, I will find another job, not in a house."

Grainger bit his lower lip.

"Julie," he said, "right now, I want to be with you more than anything else. I think I want to marry you. We can try living together and see how it goes. What I do know is that I don't want you to be hurt, especially like your mother was."

She put her hand to his mouth and slowly shook her head.

"Ken-san," she whispered, "I just want to be with you. I can wait. Maybe someday we can talk about getting married. I'm not asking for anything, except you just love only me while we're together." She smiled coyly, "Right now, my clothes are all packed."

"There's something else," Grainger said. "I talked to a fellow I know at the port. You remember the one I said had the warehouses and a lot of Japanese women working for him?"

She nodded.

"He said he will give you a job as a file clerk. He has a man who will train you, teach you what to do. It will be a good job. You can get good experience so you never have to go back to mama-san's house."

Julie's eyes flooded with tears.

"I never believe I find someone as good as you."

Grainger swallowed hard.

"You understand," he said, "I must keep my room at the BOQ so I can do my job. But I will be with you every night that I can."

Julie sobbed and smiled through her tears as they embraced.

"I got you a new dictionary today," Grainger said. "It's got both English to Japanese and Japanese to English, along with Japanese definitions."

"I am learning quickly," Julie said. "I love your eyes. I love your nose. I love your mouth. I love your ..."

She lowered her eyes and smiled shyly.

"You know," she said in a whisper and placed her hand on his thigh.

"I think it's time for us to leave," he said.

"We have to eat," she said laughing. "My man needs good food."

The next morning Grainger got a truck from the motor pool. He drove to the storage shed near the radio station and picked up two 100-pound sacks of rice and several cases of five-in-one rations. He also picked up a set of navigation charts and an American flag wrapped in plastic. He then drove to the main dock at the Port of Sasebo. The Korean conscripts, along with a tough-looking American sergeant wearing a CIB and jump wings, were waiting for him at the dock. They got on the truck and drove to Smuggler's Gulch.

One of the Koreans made a face at the sacks of American rice as they were off-loading the gear.

"American rice," he sneered and held his nose. "No good. Japanese rice, number one. You no got Japanese rice?"

"I got what you see," Grainger said. "You no like American rice, don't take."

The Korean looked down at the ground and shook his head. He bent over, lifted the sack of rice to his shoulder and carried it to the first boat where he loaded it in the cargo hold.

"Don't mind him, Captain," the American sergeant said. "He's always bitching that American rice is lousy. I notice he never skips a meal if that's all we got. These guys are spoiled. Over in our compound we buy Japanese rice by the ton. He's okay. I've been on three raids with him and he does what he's told. That's more than a lot of them."

"Where do you fit in all this?" Grainger asked.

"I'm with the 8240th Detachment in Korea, Colonel Cunningham's outfit," he said. "We use these boats for guerrilla operations on both coasts. The crews come mainly from the refugee camps. I guess it beats sittin' on your ass all day. They're screened by the Korean CIA. It's a no-bullshit screening I can tell you. If any of them take off over there and are caught by the KCIA, they're dead.

"We also use the boats to patrol for tactical intelligence. Whenever we can, we help downed pilots in escape and evasion. It's a kinda loose operation. You're not going to find the same discipline you get in a regular outfit, not even close. I volunteered because I hope to sign on with the CIA when this war's over."

One of the Koreans, wearing sergeant chevrons, tapped the American sergeant on the shoulder and spoke rapidly, pointing back to the boats.

"My engineer tells me," the sergeant said, "that we've got some engine trouble. He says he can fix it, but we'll have to lay over tonight and leave early in the morning."

"That's bullshit, Sergeant," Grainger said. "We brought those boats in here yesterday and there wasn't a damn thing wrong with them."

"I'm no engineer, Captain. If I don't agree we have to lay over so he can work on it, he'll probably fuck it up real good and it'll take a week to get it fixed."

"Where are they gonna stay?" Grainger asked.

"Right here," the sergeant said, "in that building or on the boat. They've all got sleeping bags in their rucksacks. This happens all the time. Some of these guys have got relatives around here and they like to get out for a visit. They'll get back on time."

"What if some of these guys take off?" Grainger asked.

"It has happened," the sergeant said, "but rarely. I stay here with them. I let a couple of them go for a visit the last time I was here. They both showed up the next day."

"I don't like it," Grainger said. "Doutter never mentioned this. Are you sure he went along with what you're saying?"

"Yes, sir," he said, "more than once. It'll be okay. We'll be gone first thing in the morning."

"I'll be here in the morning, too," Grainger said. "I'll bring one of the engineers off a PT boat to check things out. I don't want any more engine problems."

Grainger went back to his office and called Perkins' office.

"Lieutenant Grippa, sir," the voice said.

"Is Major Perkins there? This is Grainger in Sasebo."

"No, Captain," Grippa said. "He's at a meeting with Mr. Church. Can I help?"

"Tell him we had some engine trouble with one of the boats," Grainger said. "The crews will lay over tonight and leave first thing in the morning."

"I'll tell him, Captain," Grippa said. "Doesn't sound too serious. I heard about it happening before. The major gets upset, but as long as no one takes off he's all right."

Grainger could hear the dull putt-putt of the flathead engine as he approached Smuggler's Gulch the following morning at 0530. The sergeant was grim-faced when Grainger drove up to the corrugated tin building.

"What's the problem?" Grainger asked.

"Four of our people took off last night," the sergeant said.

"You mean they're late checking in?" Grainger asked.

"No, sir," the sergeant said, "they took off with all their gear and some of the five-in-ones."

"Has this happened before?" Grainger asked.

"Actually, yes, sir," he said. " Couple of times I lost one, once I lost two, but never four."

"What do you usually do?" Grainger asked.

"Well, Captain Doutter would handle it. I'm not sure what he did. Guess he notified the police," the sergeant said.

"Are you sure?" asked Grainger.

"No, sir, I'm not," the sergeant answered.

"Do you have an engineer? Can you or someone navigate? Can you get these boats back to Pusan?"

"Oh, yes, sir. I have someone who can drive the boat, and I can navigate. I made this particular trip eight times now. Lost my honcho, though, the guy with the bad attitude. He has been sounding off more than usual lately. Shoulda tied him to that post over there."

"Before you go, I want a list of the people who came over here," Grainger said, "and I want you to check off those who took off. If you can add anything by way of description, do that, too."

The sergeant nodded. He sat down and made a copy of the roster he had in his field jacket and added some additional notes.

"If there's nothing else," Grainger said, "you guys take off and smooth sailing."

"Yes, sir, and thanks. Sorry about the snafu," the sergeant said.

Grainger watched the boats round the bend and sail toward the open sea.

Damn, he thought, *now I get to call Perkins. This will not be a good day.*

"What do you mean you lost four men last night?" Perkins roared. "How is that possible? Damn. And what the hell happened to Dye? Some Japanese guy dropped him off at the Camp Sasebo hospital all beat to shit. He says he got mugged by three guys."

"If that's his story," Grainger said, "he can tell it however he wants."

"I can't believe you let those Koreans get away," Perkins said. "The first time you're asked to do anything and you screw it up."

"I understand it has happened before," Grainger said.

"We never lost four before," Perkins said.

"Is there anyone down here I'm supposed to notify?" Grainger asked.

"Absolutely not!" Perkins shouted again. "You just let four illegal aliens loose in someone else's country? You don't advertise that kind of information. Japanese immigration will file an official protest. You don't say anything. I'll do what I can from here. Is that clear?"

"That's clear, Major," Grainger said.

"And the next time you call with this kind of information, use the secure phone. You know they have one at the Camp Sasebo Headquarters. Next time use it."

Perkins slammed down the receiver before Grainger could respond.

Grainger sat thinking for a few minutes. He remembered Doutter's admonition about getting some help if things turned to manure and he remembered Roberto Salencio at the CIC office. He made his call.

"Major Salencio," Grainger said. "We haven't met yet; I took over Jerry Doutter's job here in Sasebo. Jerry said that if things start to unravel I could get some unofficial guidance. Is that possible?"

"Yes, it is, Captain," Salencio said. "Jerry did call and told me something about your being assigned down here. I also know Major Perkins. Is, uh, he the source of your little problem?"

"In a way," Grainger said. "That's part of it. Are you available now for a visit?"

"I'll be here," Salencio said.

Major Salencio stood when Grainger entered his office. They shook hands and Salencio motioned to his small conference table.

"Let's start with you calling me Antonio," he said. "Jerry and I were good friends and I remember when he had that same edge in his voice. You want to keep this off the record, right?"

Grainger nodded and smiled.

"Thanks," he said. "We had a situation last night in our small boat operation. Four of the Koreans, part of the crews sent over here to sail the boats back to Pusan, took off. Major Perkins is upset, to put it mildly, and I need some guidance."

"I assume Major Perkins did not suggest you seek my advice," Salencio said.

"Just the opposite," Grainger said with a wry smile.

"I thought not," Salencio said. "He really doesn't like to talk with anyone except the CIA. He and Art Church are really good buddies. That's not a secret in the Intelligence community. Do you have the names of the ones who took off?"

Grainger nodded and handed Salencio a list with names and physical descriptions.

"This'll help," Salencio said. "We can get this to the right people in the police department. They'll send out an APB, All Points Bulletin; the term's a little dated, but you get the idea. The word goes out that these guys are illegal aliens and wanted in connection with criminal activity. Once the Koreans have spent a few days in a Japanese jail, or 'monkey-house,' as they call it, they'll be begging to be deported."

He hesitated.

"Jerry told me you weren't Perkins' first choice for the job. If it had been an Intelligence job, I would have agreed, but this is a liaison thing. There's no Intelligence collection effort involved. Did Jerry brief you on that agent insertion operation he was so worried about?"

"Not really," Grainger replied. "I'm surprised he mentioned it to you. It's supposed to be so top secret he couldn't tell me about it. He really never got the chance. He hoped it wouldn't happen."

Grainger decided not to mention the file and got another surprise from Salencio.

"So you never read the file?" Salencio asked.

"No," Grainger said. "I didn't, did you?"

"Nice going," Salencio said. "I'll bet with the proper training you would make a good Intelligence officer. No, as a matter of fact I have not read it, but I do know the general idea is to get agents into China," Salencio said. "Frankly, I didn't agree with Jerry. I'm not sure why he thinks it's bizarre. I agree with the concept. We have to continue trying to get agents into China.

"What I do not agree with," Salencio continued, "is having the Far East Command Liaison Group involved in the operation, running some kind of interference for the CIA.

It's completely beyond the charter of your Group. The Group should never be listed as the primary agency for the mission. That really is bizarre. That's probably Fellinger's idea to protect Church in case the thing goes sour. Stick it to an Army officer."

Grainger shifted uncomfortably.

"I'm getting the feeling that everyone knows more about this than I do."

"Just go slow and watch your rear. Perkins is a very ambitious guy. He's supposed to be some kind of self-appointed expert in unconventional warfare. I'm not sure how he got to be an expert. And I don't know if he is, but I do know that when it's his game there are only his rules. Don't count on him playing fair."

"Well," Grainger said, "I just intend to do my job to the best of my ability, finish my tour, and go home. I really don't give a damn about any of the office politics or whatever it's called."

"It's called empire building," Salencio said. "I knew a guy like Perkins in the Pentagon. He was mean and dumb and that made him dangerous, but more importantly he had some powerful friends, just like Perkins.

"I stopped the guy at the Pentagon, but his mentors saw to it that the youngest major in the U.S. Army would probably retire as the oldest."

Salencio smiled ruefully.

"You have one thing going for you that I don't have," Salencio said. "Your record in combat is the kind that opens assignment doors and puts you on a fast track. Right now you're on a siding, like they do with railroad cars that are not in use. I understand you're Regular Army so my advice is for you to get back to the real Army as fast as you can. The Far East Command Liaison Group that Perkins is involved in isn't the real Army. If you plan on spending any time in the Army, you should know that assignments with unconventional warfare organizations will hurt you badly in the conventional Army. Our Army is very conventional."

"I've already got some guidance along those lines," Grainger said. "Right now I'm not sure what I'm going to do. I may even get out and go back to school and complete my education. In the meantime ..."

"Does this have anything to do with a certain Japanese national, named Julie?" Salencio asked.

"No secrets in a small town," Grainger said, "are there?"

"Not exactly," Salencio said. "You really haven't been sneaking around, you know. I am supposed to know what's happening in this area. In the meantime, keep a journal or a diary, some kind of record of everything that happens in this assignment. Write down everything you do. Then pray you'll never have to use it." ✦

NINE

The intercom on Major Perkins' desk buzzed.

"Perkins," he said.

"Sir, this is Lieutenant Grippa. Colonel Kim's on the telephone. He says he needs to talk to you. I told him you were getting ready to go into a meeting, but he said it was urgent."

Perkins switched off the intercom and picked up the telephone.

"Good morning, Colonel Kim, are you calling from Korea?"

"No," Kim replied. "I'm back in Tokyo. Art Church called and said we have to get together. He mentioned some bad news. Do you have any idea what it is?"

"No," Perkins said. "He hasn't called me. I guess I should expect to hear from him."

"Hmmm," Kim mused. "We'll find out soon enough. By the way, I understand your war hero in Sasebo had some of his chickens fly away from the coop."

Perkins looked toward his office door, then lowered his voice.

"I thought only two were supposed to leave."

"I owed my uncle a favor," Kim said, laughing. "You know how it is. Besides, what difference does it make? Is Colonel Beane now less impressed with the young captain?"

"That part worked out just like it was supposed to. The look on Beane's face when I told him about the mass exodus at Smuggler's Gulch made me feel better than I have in weeks. He even mentioned that it may be time for him to retire. He's right about that. The old bastard is living in the Stone Age. One more screw-up by Grainger and I can ship him up to Hokkaido where he'll be running up and down the hills, ass-deep in snow."

"I told you I'd take care of things," Kim said. "You have to learn to trust me. Art should call you since he said something about getting together later in the day. If he gets things worked out and we don't meet, I still want to have dinner with you tonight."

"Okay," Perkins said. "I don't have anything planned, but in the future it will help if I know when you're in town."

There was a knock on Perkins' office door.

"Yes," he shouted, "what is it?"

"Sir," Lieutenant Grippa said, "I didn't want to bother you, but your intercom was off and Mr. Church called. He asked that you call him back on his private line."

"Perkins?" Church said when he answered the phone.

"Yes, Art, what's up?"

"We seem to have sprung a leak in a certain ship," he said. "We need to talk about it. Can you come over this afternoon?"

"Yes," Perkins said, "Kim just called and said you had a problem. I can get over there, but it's going to be late, like about 1500."

"See you then," Church said.

Perkins frowned as Church hung up.

114

The office of the CIA Station Chief in Tokyo was on the 14th floor of the Wanishio Building. The elevator was rigged to stop at a security desk on the 12th floor before being allowed to proceed.

Church was at his desk when his secretary ushered in Perkins. Colonel Kim, already seated in a pale-blue wing chair, barely looked at Perkins as he entered. Church remained seated and pointed to an empty chair.

"We've got a serious problem," he began. "It seems that one of the four-man team of agents we've scheduled for the *Kochi Maru* may not be who he says he is. Worse than that, it now seems quite possible that the bastard's a double agent. We don't have definitive proof now, but I will have it in a very few days."

He handed Perkins a picture of a Chinese man in a suit and tie. From the angle of the subject, it was evident that someone took his picture without his knowledge or consent. The print was enlarged to the point that it was grainy.

"I got this 8 x 10 yesterday," Church said. "Look on the back."

Perkins turned the picture over and read aloud, "Sooman Ming, Shanghai waterfront area, 11 January 51. Chinese Army Intel."

Church then handed Perkins a 5 x 7 photograph. The two men did resemble one another. The hairlines were similar, and they both had narrow chins and flat noses.

"This," Church said, pointing to the 5 x 7, "is Yosh Chen. He's one of the four agents now waiting in Sasebo for the *Kochi Maru* to arrive from Korea. Based upon our interviews we selected him to head our little delegation going to Shanghai. In one of the vetting sessions, he swore he hadn't been back to his home in Shanghai since the Korean War started."

Perkins inhaled sharply at the implications of Church's revelation.

"Are you sure?" Perkins asked. "Are you sure it's the same guy and that he's one of theirs?"

"We're pretty damn sure," Church replied. "We had our photo interpretation guys study the two pictures. They gave it a very high probability and that scares me.

"Since the destination of the ship is Shanghai, we thought it was lucky that our smartest guy was from there. But, in our world, if it's too good to be true, it probably is not true."

"I say we kill the sonofabitch," Colonel Kim growled. "Give him to me for an hour, and I'll get his whole life history. Then I'll kill him."

"Dammit, Kim," Church said. "I told you it's not that easy. First of all, we're still doing some field checking on where he went to school in California. He couldn't be in Shanghai in January of '51 and going to school in Los Angeles at the same time. Also, and this is very important, we have an agent in place in Shanghai who could come under suspicion if Chen or Ming, or whatever the hell his name is, doesn't check in or winds up dead."

"How could that happen?" Perkins asked.

"Because, according to our source," Church said, "there are only two people who know that Chen or Ming, if that's his real name, was trained to infiltrate the CIA. And only those two know that he landed an assignment that puts him on the *Kochi Maru*. If his cover is blown now it could put suspicion on our source and we simply can't have that."

"He could be run over by a car or a train," Kim said. "Accidents happen all of the time."

"I can't take the chance of losing our asset in Shanghai," Church said. "It could just be that the guy is a look-alike and not this Ming fellow. I'm not going to order that Chen or Ming be terminated until I get solid proof that he's one of their guys.

"Even then, I want it set up so that it looks totally accidental. Our guy over there has to be protected. He's been there a long time and is just now starting to pay dividends. A bird in the hand is a helluva lot more valuable than four in the bush."

"Do the other three all check out?" Kim asked.

"Yeah," Church said. "There's no question about any of them. Chen is the only question mark. The problem is I have to assume they know our ship is the *Kochi Maru*."

"Frankly," Perkins said, "I like Kim's idea. Let Kim and his people work him over."

"It may come to that," Church said. "I hope it doesn't. We still have a little time before the mission is supposed to start. We'll delay as long as possible. Right now Fellinger down at Atsugi thinks we should abort the whole plan."

"Why not yank Chen off the ship and just send the others?" Perkins asked.

"We can't," Church replied. "I just told you they probably know the name of the ship. Besides, Chen, as the leader, knows stuff the other guys haven't been told. He also is supposed to have some contacts in Shanghai the other three don't. They would just stumble around and get picked up. If Chen is really theirs and the ship shows up without him, they'll be on the lookout for our three guys. If Chen doesn't go, for whatever reason, we abort the whole operation."

"Besides," Perkins added, "if Kim and his people work this guy over, and he turns out to be on our side, he wouldn't be any good as an agent any more."

Church resisted the impulse to raise his eyebrows to see if Perkins was serious, but a small frown appeared.

"What can I say?" he said. "I don't control these things. The guy in Shanghai belongs to the Deputy Director of Central Intelligence. He helped get him in place more than 10 years ago and is still very interested in what happens to him. I was told 'hands off.' I had to get special clearance to tell you as much as I have. Hell, Temp, you know about the 'need to know' rule. Just because you got clearance doesn't mean you're in on everything.

"Don't forget," Church added, "you've got something else riding on this. You remember what Fellinger said at Atsugi when we went to get the money for scrap metal."

Perkins walked over to the coffee urn, filled his cup, then turned to face Church.

"Yeah, I remember he seemed to be pissed off about everything, from Kim's pistol to the turnaround time for processing scrap metal."

"He didn't get that high without becoming an expert at covering his ass," Church said. "That was just vintage Fellinger. I remember his words very well, 'Let the record show that Major Perkins just walked the plank.' He was relying upon the due diligence of the Liaison Group when he gave his support for the mission."

"How in hell can he blame me?" Perkins whined. "I had no way of knowing that one of your agents was going to turn out to be a double."

"Maybe he isn't," Church said. "There's no way any of us know right now. I just don't want anything getting back to Colonel Beane that his Group was supporting one of our covert jobs that you didn't fully brief him on and that it turned sour because we discovered a double agent. In the meantime, this thing isn't a failure yet, so let's let the process work its way out."

Colonel Kim shook his head and pounded the arm of his chair with his fist.

"We can clean up this whole mess by getting rid of all of them," he said. "Sanction the whole lot. My people will go on board and take care of the problem."

"Damn, Kim," Church said. "I've got three trustworthy Chinese agents on that ship. I need them. If we have to abort, we'll find some other way to get them into China, in a different way. This doesn't queer the whole deal."

Colonel Kim exhaled loudly.

"Sometimes, Art," he said, "you complicate things needlessly."

"This is not complicated," Church said. "There is simply one small problem that has to be taken care of, and it will be. The *Kochi Maru* is due in Sasebo tomorrow. It will take a couple of days to load the scrap metal. After that, the Navy made it clear that they don't want that old freighter hanging around. I've made arrangements for it to lay over at Nagasaki. That's a civilian port and there won't be any questions about a freighter being anchored there. Kim, you can tell the captain that he's going to Nagasaki to wait for some additional cargo you want to load, spare parts or some damned thing."

Kim nodded.

"Just make sure he knows he is not to move one inch out of Nagasaki without your personal say-so."

"I will be there in person," Kim said. "The ship will stay there until you finish your investigation."

"You know," Perkins said, "if this operation doesn't go, we can still sell the scrap metal and use the money to infiltrate agents in another way."

"I like the way you think, Major," Kim said, smiling. "You must have some Korean blood in you."

"Nice try," Church said. "There's no way Fellinger will go for that. If this thing doesn't go, Fellinger will want us to dump the scrap metal and give him back his dough. Besides, we'd have to sell the stuff in Japan. Right now we have to assume that the *Kochi Maru* is a marked ship. If Chen belongs to them and that ship shows up in China without him they'll confiscate it for sure. How would that sit with your guys in Seoul, Kim?"

Colonel Kim shrugged.

"We know the Chinese are a bunch of thieving bastards," Kim said. "This would just prove it."

"The DDCI had a suggestion," Church said. "It was a little far out, but we can keep it in mind. If it ever got to the point where the shit was about to hit the fan, we do have the capability for radical surgery.

"In an absolutely worst-case scenario we could talk to some of my Navy friends on board the *Dixie* in Sasebo. They could have an Underwater Demolition Team drop that baby right in the harbor."

"How could you do that?" Perkins asked.

"Simple," Church said. "We just tell them that we have absolutely reliable sources who informed us that the captain of the *Kochi Maru*, Chung Tuwan, is a known Korean smuggler. He's a renegade and a gunrunner. We just learned that he has two holds full of weapons and ammunition. We don't know where he got them, we just know he's going to sell them to China."

"How are we supposed to know that's his cargo and destination?" Perkins asked.

"That's not difficult," Church said. "We'll just say that he got drunk and talked to some of our people in Sasebo. We got an agent on board and confirmed the story."

Kim stood up, adjusted his starched fatigues over his patent leather boots, and began doing stretching exercises.

"Now you're on the right track, Art," Kim said. "Sometimes I think you worry too much. Tuwan's third mate, Park Sun, told his girlfriend in Pusan where they were going. She happens to work for me and she will say whatever I tell her to say. If you want a story about a bunch of guns being on the ship, she'll spread the word. Let's load some crates of guns on the ship."

"Good idea, Kim," Perkins said. "That might be necessary in case the Navy wants some kind of additional proof?"

"They may," Church said. "That's the tough part. We have to be very careful and not leave any kind of a paper trail. We could lose a lot of credibility on this."

"Don't worry about that," Kim said. "I like your idea about the demolition team. I was beginning to think you were getting a little soft, Art."

"Wait a minute," Church said. "I said this was the idea of the Deputy Director and it's only for an absolutely worst-case scenario. Personally, I don't care for the idea. Too many things can go wrong. But if we do blow it up, we don't say anything. We stay away. We don't claim salvage rights or anything. We just let the Japanese handle it. We don't know anything about it.

"By the way, I'll need a letter from you, Kim, saying that you fellows own the ship and let the captain haul cargo when you don't have a specific mission. You're as pissed off as we are that he would sell guns to the Chinese and you have no objections to the ship going down."

"We don't," Kim said. "Go ahead and do it."

"Dammit, Kim," Church said, "it isn't that simple. There's no way you're going to keep this thing local. The Navy guys are going to have to justify an operation like this to the Chief of Naval Operations. He's not going to make that decision and that means it'll wind up on the agenda of the Joint Chiefs of Staff, and I guarantee you the subject will not be put on the consent calendar.

"Don't forget, not only will you have bodies floating in the bay, you are taking the risk of collateral damage in the territorial waters of a sovereign nation. Shit. Just talking about it scares the piss out of me. Come to think of it, Kim, you probably shouldn't be visible in this operation."

"Why not?" Kim asked.

"Because Andy McConnell, the Navy captain who directs such operations, made some unflattering comments about you the other night when your name came up."

"I don't even know him," Kim said.

"Well, he knows you. He said you are one arrogant, ruthless sonofabitch. He wouldn't trust you as far as he could throw you by your tallywacker."

"I'm honored," Kim said. "I'll remember Captain McConnell if he ever comes over to Korea."

"What the hell does that mean?" Church asked.

"Nothing," Kim replied. "I'll just invite him to dinner to show him I can be a charming sonofabitch."

He laughed, but it was a mirthless laugh.

Church frowned and shook his head.

I wonder if Kim ever blew up in front of Church like he did with me, Perkins thought.

"The whole idea about blowing up the ship is crazy," Church said. "It would never work. Someone will recall that the ship pulled into Sasebo empty and they took on a cargo of scrap metal. That would blow the guns and ammunition story."

"Not necessarily," Perkins said, "if we do like Kim suggested and load some crates of guns on board in Nagasaki."

"Where are you going to get them?" Church said. "Am I the only one who knows how bizarre this sounds? Besides, what about survivors?"

"Leave those to me," Kim said. "I'm an expert on handling survivors."

"That's exactly what Captain McConnell meant," Church said.

"I'm serious," Kim said. "Any of these guys get picked up, they're going to talk about the cargo. Shit, a salvage team will confirm that there were no guns on board. That blows the whole scenario. The Japanese sure as hell aren't going to allow a Korean salvage operation in their backyard."

"I can help get the survivors out of there," Perkins interrupted. "I've got people in a liaison detachment in Sasebo. We've got PT boats that can get to Nagasaki. We load up the survivors and ship 'em back to Pusan."

"Oh yeah," Church said. "What makes you think that Japanese immigration officials are going to cooperate with you and turn over a bunch of Korean merchant seamen found floating in the bay at Nagasaki?"

"The chief of police in Nagasaki is well known to me," Kim replied. "I've been feeding him money for a long time. I believe I can talk him into giving us the survivors and save himself a lot of trouble with immigration officials. It's about time he earned his keep. I'll take care of the problem myself if he won't cooperate."

"I don't believe this," Church muttered.

"Art, I'm serious," Kim said. "Dead men don't talk. There's no one to say what the cargo was if there are no survivors. The stuff salvaged could be weapons and scrap metal."

"That's wishful thinking," Church said.

"Wait a minute," Perkins said. "If the ship is anchored in the outer harbor, it could take a while for them to get it salvaged. I would also imagine that if they blew the bottom out of the ship that stuff will be scattered all over hell's half acre. A salvage job just may not be economically feasible."

"This won't work," Church said. "What are we talking about? Right now I've got them scheduled to anchor in close. How do we change that and then blow up the ship and avoid accountability? I take back what I said earlier, this is unbelievably complicated. For Chen's sake, this better be a case of mistaken identity." ✦

TEN

While Perkins, Church, and Kim were considering their courses of action, a different assessment was going on back at the headquarters of the 8240th, Far East Command Liaison Group housed in the Mainichi Building.

Personnel assigned to work at that building, including those in FEC/LG, parked their cars in a fenced, but unguarded parking lot. It was an easy walk to the rear entrance where a security guard checked their ID badges. On this day, those entering through the rear door were being watched through a high-powered telescope from an adjacent office high-rise.

She was like a hunter stalking prey. She watched closely as civilian government workers and those in the military walked from their automobiles to the rear entry. Not only was her prey restricted to those in the military, she also confined her attention to men only.

There! Like a cat tensing before a strike, she rose partway from her chair. *Yes.* He was perfect.

She quickly flicked the telescope back to the old Chevrolet from which he emerged to make sure she could identify it later and then resumed her surveillance.

He was short, about 5'6," dark hair, built like a fireplug, carrying a large briefcase. What caught her attention was that his head never stopped swiveling left, then right, trolling for his own kind of game. Unlike the huntress who watched him, this fellow's selection process had a different criterion. He avoided looking at any of the men. His prey was strictly female.

If one could earn degrees for ogling, this young officer would have a doctorate. He directed his gaze to the lower half of each prey's anatomy. However, if she happened to turn and face him, he switched his focus to her chest. He virtually ignored facial characteristics.

Second Lieutenant Angelo Grippa loved being in the Army. He was on his own for the first time in his life, away from a doting mother in a single-parent family. He was too shy to communicate on a peer level despite his overwhelming interest in the opposite sex and spent his frustrating high school years without once mustering the courage to ask a female classmate for a date.

In college, he enrolled in the Reserve Officers Training Corps, hoping that the uniform would end the glacial stares he received when the idea of an after-class liaison was broached. He had a few minor successes among many dismal failures.

Grippa managed to escape a combat assignment after graduation with an ROTC Reserve commission and acceptance of a tour of active duty with the U.S. Army, owing to an assessment by Major Templeton Perkins that Grippa would be an ideal choice to fill the job of resident gofer for the Far East Command Liaison Group.

At first Grippa was terrified of the major. Then, he came to regard him as the father he never knew and the most brilliant Intelligence officer in the entire Army. Grippa began to manifest a similar kind of arrogance in dealing with enlisted personnel and anyone under his boss's control because of his favored position at the right hand of "God."

Grippa never had any money. He would tell you his love life was great in Japan, but the fact was his female companionship was all purchased. Consequently, the second half of each month saw him taking his meals at the officer's club where credit was extended to those using the dining facilities.

On this sunny afternoon, Grippa noticed a well-built blonde walking toward him when he left the Mainichi Building to get his car. He was mesmerized by the up and down movement of her blouse as she stepped jauntily along the blacktop.

Suddenly she stopped and looked down.

"Oh, no," she cried.

"What's the matter?" Grippa asked.

"Oh, look at that," she said, pointing to a deflated right rear tire.

She walked around to the flattened tire. As she bent over to examine it, her loose blouse fell open and confirmed Grippa's suspicion that she wasn't wearing a brassiere. She stayed in that position while Grippa feasted on the delectable sight.

It took a few moments for him to move his eyes to her face. She waited and rewarded him with a becoming smile. Grippa could not believe the good fortune that had placed her in such close proximity and in a seemingly vulnerable position.

"I've got a spare tire and a jack in my trunk," she said, "but I've never changed a tire before."

"I have," Grippa said.

"Oh, could you?" she asked.

Then she sighed.

"Yes … uh, yes, I could do it," he said, haltingly.

"Oh, what a dear man," she said.

She kissed him lightly on the cheek. Her breasts brushed along his right arm as she did so. She reached out with her left hand and grasped his right arm.

"Oh, what big muscles you have," she breathed.

Grippa was now completely tongue-tied.

It must be the uniform, he thought.

She opened the trunk and pointed to the spare tire sitting in plain view, unsecured and ready for mounting. The jack was also in the ready position. The signals would have jangled like fire alarms for any Intelligence officer in his right mind, but she knew this would not describe Grippa's state of mind.

"My name's Jane ... Jane Farnsworth," she said. "My father's in the import-export business. He travels all over the world. Right now he's flying back home to New York on business. I decided to stay here in Tokyo for a while to see the sights."

Grippa busied himself adjusting the jack. He didn't have a clue what to talk about.

This will have to be visual, Jane thought. *Oh, well, I have to start somewhere. He could lead me to bigger fish.*

She sighed again.

"Do you work in this building?" she asked, pointing to the Mainichi.

"Yes," he said.

"Oh, what do you do?" she asked casually.

"I work for Major Perkins."

"That sounds interesting. What does he do?"

"Well, our work is in Army Intelligence. I really can't talk about it."

"Oh, no, of course, I understand. I didn't mean to pry," she said. "Gee, you're not only handsome and very nice for helping me, you are also doing important work for our country. Thank you."

"You're welcome," he said.

Handsome? He thought. *I do remember reading that everyone has an ideal mate somewhere in the world, if he could only find her.*

127

"I wish I were not so helpless with mechanical things," she continued. "I think men just have a natural aptitude with cars and motors."

Grippa nodded and smiled.

Jane watched him as he struggled with the lug wrench. *This one is really* durak (stupid, dumb-ass), she thought. *I think I know how to put a little sand in his gut.*

She eased past him into the space between the cars where he was kneeling trying to get the lug nuts on the wheel loosened. She squatted, hiking her skirt above her knees. His eyes were riveted on her slim and muscular thighs. Perspiration began to form on his upper lip as he strained with the lug wrench.

"Oh, you're sweating," she said. "Here, let me dry you off." She stumbled and her legs parted for a brief second as she started to rise.

Oh, my God, he thought. *No panties. She's a real blonde.*

His concentration broke. The lug wrench slipped and came off the octagonal nut. Grippa fell back against the fender of his car.

It was not a severe blow, but the contact made him wince.

"Oh dear," she said. "Did you hurt yourself?"

"A little," he said.

"I feel so terrible," she said. "You're my Good Samaritan, and now you get hurt helping me."

"It's okay," he said. "I can finish."

"Well, the least I can do is take you to my apartment and let you get cleaned up. Maybe I could massage your back where it's hurt."

Visions of this angel leaning over him with her loose blouse, massaging his back, were enough to blot out all rational thinking about the improbability of this situation.

She once again kissed Grippa on the cheek when he finished changing the tire, this time pressing her body against his.

"Let's take my car," she suggested. "After you get cleaned up, I'll bring you back. I live very near here."

"That would be great," he said. "Major Perkins said he wouldn't be back today, so I don't have to be at the office."

She opened the passenger door of her sports car. He eased himself in and turned to watch her squeeze into the driver's seat. He smiled in appreciation as she hiked her skirt up to her crotch and got behind the wheel. He stared at her naked golden thighs as her foot pumped the clutch pedal when she shifted gears. He tried to lean his head forward for a better look and cracked his head on the windshield.

"It's a little tight in here," she said with a wink.

What happened at her apartment was as predictable as a falling object succumbing to Newton's Law. Step by agonizing step, Jane led Grippa to the unbelievable conclusion that she found him irresistible.

It was only his utter lack of experience that allowed him to accept that this beautiful and enthusiastic woman not only wanted him, but was practically a virgin as she described her "one and only" sexual experience many years ago at a summer camp.

He strutted with pride when she told him he was much bigger than the boy at camp, asking him to be gentle. Grippa marveled that she seemed game for anything and thrilled when she led him to her bed.

"Do what you want to do, do anything. You are wonderful."

He wasn't sure whether he should offer to pay her something when she was ready to drive him back. He had purchased every other sexual liaison he ever had. He looked around the apartment and realized that she was rich, or, at least, her father was. He decided that an offer of money would be misunderstood, especially if he offered too little; besides he had fixed her car.

"Did you say you lived here alone?" he asked.

"No," she said. "My father lives here, too. But, as I said, he's on his way home. He'll be gone for at least another two weeks. I hope I can see you again before he gets back."

"I'm free anytime," he said. "How about tomorrow night?"

"That will be fine," she said. "Just in case, why don't you give me a call first and make sure I'm home before you come over."

Later, soaking in a tub of the hottest water she could stand, Jane reflected on the sacrifices she made for her country.

Arkady, General, Sir, your little Milaya, Svetlana, is singing her legend like a songbird. What I am going through for Mother Russia is beyond value. When this assignment is over, you better buy me the finest sable coat in all of Russia, or I'll cut off your balls and defect to England.

She smiled, added bath salts, and turned on the hot water faucet.

During their third liaison Grippa began to talk about a Korean freighter going to China. The combination of cognac, platitudes, praise, and questions about the important work he was doing finally produced information that Svetlana felt might be of Intelligence value. Grippa told her that Major Perkins was very happy when they got the money for scrap metal. This would help them do important things in China. The result would mean promotions for everyone.

I better radio that information to General Petrovsky's headquarters tonight, just in case it's too important to hold until the end of the week. What did he say was the name of that ship? Oh, yes, the Kochi Maru.

Her mind drifted to the coming dinner she had promised Grippa when he returned that evening.

Oh, shit, she thought, as she took her ritual bath and sank under the layers of bubbles. ✦

ELEVEN
Moscow, Russia

Major General Arkady Petrovsky was in an expansive mood. The head of the Soviet General Staff's Far East Intelligence Department had just received a radio report from his top graduate from the Illegals Training Program.

Petrovsky had been a regimental commander for eight years with the 48th Infantry Division. In 1931, he transferred to the Department of Combat Training of the General Staff and helped to develop its training doctrine. He joined the Communist Party that same year. From 1936 to 1938 he attended the newly formed General Staff Academy and became the protégé of Marshal Shapnikov, who happened to be his father-in-law.

During World War II, Petrovsky was one of only 11 Soviet commanders to receive the diamond-encrusted Order of Victory. He earned two Crosses of St. George and was twice awarded a Hero of the Soviet Union medal.

Petrovsky was a warrior in the Russian military tradition. He earned his early promotions in the field the hard way—in combat—despite his obvious political connections. Multiple scars attested to his tenacity, courage, and well-honed survival instincts. One scar, livid and dark red in the cold of winter, extended from the center of his left ear, bisecting his cheek, to the corner of his upper lip. It was a souvenir from a vicious bayonet attack during a rear-guard holding action. A German sergeant, anxious to bag a Russian officer, swung his bayonet wildly, opening Petrovsky's cheek moments before he was practically decapitated by the Russian officer's saber. The scar gave him a ferocious appearance and contributed to his stature and reputation as a no-nonsense commander. His favorite, oft-used expression adopted by many of his subordinates, was *"ne mash khuem pered mordoi"* (stop dragging your penis in front of my face).

On this day, in his Moscow office, with his feet propped on his desk, he roared with laughter as he discussed Svetlana's exploits with his Chief Deputy, Colonel Vasily Proloff.

"I feel sorry for the Americans," Petrovsky proclaimed. "Little pussy cat Svetlana has landed in Tokyo. She's already hooked one fish, a little one to be sure, but he's with that Liaison Group that has the partisans in Korea. They killed a lot of our boys at that radar station on the east coast. I told her to start there and see what she could do.

"We'll stay with the Liaison Group until we find out what they're up to. Then Svetlana can get herself a colonel or maybe something better.

"The Americans apparently have something going with a Korean freighter, the *Kochi Maru*. We got a report it's in Sasebo now, being loaded with scrap metal. Our agent reported it because the Americans usually don't allow civilian ships to dock in their area. He said the ship looks like it's at least 30 years old.

"Svetlana doesn't know the tie-in yet, but she thinks it's connected to a plan to get agents into China."

"She's pretty damn smart," Proloff said. "Does she have any idea how many agents?"

"No, but she's smart enough to figure out that it has to be something like that. She didn't give a number, but she'll try to find out.

"Tell Olga to get my driver," Petrovsky continued. "I want to shoot some skeet this afternoon. Contact Fyodor in Sasebo, see if he can get any more information about this ship ... *Kochi Maru.*

"I don't get the Army's involvement in this thing. See if she can find out why they're involved. I'd be very interested to know. My nose smells CIA. The Army doesn't infiltrate agents. This has got to be a CIA operation."

He paused, frowned, and stared at Proloff.

"She says the lieutenant talked about them getting the money to buy scrap metal. Where did the money come from? Let's assume the money came from the CIA, but why the hell would they give it to the Army to buy the scrap? Something's wrong here."

Petrovsky shrugged.

"They got the money from Fellinger, at Atsugi," he smiled. "They got enough money to buy anything they want. But the Army? I think her little lieutenant's confused. It's the CIA, I'll bet a case of vodka. Have Fyodor check the registration of the ship. With that name it could be Japanese, but I'll bet it's not. It's probably Liberian or some damn thing. Have him follow some of the crew to the bars and see if he can get anything."

The following afternoon, Grainger looked up in surprise when Jerry Doutter opened the door of his office.

"I didn't think Perkins was going to let me come back for my stuff," Doutter said. "I almost called to ask you to put it in a duffel bag and ship it for me."

"How long have you got?" Grainger asked.

"Perkins gave me one day. I'm scheduled to go back on the PBY tomorrow afternoon."

"Is he still upset about the Koreans taking off?" Grainger asked.

"Are you kidding?" Doutter asked. "He's thrilled. He's telling everyone who'll listen that he knew you were a screw-up from the day you walked into the place. He's happy about them taking off. Edna told me he ran up to complain to the old man right after your call. He griped again that you shouldn't have been selected. I reminded him that guys took off on me too, but he wasn't interested. It was like talking to a wall."

"What are you going to do when you get back home?" Grainger asked.

"Go back to the Sheriff's Department. One thing I ain't gonna do is get back in the Reserves. First, War II and now Korea. I'm a two-time loser. My wife would shoot me if I got into a Reserve outfit."

"What's wrong with the Reserves?" Grainger asked.

"Well, just before Korea they put an Army Reserve Military Police unit in Fresno. All the guys in the Fresno PD and the Sheriff's office joined. No way we would ever get activated, right? Wrong. Our unit was among the first re-called to active duty. They pulled me out for the Liaison Group because I'd served in 'Wild Bill' Donovan's Office of Strategic Services."

"What did you do in the OSS?" Grainger asked.

"Some behind-the-lines stuff in Europe, but nothing as bad as Korea. It's hard to do behind-the-lines stuff when you got round eyes and you're sitting on a little island with no room to maneuver. Mostly we hid from the North Koreans. If they caught us, we'd be lucky to just get a bullet. We hid in caves during the day, lived like moles on this island.

"Once a month one of the detachment's boats would take us off the island to a destroyer sitting just over the horizon. I lived for that monthly hot bath."

"Was Perkins with the Group then?" Grainger asked.

"Yeah, but he was always back at headquarters. He never did any time on the islands. He joined about halfway through my tour. I was already scheduled to get the detachment before he got there. At least he couldn't complain about my credentials. You just need to watch your ass, Ken. He's really got it in for you."

Doutter paused, deep in thought.

"You know, Perkins said something funny to me about one of the CIA guys getting disgusted and quitting. The guy apparently wrote some exposé letters to the *New York Times* about conditions here in Japan. He said the guy set out to tour Japan before he went home. They found him a week later with his head stoved in. Perkins laughed and said, 'Just because you're paranoid doesn't mean they're not out to get you.'"

"What the hell does that mean?" Grainger asked.

"I don't know," Doutter said. "I think he's seen too many war movies."

Later, as they drove to the hotel, Grainger decided to tell Doutter about his meeting with Salencio.

"I told him about the missing Koreans," he said.

"I don't blame you," Doutter said. "I kinda hinted around about *Kochi*, but I didn't let him read the file. I also told him about the guys who took off when I was here. We never did find the guys who jumped. Colonel Kim of the Korean CIA said they found two of them in Kobe. When I asked what happened, he said, 'They're still there, six feet under.' I don't know if it's true or not. Frankly I doubt it. That bastard's ruthless. He would proably find a way to have them work for him here in Japan.

"One other thing," Doutter said. "I'm supposed to bring back the *Kochi Maru* file. But, I'm gonna forget it. If anything comes up about that ship, read the file and then hide it. If that operation gets screwed up, Perkins will find a way to make you the fall guy and, Regular Army or not, it will kill your career." ✦

TWELVE
Nagasaki, Japan

It was Aki Nomura, the security guard at the Port of Nagasaki, who first noticed something amiss. A severe storm had kept him at home on his day off, and he answered the call to fill in for an ailing guard during the night shift.

The Chief of Security at the port was a little surprised when the normally compliant Nomura initially demurred.

"Why is it I get called first every time there's a problem?" Nomura grumbled.

He pinched the bridge of his nose and listened with his eyes closed as the Chief recounted that almost a third of his force was out with the flu.

"Okay, okay, I understand," Nomura said, "but I've got to catch a taxi. My car won't start and I can't get a mechanic until tomorrow. It's this damn storm."

He hung up and dialed the taxi dispatch number. The line was busy. After four unsuccessful attempts he slammed down the phone, pulled on his raincoat and stumbled down the narrow stairway of his apartment house on to the rainy street, all the while cursing the ailing port security officer.

Nomura's eyes stung from the bitter cold as he leaned his head forward into the icy wind. In his haste and anger, he forgot his rubber overshoes. By the time he slogged six blocks to the taxi station, his shoes squished with every step. When he reached the Port of Nagasaki he was soaked and in poor humor.

His lips puffed out in a pout as he hastily scribbled his name on the sign-in roster and barely nodded at the departing security guard. He walked downstairs to the employee's locker room and dialed his combination. After toweling off, he changed into a dry uniform and checked himself in the full-length mirror next to the bathroom entrance, frowning at the fact that his compact build and short stature gave him such a squat appearance.

He shuffled to the third-floor picture window in the operations room that fronted on the ships anchored in the harbor. He scanned the ships in the inner harbor, noticing that one of them had not turned on its deck lights. There was a light in the captain's cabin at the rear of the vessel. Glancing down at the mooring chart he made note of the ship's name, *Kochi Maru.*

No deck lights. That's bad seamanship. I remember that old freighter with the Korean flag; that's the one whose captain always stinks of kimchee. Why didn't they make him anchor in the outer harbor?

Nomura's eyes widened as lightning surged across the slate-gray sky, zigzagged in his direction, then darted to stab the earth near a copse of pine saplings across the harbor. Moments later he shivered uncontrollably as the deep rumble of distant thunder echoed across the water.

As Nomura fussed, a man in a black diver's wet suit crouched on the deck of the *Kochi Maru.* He had turned off the deck lights earlier and now moved duck-walk fashion along the starboard side of the sleeping old freighter. From time to time he paused, checking the dimly lighted bridge to be sure he was not observed. Then, easing over the side, he climbed down the anchor chain into the rippling harbor waters and swam away to a gently rising promontory jutting into the bay.

He reached the shore and struggled up the slippery slope. Crouching low he worked his way to a row of shrubs and changed into dry clothes from the waterproof oilskin bag slung over his shoulder. A dark-green military poncho provided some cover from the rain, which had slacked off considerably. Placing his wet suit in the oilskin bag, he eased past the *Glover House*, a closed memorial made famous by Puccini as the setting for his fictitious tale of Madam Butterfly. His canvas tennis shoes sank into the soft earth as he circled around the left side of the house, away from the light standard at the edge of the road. He scanned the driveway from behind a large oak tree and noted the absence of any vehicles or foot traffic. Once out of the shadows and on to the right side of the macadam road leading to Nagasaki, he stamped the mud off his shoes and was soon enveloped by the darkness.

Two hours later, three muffled explosions aboard the *Kochi Maru* rocked the harbor. The stern of the *Hideki Maru*, anchored nearby, lifted out of the water, turned, and smashed down 50 feet from its original mooring. Smaller vessels rolled and twisted in the raging waters, one nearly capsizing. Loose cargo slid across decks. Larger freighters bucked wildly as waves caused the flukes and crowns of their anchors to ball with mud.

Windows at the port administration building rattled. Two of them shattered. The pilot launch, tethered to the pier, was heaved over the dock by a five-foot wall of water. The resulting crash, as the boat smashed into the raised pilings, resounded throughout the harbor.

In the bowels of the stricken Korean freighter, the worst nightmare of seafaring men became a reality. Some were knocked unconscious by the explosive charges and drowned. Men in the engine compartment slammed against steel bulkheads and plunged brutally into the black rampaging water flooding the engine room. Crewmen struggled in vain and died in agony.

Three Chinese-Americans, wide-eyed with terror, crouched in a small room below decks fitted with four makeshift bunks. They watched in fear as their quarters flooded. Blankets were crammed into the top vent and the opening below their door, in a futile attempt to stem the flow of water.

One man clutched a small metal box to his chest as if it contained some miracle that could save his life. He was wrong. The men succumbed in their steel coffin choking, thrashing, sucking seawater.

The seismography at the University of Nagasaki recorded three sharp jolts comparable to small earthquakes. The clock attached to it registered the time as 0259.

Eyewitnesses reported a large cloud of smoke hovering over the stricken ship. They expressed surprise that there were no flames.

The *Kochi Maru*, loaded with scrap metal, took a scant eight minutes to settle to the bottom of Nagasaki harbor.

"It was like a giant bass drum. Boom, boom, boom, kinda hollow sounding," a merchant seaman said later. "I thought our main mast gave way and was bouncing on the deck."

Nomura placed an emergency telephone call to his superior 15 minutes after the incident. He described the explosions as "rhythmic," and the sinking of the ship as "almost surgical."

The tips of two of the *Kochi Maru's* masts rested just below the surface of the water, hovering like grave markers. Twelve bodies, along with flotsam, danced in the swirling waters. The plaintive wail of police sirens had older residents recalling wartime air raid warnings. They shuddered at the memories. ✦

THIRTEEN

Sasebo, Japan

Grainger had just left Julie in their apartment and gone back to the BOQ when there was an insistent knocking at his door. He glanced at the clock on the nightstand. It was 0500. He opened the door.

"Sir, I'm Lieutenant Silva, Duty Officer over at Camp Sasebo Headquarters," the fresh-faced shavetail said. "I've been checking your room every 15 minutes for the past hour. There's an emergency message for you. Major Perkins called from AFFE G-2 in Tokyo. He says the hotel people couldn't wake you up. He ordered me to keep trying until I got you. I'm supposed to tell you, 'Secure telephone, now.' He said it was a three-word message. He really seemed upset and had me repeat his words exactly."

"Okay, thanks, Silva. Don't worry about it, I got it." Grainger said.

Perkins answered on the second ring.

"Major Perkins," he said.

"Grainger, Major."

"We've got a problem," Perkins said. "I don't want to have to say this more than once, so listen carefully."

Grainger grabbed a notebook lying on top of the desk and began taking notes.

"No notes," Perkins said, as though he could see him. "This is top secret."

Grainger decided to ignore the admonition. The notes could be burned if not needed.

"We just had an operation go sour," Perkins began. "We hired a Korean ship captain who owned an old freighter, the *Kochi Maru*, to deliver a load of scrap metal to Shanghai. He could sell it and keep the money as long as he allowed four of our agents to sail as crewmen."

Grainger heard the alarm bells ringing with the words *Kochi Maru*.

"The Group hired him, sir?" Grainger asked.

"Never mind," Perkins said, "just listen. I said there were four agents. They're CIA, we're working with the Agency on this one. Now, goddamn it, don't interrupt me again."

Grainger scribbled rapidly: *CIA Operation went sour. Kochi Maru-Korean ship-4-Agents-Scrap metal to Shanghai-Agents: Crew members. Leave ship in Shanghai?*

Perkins hesitated.

"Okay, here's what happened. We're pretty damn sure our Korean captain got cold feet and sabotaged his own ship. There's no other possible explanation. Right now the ship is at the bottom of the harbor in Nagasaki."

"When did he blow up his ship?" Grainger asked.

"A couple of hours ago," Perkins said. "About 0300. We think there are survivors."

Grainger scribbled again: *Captain double-crosses-sabotages own ship. 0300-Nagasaki-Survivors. How did Perkins find out so fast?*

"Were we involved in a CIA operation, Major?" Grainger asked.

"We work on their projects all the time," Perkins said. "Look, Grainger, we're on a real short fuse here. We've got a major problem with survivors. I don't have time for a lot of bullshit questions. It's time you earned your pay. I've gotta have someone to take care of the damage control and you're appointed."

Perkins paused.

"Someone at the Port of Nagasaki called; the duty officer didn't get his name, but called me and gave me the message."

Grainger made a quick note: *How did Japanese duty officer at port know to call Perkins? That can't be top secret.*

"How did they know to call you at our headquarters?" Grainger asked.

"I have no idea," Perkins said. "We'll get that sorted out later. I called the Port of Nagasaki and they confirmed that a ship blew up in the harbor. They said it was the *Kochi Maru* and that there were survivors. That's our ship."

Grainger made another note: *Perkins-BS. These not TS notes.*

"What do you want me to do?" Grainger asked.

"You've got a pile of yen in your safe. Get it and get up to Nagasaki."

"Uniform or not?" Grainger asked.

"Go in uniform," Perkins said. "It gives you official status."

Nagasaki-uniform-yen-all ($5,000).

"When you get to Nagasaki, go directly to the Police Station and ask for Shiru Yamamoto. He's the chief. He's done work for us in the past. Talk to him in private. Tell him that the crew, those still alive, worked for us in Korea and we want to get them back there. We don't want any trouble or have to answer a lot of questions from Japanese immigration.

"Tell him the survivors are just stupid crew members. They don't know anything. Give him the yen, the whole bundle."

Police Chief Yamamoto police-5K-yen-get survivors.

"You drive up there in your jeep, you'll get there sooner. Send both of your PT boats. Tell CPO Michaels he's in charge of the two boats. We can trust him to keep his mouth shut. Tell Michaels to go right into the harbor, the main dock by the Port Headquarters. That's where you can meet him. Tell him to get back to Pusan ASAP."

Two PT boats-Michaels in charge-survivors to Pusan.

"Suppose the police chief won't go for it?" Grainger asked.

"He'll go for it," Perkins said. "If he gives you any trouble just tell him that Colonel Kim is in Nagasaki and will see him after the survivors are released. Be sure to say Colonel Kim. That and the yen are all the insurance you'll need."

"What if some of the survivors are badly injured and shouldn't be moved?" Grainger asked.

"I don't give a shit if they're unconscious. I want all living survivors on the PT boats. Damn, Grainger, I'm giving you a simple job to do. The whole thing is already greased. Get up there, now!"

"Major, I'll be there in about an hour and try to do what you want. When I get back I would appreciate being briefed on what's going on. You said the CIA is giving scrap metal to the Chinese who are killing our guys in Korea?"

"Someone with a lot more rank than you made that decision, Captain. Someone who understands the strategic Intelligence situation and has been doing it longer than you've been in the Army."

"I understand, Major, but I can't help thinking that it stinks. There had to be a better way to do what they wanted to do."

"I'm not interested in what you think, Grainger," Perkins said. "If you knew anything about Intelligence, you would know that there is always a good reason for covert operations. You have no idea what this operation is about or what's at stake. You're a square peg in a round hole. Just follow your orders. Did you think Colonel Beane was hiring you to take VIPs to the PX?"

"No, sir," Grainger said. "I thought I was to support our guerrilla operations in Korea. I'll do what you are ordering me to do, but I am requesting that you put these orders in writing. I believe I have a right to ask for that."

"Right?" Perkins stormed, "This is a classified operation. What makes you think you have any right to demand anything, Captain? I'm giving you a verbal order. For your information, you don't put top secret orders in writing. We're fighting a war. This is not a Sunday school."

"That's pretty obvious, Major," Grainger said. "I'm supposed to get people out of a hospital even if they are seriously injured and shouldn't be moved. I believe my request to have these orders in writing is reasonable."

"We'll argue about this later, Grainger. Right now I expect you to carry out the order you received. Is that clear? You're wasting valuable time."

"Is this something Doutter worked on?" Grainger asked.

Damn, Grainger thought, *why did I mention Doutter?*

Perkins' tone changed immediately.

"What are you talking about?" he asked. "Did he tell you anything about this operation?"

"Not in any detail, sir," Grainger said. "He did say he was concerned about an upcoming operation that he thought was poorly planned. He hoped it would not be carried out and used the word 'unbelievable.' What you're talking about now seems unbelievable, so I asked."

"I don't have the slightest idea what he was referring to," Perkins said. "No more questions. I want you to get to Nagasaki. Get there before the PT boats."

He hung up.

Grainger added a few more notes: *Get written orders-read classified document-ask to see Beane-Request transfer.*

He opened the safe and took out the bundle of yen. The money was under the tan envelope with the document that Doutter had told him to read and hide.

I wish I had time to read this right now, Grainger thought. *I'll read it when I get back. This really is unbelievable. I've got to get going. I should take this over to Salencio for safekeeping. Damn, I don't have time.*

Perkins' next call was to Art Church at his home in Washington Heights.

"I have to see you this morning, Art," Perkins said. "We may have a big problem on our hands."

"Can you give me an idea of what it is?" Church asked.

"Well," Perkins said, "it pertains to a certain ship that sprung a leak and to a person you once called a 'loose cannon.'"

"Oh, no, oh, shit," Church said. "Did it go down?"

"The bottom of the bay," Perkins said.

"That stupid SOB," Church said. "I was afraid he'd go off on his own. My office, one hour."

Perkins lowered his eyes when Church nodded at him in the outer office of his suite.

"You're sure it's Kim, right?" he asked as he led Perkins into his office and closed the door.

"Yes," Perkins said.

"How did you find out?" Church asked.

"He called me at home," Perkins said, "and told me there had just been a terrible accident. He laughed and said now there were no more problems."

"He's absolutely nuts," Church stormed.

Church flipped on the intercom switch. "Bring us some coffee, will you, Martha?" he said to his secretary.

Church stared at Perkins. "You know, this is just not possible," Church said. "How could he blow up the ship? We know why he would blow it up. Because he's a psycho. But how in the hell could he get it done so fast? It went down this morning. Did he say anything else when he called?"

"It went down at 0300," Perkins said. "He woke me up an hour later to tell me his good news."

"His good news?" Church said incredulously. "His good news?"

"I know," Perkins said. "He said, 'I have taken care of the problem. I told you not to worry, I would take care of it.'"

"That stupid bastard," Church said. "If we had one more like him we could lose this war. Anything else?"

"He was in Tokyo three days ago, and he did say that he warned you there was only one way to solve the problem of the double agent. We had to kill all of them. You know his favorite line, 'Dead men don't talk.' He said you were too faint-hearted to deal with the problem head on ..."

"That sonofabitch," Church said. "We still don't know for sure about Chen. But, it appears they didn't recognize him from his description at the California college. Even so, good God, he killed three loyal, trained agents. You don't need a cannon to kill a rat.

"Do you know how Kim did it?" Church asked.

"He had to have used Koreans," Perkins said. "There's a U.S. Navy Underwater Demolitions Team (UDT) stationed in Pusan. The other day I talked to Cunningham, you know, our guy in Korea. He mentioned that Kim talked the UDT team leader about training some Korean Navy guys to prepare and set underwater charges."

"There's got to be more to it than that," Church said. "There's no way American UDT people are going to train Koreans without a recommendation from an American senior officer."

Perkins looked down at the floor and slowly shook his head.

"Do you think Cunningham okayed the training mission?"

Perkins swallowed hard.

"I'm not sure," he said, "but I would doubt it."

Church fumed.

"If there is anybody in this world I'd like to terminate with extreme prejudice," he said, "it's that arrogant sonofabitch."

The secretary brought in a tray with a coffee urn and two cups.

"What are you doing about damage control?" Church asked.

"I've got my Sasebo detachment guy on his way to Nagasaki," Perkins said. "He's brand new, has no training or background in Intelligence. He doesn't know anything about the mission."

"How do you know?" Church asked. "Is this the same guy that beat the shit out of Dye down there?"

"Yeah," Perkins said. "So far I haven't raised that as an issue with him because Dye at first insisted that he was mugged by three guys. Grainger hasn't volunteered to tell me about it."

"Hrummp," Church snorted. "Dye finally told my deputy that he and Grainger got into a fight over some whore and that Grainger hit him with a sucker punch."

Church shook his head vigorously.

"Sucker punch, my ass. He beat the hell out of him. We had to ship Dye back to the States for reconstructive surgery."

"Grainger is a physical type," Perkins said. "I sent him up to Nagasaki because Kim wanted all the survivors picked up and taken back to Pusan. That part I did agree with and I knew you would, too. I sent our PT boats up there. Grainger's driving up there in his jeep right now. He'll get there before the boats. I told him to pay off the police chief in Nagasaki and get custody of the survivors."

"I don't know," Church said. "I think that's going to put our fingerprints all over this mess. We need to get the survivors out of there, I agree with that. Just in case any of them knows more than he should. You think your guy is going to be able to get those survivors out of the custody of the people up there in Nagasaki?"

"That shouldn't be too tough," Perkins said, smiling. "Kim already has the chief in his pocket, but, for the record, I want Grainger to be the front man. He's the one who will have to answer all the questions and he only knows what I tell him."

"Well, what did you tell him?" Church asked.

"Nothing, really," Perkins said. "I told him that the Korean ship captain worked for us. He was supposed to haul a load of scrap metal to China, and we were going to insert some agents. I said that the Korean captain double-crossed us and decided to blow up his own ship for the salvage value of the ship and scrap. I told him that the captain got cold feet because he was afraid that if the agents were picked up in China they would name his ship and that would be the end of him."

"I don't know," Church said. "You may have told him too much. Do you think he believed that crap?"

"He believes it for now," Perkins said. "That's all I care about. By the time he gets back, I'll have him ready for a transfer back to his beloved Infantry or maybe all the way home."

"Back home is good," Church said. "He'll probably be glad to forget the whole mess. In the meantime, I've got to do some serious political damage control and try to keep this as low profile as possible. This thing could get blown way the hell out of proportion and wind up on the front pages as an international screwup. Our ambassador is going to go ballistic. He's really a worry-wart. I'll dump this whole thing on the KCIA. We have to cover for some aberrant behavior on the part of one of our allies in the KCIA.

"We used an American officer simply in an effort to minimize the impact on our allies. The young officer had no idea he was circumventing Japanese immigration laws. He is, by nature, an aggressive young man who meant well, but exceeded his authority. He's been transferred back to the United States for disciplinary proceedings.

"By the time our silver-tongued ambassador gets through, the Japanese will believe that it was the old freighter's boiler that blew up or some damn thing. You sure you can get all the survivors back to Korea?"

"If there are any too badly wounded to travel," Perkins said, "knowing Kim, I don't think we have to worry about them saying anything, even if they know anything, which I doubt."

"Hmmm," Church mused. "Maybe this will work out okay. Officially, we don't know what happened. Unofficially, we'll blame it on the Koreans. It was their idea all along. As long as there's no way to tie this back to us, we just sit back and let nature take its course. Our people will make sure Colonel Kim gets 'decorated' one way or another when this cools down. I should have taken him more seriously when he was here waving the bloody shirt about killing all of the bastards. I thought he was just blowing off to hear himself talk. That guy is more than a loose cannon. He's dangerous."

Church poured another cup of coffee.

"What about the agents?" Church asked. "Do we know if any of them survived?"

"Not yet," Perkins said. "I told Grainger to get all of the survivors on our PT boats and get them back to Pusan. Cunningham will find out very quickly if any of them are the agents. If any survived we can get them flown back here."

Church stood and began pacing the room.

"You know," he said, "my gut instincts tell me that if Chen survived, there's no way we're going to see him again. What about the file? Did your other guy bring it back?"

"No," Perkins said. "But I've got that base covered. I've got a contingency plan to charge Grainger with mishandling classified documents. I'll run his ass right out of the Army."

"What the hell did he do to you," Church said, laughing, "screw your mistress?"

"He upset about six months of my planning," Perkins said. "And I just don't like the cocky bastard."

Grainger arrived in Nagasaki shortly before 0800. After enduring a great deal of head-shaking and sucking sounds, he finally persuaded the officer on duty to call the chief of police at his home. A very upset Chief Yamamoto, who had just gotten home from the harbor after the explosion, screamed at Grainger until he said two words: "Colonel Kim."

"*Chotto matte kudasai*" (Just a minute) was all Yamamoto said. Then, in broken English, "I will come to my office. You can be there."

The chief walked into the station 15 minutes later wearing a sweater over his uniform shirt, carrying his jacket and cap. He motioned Grainger to follow him to his office.

"What about Colonel Kim?" he asked after they entered his office and closed the door.

"He wanted me to give you this," Grainger said, taking the huge wad of yen from his overcoat pocket and slapping it on the chief's desk.

The chief's eyes bulged.

"Were there any survivors from the explosion?" Grainger asked.

"Survivors?" the chief repeated. "Koreans?"

"Yes," Grainger said.

The chief held up eight fingers.

"Those are Colonel Kim's men," Grainger said. "He wants me to take them to Korea, *ima*" (now). "Go Korea, *ima*."

The chief nodded, but sucked in his breath.

"Korea, *ima*, no good," he said.

Grainger put his hand on the stack of yen.

"Colonel Kim say, *ima*," Grainger repeated.

The chief took out a small dictionary from his desk and pointed to a word.

"Hospital," it said.

"Very bad," the chief said, shaking his head.

"Colonel Kim, *koko*" (here in Nagasaki), Grainger said, pointing at the desk.

The chief swallowed and worked his mouth like a man trying to swallow his lower lip.

"Colonel Kim, *koko*," Grainger repeated. "Nagasaki."

First the chief shook his head. Then he nodded.

"How Koreans go Korea?" he asked.

"Boats," Grainger said. "At port, I have two boats."

The chief picked up his telephone and rapidly shouted orders to someone. The only word Grainger was able to pick up was *torakku* (truck).

Great, Grainger thought, *with a truck I can get those guys down to the port and out of here.*

"Koreans go home," Grainger said. "No problem."

The chief ground his teeth, then rubbed his jaw in thought. He grabbed the bundle of yen and shoved it into his desk drawer, locked it, and motioned for Grainger to follow him.

Yamamoto barked instructions at the officer perched behind the elevated desk in the lobby. The officer reached down and took a form from a desk drawer and handed it to the chief.

The officer smiled and bowed briefly to Grainger. Grainger bowed in return, wondering what the chief had said.

Grainger followed the chief to the rear exit. Someone had driven his jeep to the back of the building. He noticed a policeman with a notepad jotting down his bumper markings.

*It may not do any good, but I better get those changed when
I get back.*

The Koreans were in an isolation ward at the hospital.
When the chief and Grainger entered, two of them immediately sat up in bed.

Yamamoto addressed the older of the two in Japanese.

"Do you speak Japanese?" he asked.

"*Hai*" (yes), came the reply.

"What happened to your ship?" the chief asked.

Making a loud noise, the man threw his hands out to
simulate an explosion.

"Do you want to go back to Korea now?"

"*Hai*," was the reply.

"Okay," Yamamoto told him. "It will save you a lot of
trouble. I don't think you want to be in my jail, do you?"

The Korean shook his head.

"We all want to go," the Korean said.

"Good," Yamamoto said. He pointed to Grainger.
"American take you to Pusan."

"*Hai*," the Korean said.

Yamamoto pulled out the piece of paper he received
from the officer at the station, placed it in front of the Korean, and handed him a pen.

The chief raised his voice and began shouting when
the man balked at signing.

The Korean bowed twice and hurriedly scratched his
name on the paper.

By now all the Koreans were awake, some of them still
disoriented and in shock.

The Koreans moved slowly to the table and began to
put on the hospital bathrobes that the chief had ordered.

The chief stood there and watched. His stony face and
rigid stance discouraged any further comments from the
Koreans.

A few of the injured Koreans needed help from their friends to get dressed. They stood weaving back and forth. Grainger was concerned that some of them would collapse before he could get them on the boats and on their way back home.

Grainger's jeep with the chief in the front passenger seat led the truck carrying the Koreans to the main dock in front of the Port Administration building. The port was coming to life and the two vehicles, with the chief clearly visible, were incongruous enough to attract many curious stares.

The Koreans, including those who needed help from their shipmates, quickly disappeared through the hatches of the PT boats.

Grainger spoke briefly to Chief Petty Officer Michaels.

"We've got four in each boat," Michaels said. "There won't be any problems. Some of those guys look pretty shaky. We'll get them to the bunks below. Major Perkins said he would alert Colonel Cunningham in Pusan," Grainger said. "You know where to take them?"

"Yes, sir," Michaels said as he waved a salute.

The PT boats edged away from the dock and picked their way through the vessels at anchor, giving the mastheads of the sunken *Kochi Maru* a wide berth.

Aki Nomura, the security officer filling in for an ailing associate at the Port Headquarters, watched the entire proceedings. It had been an eventful tour. He could not believe his eyes when he saw the chief of police riding in an American jeep and directing the unloading of a police truck.

What is going on, he wondered. *American patrol boats? American Army officer? Chief of police? Most unusual. I must put all of this in my report.*

Aki made notes about the Koreans who survived the sinking of the *Kochi Maru* and noted the condition of many of the Koreans who seemed to still be in shock following their harrowing experience.

I wonder who will read this report? he thought. *With the chief of police involved they bury any notes about these suspicious things. Very suspicious. They don't appreciate me here. No one will even read my report. Oh yes, I promised Suziko I would be at her apartment by 0900. I'm already late. I'd better call her now.*

"*Moshee mosh,*" came the response, cool and distant.

"Yum Yum," he said, using the nickname he had given Suziko.

"Oh, Aki," she said, "I've been thinking about you all night. How long before you can be here? Are you on the way?"

"I may have to stay a while and write a report."

"Oh, no," she began to sob. "Aki, I made a special breakfast for you. I wanted to surprise you."

Aki lowered his head.

"You're right," he said. "This is important, but not that important. It's not like it's a matter of life or death; I will write the report later."

"Oh, thank you my love," she said. "I wanted the meal to be special for you."

He folded his sheets of paper and put them in the shirt pocket of his security officer's uniform.

From across the harbor, Colonel Kim had watched through binoculars as the Korean survivors were helped off the trucks and loaded onto the PT boats. He smiled as he noticed that the chief of police nodded but did not bow to Grainger. Then Colonel Kim glanced toward the Port Headquarters building and frowned as he noticed the security officer furiously writing notes.

Colonel Kim put down his binoculars, his chin thrust forward and he squinted. He moved quickly across the grassy knoll and got into his car. Minutes later he positioned himself near the main entrance to the Port Headquarters.

When Aki walked out the gate toward the pickup point for the shuttle bus that ran from the port to downtown

Nagasaki, Colonel Kim pulled alongside the curb, lowered the window, and asked in flawless Japanese whether he could give him a lift downtown. Aki Nomura hesitated a moment, saw that no bus was in sight, and thanked the pleasant-looking, well-dressed Korean for his courtesy.

"Thank you," he said. "My car is in the garage. The motor was flooded in that storm we just had. You'll save me a lot of time."

"Some interesting things going on at the port these days," said Colonel Kim.

Nomura nodded, pressing his lips together.

Just beyond the built-up area and before they reached any houses along the road, Colonel Kim slowed down, leaned over and looked to his right, through the door window. He spoke to his passenger.

"What's that?" he asked, pointing to the right.

Aki turned his head.

In an instant, Colonel Kim pressed a silenced .32 caliber Walther PPK against Aki's shirt front and pulled the trigger three times. The faint sounds could barely be heard outside the car.

Aki Nomura's body jerked straight up, his head hit the roof of the car and he sagged down, face frozen in shock and dismay. Three small perforations shaped a perfect triangle on his left front shirt pocket, directly over his heart. As he died, his shirt blossomed with a thick, slow flow of blood that moved over his belt and into his crotch.

Just before Colonel Kim was about to shove the security officer's head down between his legs, he reached over, checked his jacket pockets and emptied the shirt pocket stuffed with notes. He slipped them into his jacket pocket. Reaching back, he grabbed his overcoat from the back seat and pulled it over Aki's inert form.

I'll find a place for you, my nosy friend, Kim thought, *then I have to get that flight to Pusan so I can clean up another mess.* ✦

FOURTEEN
Moscow, Russia

Colonel Proloff knocked and entered General Petrovsky's office.

"What is it?" Petrovsky asked.

"You remember that ship, *Kochi Maru*, that Svetlana told us about in her report?"

"Of course, the one taking agents to China."

"Well, it won't be going."

"How do you know?"

"Because it's sitting on the bottom of Nagasaki Harbor."

"What happened?"

"We don't know," Proloff said. "It was loaded with scrap metal, like Svetlana said, and its destination was Shanghai. But Fyodor in Sasebo wasn't able to learn anything else."

"That guy couldn't find stinking sturgeon," Petrovsky growled. "Get him out of there."

"We'll get someone transferred there as soon as possible," Proloff assured his chief.

Petrovsky gestured toward Svetlana's file.

"Svetlana can find out more in one day than that clown can learn in a month," he said.

"It was definitely a professional job," Proloff said. "The ship went down in minutes."

"Minutes? How big was it?"

"Ten thousand tons," Proloff replied. "I think you were right. It smells like CIA."

Petrovsky nodded.

"Of course," he said. "I knew it."

"Yuri Kozlov was up there," Proloff said. "You remember we asked him to check on that community of White Russians in Nagasaki?"

Petrovsky nodded.

"What did he say?"

"His report said that hours after it sank, an American Army officer, a captain, showed up. He got the survivors released and loaded them on American PT boats."

"The American obviously is working for the CIA," Petrovsky said. "Did the ship captain survive?"

"I don't know," Proloff said.

Petrovsky got to his feet and began pacing angrily.

"Well, what the hell's going on?" he shouted. "I want to know about the survivors. I want to know how some American Army captain can waltz into Nagasaki and get the survivors, Koreans, out of the hospital. Where are they now? Where is this Army captain?"

Petrovsky made some notes on his desk pad.

"Who blew up the ship?" Petrovsky demanded. "And the biggest question of all—why?

"I'm not happy with Kozlov," Petrovsky stormed. "He's an alcoholic. Tell me again what he was doing in Nagasaki."

"Excuse me, General, sir, but you told me to send him there to keep an eye on the White Russians who settled there."

"I must be slipping," Petrovsky said, "I don't remember that."

"Yes, sir," Proloff said. "You said he was an alcoholic, but he only had one year to go until retirement. You wanted me to bury him there. You said that once Nagasaki got hit with the bomb, nothing would ever happen there again."

"Well, I was wrong," Petrovsky rasped. "Put him somewhere else or, better yet, retire him early. I need someone who can get the job done."

"I'll send Andropov," Proloff said. "He's smart and knows how to dig out the facts."

"Good, tell him I want answers, and I want answers fast. I just can't figure that Army captain walking right in and getting the survivors in the space of a few hours. They don't like Americans in Nagasaki."

Petrovsky narrowed his eyes.

"That CIA's got so much money they can bribe anyone. I'll bet they have half the Japanese government taking money. But, the Army? That captain's got to be CIA. Their Army doesn't have money for that kind of game."

"We'll get a team there right away," Proloff said.

"Good," Petrovsky said. "And contact Svetlana. Tell her to pump that boy wonder. We need to know everything he knows. Tell her to be thorough. Remind her of one of my maxims. The person being questioned, the lieutenant, may know, but doesn't know that he knows."

Proloff smiled.

Alex Andropov was an ambitious Soviet career agent. He was balding, middle-aged, and wore one-inch mail-order elevator shoes. His everyday apparel was cheap, ill-fitting business suits. He always wore the same dark, faintly patterned cravat. He loved that tie because he thought it made him look very dignified. He bought all six that the department store in Kobe had in stock.

Andropov had no real interests outside of his work for the Soviet Union. He would spend almost every waking hour collecting information, reading all the local periodicals, cultivating sources of information and poring over the data, honing his analysis which was generally quite accurate.

The import-export business he ran in Kobe as a front specialized in Western-style furniture and garden statuary. Despite his obvious lack of interest, the store was a success because he could get merchandise not available to other merchants.

Andropov's only driving ambition was to land the kind of assignment that would attract his superior's attention and propel him ahead of his classmates at the Counter-Intelligence Institute. He thought this might be the opportunity he was seeking when he received the lengthy coded message from Proloff. He would go to Nagasaki to get the required information.

Andropov faintly remembered a short announcement on the radio about some ship sinking at the harbor at Nagasaki, but he dismissed it as being of little Intelligence value. The first report said it was an old Korean freighter with a faulty boiler. He now recalled that the name of the Korean freighter was *Kochi Maru*, the same name as in his coded message.

"I will be gone for a few days on business," he told his secretary in the small office above the shop.

The decoded message advised in part, "Contact Larissa Shpanko in Nagasaki. She's been getting money for two years. It's time for her to earn it."

Andropov knew this meant that Larissa had been recruited from among the White Russians who fled the Soviet Union after the revolution and now lived, self-exiled, in their own small community in Nagasaki. This little settlement, miles south of the Urakami Valley where the atomic bomb had landed, was well beyond the "Red Circle of Death," described in the *Nagasaki Nippo*.

Larissa was still an attractive woman in her mid-40s. She had blonde hair, blue eyes, and regular features that belied her Slavic origins. She had, at one time, dreamed that she would find a wealthy man, marry him, and secure an education. That dream was now past and Larissa had little to hope for in the small community.

The abbreviated dossier that Proloff included confirmed that hers was a very nominal stipend. An analysis dismissed the information credited to her as local gossip devoid of real Intelligence value.

Proloff had emphasized one item in Larissa's file that he felt could be of particular interest to Andropov.

"Larissa had a disagreement with her landlord," Proloff wrote. "A young Nagasaki police sergeant named Yukio Hattori was called to the apartment house. He was immediately smitten with Larissa and told the landlord to stop making trouble or he would start regular police inspections for safety violations and the like. Larissa showed him her gratitude on a regular basis."

"He is not a good lover," Larissa wrote in her report, "but if you need to know what is happening at the police station, I can find out."

When Andropov contacted Larissa by telephone, his instructions were direct and to the point.

"Tell your police friend you heard about the *Kochi Maru* and wonder what the real story is. If you do this right, you will get a bonus. If you don't, we will have no further need of your services. I'll be back in touch in three days."

To Larissa's surprise, the assignment was easier than expected. Sergeant Hattori was a willing talker, eager to impress her with his knowledge of the incident. Her constant touches and affectionate murmurs as she massaged his legs were all the encouragement he needed.

"There were bodies floating all over the harbor," he said. "We found a couple of them in the weeds. We took them all to the hospital, living and dead. They were all Korean. Some of the young ones pretended they couldn't speak Japanese. I heard the chief of police say it was a boiler that had exploded. I don't know how he knew that. Maybe that's what the Koreans told him. A couple of the officers said privately that they thought someone must have set some bombs. They thought there were too many bodies for it to be a blown boiler."

"I couldn't do something like that," Larissa said softly. "I could never touch dead bodies. Ugh."

"It wasn't really too bad," Hattori offered, "but I know what you mean."

He smiled playfully and said, "Warm bodies are better."

Larissa laughed and slapped him on the arm. Then, growing serious again, she asked, "What happened to the survivors?"

"Ah," Hattori said, nodding his head as if ready to confide a confidence because she had asked the right question. "That's another mystery. The desk sergeant told me there were no more Koreans at the hospital. When I asked why, he told me the chief himself went to the hospital with an American Army officer and ordered all the survivors released in the American's custody. Everyone was surprised."

"Then why did he help them?" Larissa asked.

"That's what everybody wants to know," Hattori said. "But the chief is one person you never ask anything. The sergeant told me privately that he thinks the chief did it for Colonel Kim."

"Who's Colonel Kim?" Larissa asked.

"I don't know," Hattori said. "When I asked the sergeant, he told me to forget I ever heard the name. He said he shouldn't have mentioned it. Then he said he was some kind of special friend of the chief's. He thinks the chief and this colonel are in some kind of business together because one night, when they were drinking, the chief said that Colonel Kim was going to help him get an American car. The sergeant told me not to say anything about it. A month later the chief was driving a new Chrysler New Yorker."

"Do you think anything will happen to the chief for giving the survivors to the American?"

"Happen to the chief?" Hattori asked incredulously. "Are you crazy? No. He'll be the chief until he dies or retires. He's like a general; no one can touch him."

Andropov seemed satisfied with the information Larissa communicated.

"That's a good start," he said. "Now burn those notes. Never keep anything like that around. It's better to remember without writing anything. Understand?"

She nodded.

"Keep asking about Colonel Kim," Andropov said. "Any little tidbit of information helps. It's like a puzzle—a piece here, a piece there, one day you see the whole picture. Also, see if you can find out where the American is stationed."

The corners of Larissa's mouth turned down. She lowered her eyes.

"I thought I did a good job for you," she said. "Now you want me to keep asking questions. Maybe he doesn't know any more."

"You did all right," Andropov reassured her. "It's a good start, but we need a lot more details. He likes you. You told me he liked to brag about what a big shot he is. Let him brag; just nudge him a bit. You women know how to get a man to talk. If you want the bonus you have to earn it."

She crossed her arms and grimaced.

"Look," he said, "we don't have a lot of time. Moscow wants these answers fast. Once this is over, they may not ask you to do anything for months."

Andropov radioed his report to Proloff, suggesting that Colonel Kim was probably with the Korean CIA and working with the Americans. He stressed that he would try to pin down Kim's full identity for his next report since Kim seemed to engender some feelings of apprehension from his sources, perhaps because of his close ties with the chief of police.

Moreover, Andropov reported, it appears that Chief Yamamoto's job is *not* absolutely secure. Local newspapers are suggesting his handling of the matter has raised questions in high places, but the sources are not directly quoted. That means someone in the governor's office, either the security chief or maybe even the governor himself, is after Yamamoto's head. Also, it seems the security officer who was on duty during the incident has disappeared. I don't know if there's any connection, but they can't find him and his girlfriend called the newspaper to tell them he was writing an important report on the explosion the day he went missing. ✦

FIFTEEN
Sasebo, Japan

Grainger went directly to the port warehouse on his return from Nagasaki. He noticed the padlock on his door was missing as he approached his office.

"What the hell?" he said aloud.

His foot struck a hard object on the floor. It was the padlock. Someone had used a hacksaw to cut the hasp. The door was ajar.

Grainger pushed the door open carefully and looked inside.

The office was empty. He walked quickly to the safe. The door to the squat iron box was open. It, too, was empty.

The safe wasn't broken into, he thought. *That means Perkins. Doutter would have given him the combination in case of an emergency. I should have left Butch here instead of with Julie. My fault. Should have stashed the file with Salencio.*

He sat down behind his desk, feeling helpless, unsure of his next step. He clenched his fist and pounded on the desk.

I need to find out what the hell was in that file.

The long-distance operator at the telephone exchange motioned to Grainger.

"Your call's ready, sir," she said. "Booth four."

"Who is this?" a woman's voice asked.

"This is Ken Grainger, Ma'am. Is Jerry there?"

"Jerry? Who did you say you were?"

"Ken Grainger," he said. "I'm the guy who took over Jerry's job when he went home. I'm calling from Sasebo in Japan."

"You're in the Army, Mr. Grainger?" the woman asked.

"Yes. I'm Captain Ken Grainger, U.S. Army, Ma'am. I need to talk to Jerry. He knows who I am."

A poignant silence followed as Elizabeth Doutter struggled to maintain her self-control.

"You're a little late, Captain," she said flatly. "He's gone."

"Sorry I missed him," Grainger said. "Do you have any idea when I should call back?"

"You don't understand, Captain," Elizabeth said. "Jerry is dead. He was killed in a freak traffic accident of some kind."

"What!" Grainger stammered. "I can't believe this. There's no mistake?"

"That's not a mistake I would make, Captain," she said.

"Yes, of course," Grainger said. "I'm terribly sorry, Mrs. Doutter; I mean, my God, he left here two weeks ago. What happened?"

"I'd like to know what the hell happened over there," she said. "Jerry wasn't the same when he came home. He was afraid of something. He carried a gun every day after he came home."

"But wasn't he in the Sheriff's Department?" Grainger asked.

"Yes," Mrs. Doutter said, "but he wore a gun all the time, even to our daughter's wedding."

"I really have no idea, Mrs. Doutter," Grainger said. "I know he did some scary things in Korea. Working behind the lines had to be tough duty. He seemed all right during the short time we were together. I thought he was level-headed, down-to-earth, and had a great sense of humor, a straightforward way of expressing himself."

Grainger sat in the phone booth in a state of shock.

"Mrs. Doutter," Grainger said, "he had a gun here, while he was with the detachment, but he never carried it. He left it in the safe in his office."

"I thank you for that, Captain Grainger, but the fact is he was preoccupied with something he wouldn't discuss."

"Mrs. Doutter," Grainger said, "I'm terribly sorry about your loss. I liked Jerry. He was a good guy."

"He was a good guy," she interrupted. "He was a good husband and father, the neighbors liked him, everybody seemed to like him. He was my gentle giant, a big teddy bear. Did he ever tell you about his hobby?"

"Uh … no," Grainger said, "I don't believe he mentioned it. We really didn't have as much time together as we would have liked."

"He collected toy soldiers. The lead kind. He had them from all over the world. He spent a small fortune on them. Wanted to give them to his grandkids. All except his favorite, of course, the U.S. Infantry Squad, handmade in Ireland. They were made in County Cork, Ireland, in 1904. It was the only set he wanted me to keep."

"I didn't know any of that, Mrs. Doutter. I'm just absolutely floored by your news."

"Why did you say you called?" she asked.

"He worked on an operation that I got involved with after I took over the detachment. Something up in Nagasaki. There was a file he wanted me to read. I guess it got misplaced or something. I just thought he could kind of tell me what was in it. Did he, by chance, ever mention a plan involving a freighter or a ship?"

"He never discussed any ship. He never discussed anything except to say he didn't like his boss, Major Perkins. He never said much and I didn't ask. I didn't want to remind him of the stuff he did. I hoped that some day he could unburden himself, get rid of his ghosts." She paused, "He was a good man. Too many of our married years were spent apart, years when he was in the Army.

"Since you replaced him, Captain, what kind of job is it?"

"It's a liaison job, Mrs. Doutter. Jerry commanded a detachment. We help people get supplies, things they'll need over in Korea that aren't usually in the normal supply channels."

"That doesn't sound scary," she said. "What about Korea? Wait, I'm sorry to keep asking you these questions, but I'm just at my wit's end trying to cope with this."

"Mrs. Doutter, I honestly don't know anything that he did over here or in Korea that could have any connection to the accident."

"But you don't know for sure," she said.

"No, I don't know," Grainger said. "I will promise you this, Mrs. Doutter, if I find out anything that ties in Jerry's death with what we're doing, I will let you know."

"And that's a promise?" she said.

"Absolutely, yes," Grainger said.

After he hung up, Grainger continued to sit in the booth, staring at the telephone.

It's not possible, he thought. *His accident could not be related to the* Kochi Maru.

He walked out of the telephone exchange, still in a daze, and drove back to his office. Swinging the jeep into the warehouse, he made a large circle, parking next to his office with the front of the jeep protruding slightly out into the street.

He called Major Perkins' office once he got inside.

Lieutenant Grippa answered and advised him that Perkins would be in meetings all day.

"Tell him I called," Grainger said. "I'm back in Sasebo and the mission is accomplished. Tell him also that I am requesting permission to read the file."

"He'll know what file, I assume," Grippa said.

"He'll know," Grainger said. "There is one other thing. You should let him know that Jerry Doutter was killed in an automobile accident."

"Yes," Grippa said, glancing at Perkins and nodding, "he knows. We heard about Captain Doutter's death a couple of days ago."

Grainger was stunned again.

A couple of days ago? Grainger thought. *Then he knew when he sent me to Nagasaki. Our discussion about the file that Doutter forgot to bring with him to Tokyo....*

The unmistakable twang of Major Perkins' voice sounded loud in Grainger's ears.

"Where the hell did you find out about Doutter?"

"From his wife, Major. I talked to her this morning."

"Why?" asked Perkins.

"I wanted to ask him about operational issues we discussed, but didn't fully cover before he left," Grainger said. "I can't believe he's dead."

"What operational issues?" Perkins asked.

"The one I just worked on, Major," Grainger said.

"You have no business calling him about anything related to operations," Perkins said. "If you have any questions about operational issues you're supposed to call me. I would have thought you knew that."

"Speaking about what I've been working on," Grainger said, "I'd like to officially request the opportunity to read the file about the *Kochi Maru.* If you'd like, sir, I will put my request in writing."

"Permission denied," Perkins said. "Even if you did have the requisite security clearance, which you don't, you have no need to know the contents of that file. You can save yourself the trouble of putting the request in writing. You know all you need to know. We got double-crossed and the mission was effectively aborted. It never happened. It ended in the starting blocks."

"It never happened?" Grainger exclaimed. "Pardon me, Major, but I can't believe what you just said. No ship was blown up? They didn't drag 12 bodies out of the bay? I didn't bribe the chief of police to help get eight sorry-looking seamen out of the hospital and ship them back to Pusan? There still aren't other bodies in the ship at the bottom of Nagasaki harbor? And you say the mission never happened?"

"That stuff is our problem, here in Tokyo," Perkins said. "We'll do our own damage control. Everything is under control. It doesn't involve you at all, so stay out of it."

A long silence hummed on the line.

"I will do one thing," Perkins said. "I'll prepare a sanitized abstract of the file and see that it's delivered to you by our courier. That's all you need to know, and I don't want to hear about this any more."

"The police in Nagasaki know who I am," Grainger protested. "If I get any questions I'll refer them to you?"

"Do that," Perkins said. "That's the first intelligent thing you've said since you took over down there. Did you discuss the operation with Mrs. Doutter?"

Grainger hesitated.

"I don't think she knew anything of Jerry's work in the Army."

"Good," Perkins said. "For everyone's benefit, it would be best if you had no further contact with Mrs. Doutter."

Grainger made no response.

"If you do," Perkins said, "I will personally bring court-martial charges against you."

"Major," Grainger said, "are you aware that my office was burglarized and the file that Doutter had in the safe was removed?"

"There was no burglary," Perkins said. "There was a 'no-notice' security inspection of the detachment office and an unauthorized, classified document in that safe was removed. I had it brought here to avoid a security violation filed against the Group."

"Is it common to hacksaw locks off doors to conduct such inspections?" Grainger asked.

"Since you insist upon pushing things, Grainger, I should tell you there is a distinct possibility that you, personally, will be charged with a security violation concerning a top-secret document. If I were you, I would keep my mouth shut. Is that clear?"

"Major," Grainger said, "you're free to file whatever charges you want. I'll look forward to asking the same questions at my court-martial. I'm sure they'll be interested in my duties, bribing a chief of police and taking eight people out of a hospital who apparently needed medical attention; did we also disregard some Japanese immigration laws?"

"Your reaction is just what I expected," Perkins said. "You over-react to a simple order. You want to bring disgrace down on Colonel Beane and this group. You prove my point. You're too emotional for Intelligence work."

"So you are saying," Grainger said, "that Colonel Beane had full knowledge of all aspects of this operation and all of your direct orders. In that case I am requesting an appointment with Colonel Beane at the earliest practicable time. If he knows all about this operation, I really believe I should be requesting a transfer immediately."

"You don't hear very well, Grainger. I told you I would send you an abstract of the file. Until you get that, you will not have an appointment with anyone."

There was another long pause.

"Besides," Perkins added, "it just happens that Colonel Beane is in Washington, DC, on official business. I also expect that he will be retiring very shortly after his return. As far as your transfer is concerned, I'm already working on that, Captain, giving it my full and personal attention. How does the First Cav in Hokkaido sound to you, or maybe a State-side transfer?"

"That's fine with me, Major," Grainger said.

"Good. As soon as I set up some interviews, we'll find a replacement, and you can go back to the Infantry. In the meantime, there is one thing," he said.

"What's that?" Grainger asked.

"You need to visit our detachment in Korea. Colonel Cunningham has asked for help in developing an SOP for our guerrilla training operation in our camp near Kobe. It's possible he can put all your good Infantry training to some use."

"When do I go?" Grainger asked.

"I'll let you know," Perkins said. "Very soon, I expect. Lieutenant Grippa should have a draft of my instructions for your trip. I'll review it tonight and send your orders down on the courier plane."

"I'll be looking for the letter," Grainger said.

Perkins hung up.

Grainger pushed back from his desk.

This is probably the beginning of the end of a promising career, he thought, with a grim smile. *Well, so be it. It only takes one adverse efficiency report to kill a career and if Colonel Beane is up to speed on this operation, I'm dead. Somehow, I just can't believe he knew what was going on.*

Back in Tokyo, Perkins railed to his assistant.

"That sonofabitch, Wyatt Earp cowboy will be the death of me yet," he said. "Until I can get a replacement down there, I don't want anything going to him without my initials. Is that clear?"

"Yes, sir," Lieutenant Grippa said.

"He was calling Doutter," Perkins said, "because he saw the file was gone and wanted Doutter to tell him what was in it. That would be a violation of Federal law that could have put Doutter in Leavenworth. Of course he's gone now so that makes that issue moot.

"Call the CID in Sasebo," he said. "Tell them that we were running a check on the handling of classified documents, found our guy had left his safe open, and for security reasons removed the documents. Tell them we'll take the appropriate action here."

"Yes, sir," Grippa said. "Sir, what if Grainger checks and finds out that Colonel Beane has not set his retirement date?"

"He's not going to be around that long," Perkins said. "Also, prepare a memo to file on Grainger's telephone call requesting a transfer to the First Cav in Hokkaido. Cite his unhappiness with his liaison detachment duties and add a copy of our report to the CID about the open safe. By the time I get through with Grainger, I don't think the old man will even want to give our young hero an exit interview."

Perkins smiled.

"Our good captain is totally out of his element."

"Yes, sir," Grippa said. "I'll prepare the memo to file and then call the people in Sasebo."

"Grainger has screwed with the wrong guy," Perkins said.

"CIC, Coburn speaking."

"Hi, this is Lieutenant Grippa from the 8240th, Far East Command G-2. Is your boss in?"

"Our boss?" Coburn said. "You mean our Commanding Officer, Major Salencio?"

"Oh," Grippa said, "I thought they called all you guys agents, that you didn't have any rank, at least to tell people about."

"You want Major Salencio?" Coburn said. "Just a minute."

"Major," Grippa said, when Salencio came on the line, "we just had one of our security teams from AFFE G-2 go into the office of one of our people, Captain Grainger — he has a liaison office down at the port. They found the safe he uses for classified documents open. They returned a classified document that should not have been kept in that kind of safe. It was returned to our office for safe keeping."

"I see, Lieutenant," Salencio said. "Well, that sounds like pretty fast service. So, what would you like us to do?"

"Nothing, really," Grippa said. "Major Perkins just told me to call you and have you make a record of this call … letting you know what we did."

"I see," Salencio said, "He asked you to call the CIC, Counter-Intelligence Office in Sasebo, or the CID, Criminal Investigation Division?"

"Uh, … right, sir," Grippa said. "Let's see, I think it was …, it's not clear on my notes. Sorry, sir, am I calling the right office?"

"Yes, you've called the right office, Lieutenant Grippa. Rest assured we'll make the appropriate notation."

"Oh, good," Grippa said. "Thank you, sir."

Grainger called Salencio to tell him of Jerry Doutter's untimely death.

"There's a lot going on that I need to discuss with you," Grainger said. "You may be hearing some rumors about an Army captain who was in Nagasaki getting Koreans out of the hospital and onto a couple of PT boats. That was me, of course. There's a lot more. Right now I feel I'm in over my head and need some sage guidance."

"I think you're right," Salencio said. "The plot is thickening. They just made one little mistake. A Lieutenant Grippa from your Tokyo office just called. I think he had instructions to call the CID. Instead, he called us. He reported that one of the Liaison Group's security teams found a classified document in an open safe in your office. I assured him we would make note of your criminal negligence. It may not help too much, but it will buy you a little time."

"That bastard really plays dirty," Grainger said. "I kept Doutter's combination for the safe, thinking it wouldn't make any difference. That was my mistake. Perkins knew it and sent someone over to get the classified file that dealt with the operation that just blew up in Nagasaki. They sawed through the lock on my door to get into my office."

"As I told you," Salencio said, "I never read the file, but that ship was here recently and it was loaded with scrap metal. When we started asking questions we were told to stay out of it because it was a CIA operation. The ship was the *Kochi Maru*. And that's the ship that Doutter told me was going to be a problem."

"That's the one," Grainger said.

"By the way," Salencio asked, "Did Doutter ever ask you to sign for the file or any other classified documents?"

"No," Grainger said. "He asked me not to read it unless I had to, so I didn't. By the time I wanted to read it, I had to get to Nagasaki fast, then it was gone. I never signed for anything, no classified documents, not even the $5,000 worth of yen I gave to the police chief in Nagasaki, absolutely nothing."

"Frankly," Salencio said, "I don't think you have a problem. First, you're not even sure there was a classified document in the safe; you never saw it. Secondly, there's no receipt with your signature on it, there's no evidence it was ever there. You have no accountability. Perkins either isn't thinking straight, or he's trying to bluff you.

"Hell, even if you did sign for the document, someone else placed it in the safe that was provided to you by your higher headquarters. If anyone's in trouble, it would be the commanding officer of the Liaison Group, since the safe is apparently not approved for top-secret documents.

"Having said all that, cover your rear by taking a picture of the lock that was on the ground and the hasp. Turn it over to the CID at the Post Headquarters. Tell them that someone burglarized your office. The safe was open because, luckily, to your knowledge, there wasn't anything in it. You're reporting the break-in because they may want to get some fingerprints. Right?"

"Yes, sir, I understand, right," Grainger said.

Salencio smiled.

"Bueno."

"Oh, yes," Grainger said, "one other thing. Perkins is sending me to Pusan to work with the detachment there. I'm supposed to help with some SOPs on Infantry training for the guerrillas."

Salencio frowned.

"That doesn't sound right to me," he said. "It sounds like he wants to get you out of town and he's sending you to a place that's unfamiliar. I don't know how far Perkins will go. Ken, do you have a weapon?"

"Yes," Grainger said.

"Take it," Salencio said. "You've been in combat. I'm sure your instincts are well-honed. Just don't relax." ✦

SIXTEEN

Pusan, Korea

Grainger walked down the gangplank with a strong feeling of *déjà vu* when the USNS *Sergeant Muller* docked in Pusan. Like months earlier, a fine sea fog clouded the landscape, giving it a surreal quality.

Welcome back to the Land of the Morning Calm, he told himself. A brackish smell assaulted Grainger's nostrils.

I wonder if all ports stink of stale salty water, he thought. *I don't remember it being this quiet.*

Grainger's recollections were interrupted by the distinctive roar of a jeep engine. The olive-drab vehicle punched a gaping hole in the billowing mist, and a cloud of dust enveloped Grainger, the jeep, and the driver, wrapping them in a brown-tinted mock fog.

"Captain Grainger?" the driver asked.

Grainger nodded.

"I'm Sergeant Henderson, Captain. Welcome to the Eight-Two-For-Nothing AU" (8240th Army Unit).

Henderson was in his early 20s, with dark-blue eyes, fair skin, and a stocky build. In his haste to get out of the jeep to greet Grainger, the bill of his cap brushed the sun visor, knocking it back to reveal a blond crew cut.

Henderson smiled broadly and saluted.

"I know you were over here before," he said. "We heard you got a DSC." He paused and checked the rear-view mirror. "Have you ever been over to the island before?"

"No," Grainger replied.

"It's kinda different."

"How so?"

"Well, everybody on the island does some kind of Intel work. We got Navy and Air Force detachments, the CIA, and the Korean CIA. The Koreans are the worst. They act real stuck up all the time. Everyone stays away from their compound at night unless you're invited, which ain't likely. You can tell you're getting close when you get the smell from those crock pots full of kimchee they got fermentin' all over the place."

Henderson skidded to a stop next to a motor launch tied up at one of the pilings at a small dock. He nodded to a Korean in the boat, who was dressed in Army fatigues and stood as they arrived.

He reached in the back of the jeep and got a length of chain that he wrapped around the steering column and then secured to the piling at the dock. The Korean pulled the line taut as they boarded the launch. Henderson moved directly to the wheel, pushed the starter and the engine roared to life. The Korean loosened the stern line and tossed it in one of the rear compartments of the boat.

With a quick twist of his wrist, Henderson spun the wheel to the right and the bow of the small boat raised in the air as it plowed into the bay at full power. Henderson looked over his shoulder and grinned at Grainger.

"I love this shit," he said. "Maybe I shoulda joined the Navy."

He pointed to a small hill west of Pusan.

"Over there is one of the training camps for the partisans. We teach radio communications and basic map reading. We also teach some demolitions and hand-to-hand stuff. Then we ship 'em up to Seoul and drop 'em out of a balloon for parachute training."

He steered the boat in the pattern of an elongated "ess" figure, and put up his hand to catch some of the spray.

"You probably know we get North Koreans out of the refugee camps," he continued. "They sign up to be partisans. We give 'em a uniform, put 'em on the payroll, and train 'em. When they get finished, we ship 'em to Seoul. If they survive their first guerrilla raid, they get interviewed to join one of our task forces.

"We wait until after they come back from their first raid to make sure they're serious about fightin' and not just looking for a ticket home. Right now, about half stay with the program. I don't think they go back north, they just disappear in the big city."

"Is 50 percent considered to be a good percentage?" Grainger asked.

"I don't know," Henderson said. "That's not my job. I guess it's better than nothing. I do know that if one of our guys is not with the Koreans on a raid, you can't believe what they say. We found this out early. They'd come back and tell us a bunch of crap about what they did and none of it checked out."

"Really?" Grainger asked.

"Yeah, on one raid they claimed they knocked out a radar station manned by North Koreans and some Russian advisors. One of our destroyers sailed into the area, and two MIGs buzzed out. Luckily, we were able to scramble a couple of F-80 Shooting Stars that scared 'em off. Our guys said that if they did knock out that radar, the commies sure got it up again in record time.

"We've got some Navy underwater demolition types, (UDT) over at the Navy compound. They're really great guys, come over for booze a lot, lousy poker players. That's why we like 'em. They said if that radar site had been blown, no way they could get it up that fast."

"What do the UDT people do?" Grainger asked.

"UDT? Oh, they just do demolition work. They help when we need to blow a bridge or tunnel. They really know how to blow things up."

Nearing the island, Henderson pointed toward a white, three-story gabled house with stately white columns that looked like an old Southern mansion.

"That's our place," he said. "We had it built from the plans we found in the house we got in Seoul. The one up there was built by Baptist missionaries. It kinda looks like the house in *Gone with the Wind*."

There were no shrubs or flowers around the house. A small sign was nailed to the front door: 8240th AU, FEC/LD.

"This is where we live between missions," Henderson said. "After goin' out it's really good to get back, like comin' home."

Colonel Bill Cunningham was on the porch as they walked up from the dock.

"Good to see you again, Grainger," Cunningham said. "Over in Sasebo you were finding homes for K-9s. How did that turn out?"

"Pretty good, Colonel," Grainger said, saluting. "I kept the sergeant's dog, Butch. He stays with me at my place. Great dog. We're pretty sure we've got homes for all four that are coming over next month."

"Good," Cunningham said.

He smiled, and tilted his head to the right.

"Well, how's it feel to be back?"

"It's a little different," Grainger said. "I hadn't planned on visiting Korea, at least not this soon."

"I can imagine," Cunningham said with a nod.

"We'll put your gear in Doutter's old room," Cunningham said. "Damn, that was a shock to hear about his accident. Home such a short time and killed in a traffic accident, that's tough. What a waste."

"Yes, sir," Grainger said. "I really didn't get to know him that well, but he seemed like a good man."

"He was," Cunningham said. "Jerry was one of my closest friends. We served together in Europe, in the OSS. He got out and I stayed in. We worked together on some of the islands when he was recalled to duty, helping rescue downed pilots, among other things. He deserved better. I'll write to Elizabeth."

Cunningham led the way into the house that served as both living quarters and offices for the detachment.

"I've got a place set up for you to work," Cunningham said. "The training SOPs we've been using are out of date. I was delighted when Perkins asked if there was something you could help with over here. Knowing about your combat experience, updating the SOPs seemed a natural."

"I thought it was your idea," Grainger said.

Cunningham stopped and turned to Grainger.

"That's funny," he said. "I thought he told me it was your idea."

"No, sir," Grainger said.

A slight frown creased Cunningham's brow.

So, Grainger thought, *he either wants me out of Sasebo or over here, or both. The question now is why?*

"This afternoon we'll go over to look at some training sites," Cunningham said. "Our partisans don't have the same generation of equipment you used in combat, and most of it is pre-WW II stuff. To tell you the truth, this opportunity hit us so quick we're still getting set up for you."

When they walked into Grainger's temporary office, Cunningham closed the door.

"Are you getting along any better with Major Perkins?" he asked.

"Frankly, Colonel, not too well. I'm just not one of his favorite people."

"Hmmm, that's too bad. I heard there was some friction. He and Doutter never got along either, so it's not just you."

Grainger nodded.

"Perkins has been known to chew up a few subordinates," Cunningham said.

"I understand Colonel Beane will be retiring shortly," Grainger said.

"Not that I know of," Cunningham said. "Who told you that?"

"Major Perkins," Grainger said. "He told me two days ago."

"I think he's mistaken," Cunningham said. "I believe I would know since I'm the next ranking colonel in the Group."

Grainger fingered the SOPs.

"If you can stay over a couple of days," Cunningham said, "we'll be going pheasant hunting with some Navy guys. You're welcome to come along."

"I'd like that," Grainger said.

"Good. Over here you don't need a license to hunt."

Grainger smiled.

I wonder if I'm the prey, he thought.

"By the way, Colonel," Grainger asked, "did those eight Korean seamen I sent back on the PT boat get here okay?"

Cunningham's eyes narrowed.

"Well," he said, hesitantly, "they got back okay. My only job was to see if any of the survivors were the Chinese agents. None of them made it. My orders were to turn the Koreans over to the KCIA. They were waiting for them at the dock when the PT boats got here."

"What happened to them?" Grainger asked.

"Ken," Cunningham said, "that's really not our business. I was told they were being held for Colonel Kim."

"Some of them needed hospitalization," Grainger said.

"I don't know anything about that or the operation," Cunningham said. "This was strictly a CIA operation and

I'm not in the so-called 'need to know' group. I heard you were able to get those guys out of Nagasaki. You may not have done them a great favor. It's not official, of course, but the word is that Colonel Kim walked into the room where they were being detained and shot them all."

"What?" Grainger said in disbelief. "Why? What the hell for? They were just merchant seamen, crew on an old freighter that hauled junk."

"Like I said," Cunningham repeated, "I don't know about the operation. I don't know what those fellows knew or didn't know. I just told you what I heard, but it was from a very reliable source. Once those fellows got back to Pusan it was strictly the Koreans' show."

"I saw them in Nagasaki," Grainger said. "They were in sad shape. I can't believe they knew anything. Hell, most of them didn't know where their next rice ration was coming from. Some of them were still suffering from shock."

Cunningham bit his lip and looked away.

"Again," he said, "it was a CIA operation, out of Tokyo. From what I heard, our involvement was strictly nominal. Sometimes these things don't turn out like they were planned. Those are the breaks."

The evening meal at the 8240th was family style. Cunningham introduced Grainger as the Sasebo liaison officer. Grainger quickly took some good-natured ribbing about being in heaven with all those beautiful Japanese women and out of harm's way.

"What do you mean," Grainger replied good naturedly, "you consider yourselves to be in `harm's way'? The fighting's 200 miles north of here."

"Yeah, but we're only 500 yards from the KCIA compound," someone said.

There were a few snickers.

"Knock it off," Cunningham said. "By the way, Colonel Kim is coming over to discuss a raid with us tonight."

"Another radar station, Colonel?" Sergeant Henderson asked.

Everyone laughed.

At 1900 hours there was a loud knock at the front door. Colonel Kim entered without waiting for an answer and walked into the dining room.

"Good evening, Colonel Kim," Cunningham said.

Kim was clad in a heavily starched and pressed set of dark-green fatigues. The brass of his web belt gleamed and the cordovan leather of his shoulder holster shone like glass. Grainger noticed that the exposed wooden pistol grip on his Colt .45 was carved in the shape of a rattlesnake about to strike. The ammunition clip had an unusual oval-shaped plastic cover with a series of filed notches.

I wonder if any of those are for unarmed merchant seamen? Grainger thought. *Kim looks about like the way Doutter described him. From what he said, the rattlesnake grips suit him to a tee.*

Kim scanned those at the table. He paused briefly when he saw Grainger.

"Ah, Colonel Cunningham," Kim said. "You have a new officer."

"Captain Grainger is just visiting from Sasebo," Cunningham said. "He commands our detachment there."

"Oh," Kim said, "one of Major Perkins' officers. Is this your first trip to Korea, Captain?"

"No, Colonel," Grainger replied. "I've been here before."

"Grainger has an excellent record from when he fought here earlier in the war," Cunningham said. "He's an experienced Infantry officer. He's going to review the training SOPs for the partisans."

"Good," Kim said. "We need to improve their training. They need direction. What is it you say, Colonel Cunningham, your six Ps? Prior planning prevents piss-poor performance."

Kim threw back his head and laughed.

"Exactly how long is this short visit, Captain Grainger?" Kim asked.

"Not long," Grainger said, "a few days."

"As Americans like to say," Kim said, "if you need help, don't hesitate to call."

Grainger nodded.

"There is one thing," Grainger said. "I recently sent over two PT boats with eight Korean seamen from a ship that went down in Nagasaki. Would you have any idea what happened to them?"

The smile faded from Colonel Kim's face.

Colonel Cunningham looked up quickly.

"I don't think this is the right time," Cunningham said, looking at Grainger.

"No, Colonel," Kim interrupted. "I'll answer your brash young captain's question. That little matter has been disposed of. I took care of it personally."

He smiled broadly.

"What exactly does that mean, Colonel?" Grainger asked.

"Grainger," Cunningham admonished.

Kim's nostrils flared, his cheeks reddened, and his eyes narrowed to slits.

"What that means, exactly, my young warrior Captain, is that it is none of your business. Dead men don't talk."

He laughed a mirthless laugh as he stared at Grainger.

Grainger shook his head in disgust.

"If you intend to make a career in the field of Intelligence, my young Captain," Kim said testily, "you're going to have to get a little more sand in your gut."

"Really, Colonel," Grainger said, "I need sand to do exactly what?"

Kim turned to Cunningham.

"It seems you have some training to do as well, Bill," Kim said. "Now if you will excuse me, I have something else to do. Perhaps your captain and I can discuss strategy some other time."

He spun sharply and strode to the door.

Cunningham jumped to his feet and followed Kim to the door.

When he returned, he motioned for the others to leave and waited until the door was closed.

"That wasn't too smart, Ken," Cunningham said. "I'm not sure why you baited him, but if you wanted to make an enemy, you succeeded. If you leave the Regular Army, I wouldn't recommend the diplomatic corps."

"I apologize, Colonel," Grainger said. "I know I was out of line, but that whole mess in Nagasaki really upset me. Those seamen were not a danger to anyone. Why kill them?"

"Frankly," Cunningham said, "I'm surprised you got to him that fast. He's normally pretty controlled. He practically confirmed the rumor. There's obviously a lot more to this. You may have opened a Pandora's box. Watch yourself. That man can be ruthless, and I doubt he has any scruples about murder."

"Maybe Doutter was right," Grainger said. "This job can make you paranoid."

"The fact is," Cunningham said, "Kim's right. Those Koreans really aren't any of our business."

"Then I don't understand," Grainger said. "If we're going to condone the murder of people who are presumably innocent, what are we fighting for?"

Cunningham shook his head.

"Whatever it is," he said, "we're not going to solve it tonight. You know I'll have to report this little exchange to Colonel Beane. I'm not going to mention it to Perkins. I'll wait until Beane returns. Even so, I'd bet that Kim will complain to Perkins. Don't ever underestimate that guy."

"You mean Kim or Perkins?" Grainger asked.

"I mean Kim," Cunningham said. "He's in a class all by himself."

Grainger walked out to the front porch. Sergeant Henderson was sitting in a wicker-weave chair smoking a pipe.

"Whew," Henderson murmured, "that's a different side of Colonel Kim. Usually he's laughing all the time and not saying a whole lot. You really got to him."

Grainger was silent.

"Them Koreans are just different, Captain. They don't give a shit about life. The way they treat their own guys would just knock you over. I hope I never have to be interrogated by one of them. The only one worse would be the Englishman."

"Who's the Englishman?" Grainger asked.

"He's a guy who stays here," Henderson said. He looked down at his wristwatch. "Oh hell, I gotta go. I'm on the Seoul run tonight. If you're gonna be here tomorrow night maybe we can talk about him. He's really one weird dude."

The rising sun appeared in a cloudless blue sky the following morning and bathed the island with a golden glow. There was an air of excitement at the detachment. Shotguns were oiled, bolts drawn back and released, thermos bottles were filled with steaming coffee and lined up on the kitchen counter along with box lunches. Cunningham paired Grainger with one of the Navy UDT lieutenants. From the beginning Grainger liked the red-haired, freckle-faced young officer who talked nonstop about any and all subjects.

"Name's Shaw, Parnell," he said, "but everybody calls me 'Red.' I never cared much for Parnell, anyhow.

Remember now, lieutenants in the Navy are the same as captains in the Army. Don't expect me to wait if a bird gets between our sectors.

"The way we do it here, we'll just head out and go straight for about 300 yards. Anything on the left, I'll take; anything on the right, you take. If the bird comes from the left and crosses to a line between us, it's your shot and vice versa."

"Got it," Grainger said.

At that moment two birds were flushed from the far right. Grainger raised his shotgun and fired twice. Both birds went down.

"Wow," Red said. "Nice shootin'."

They continued on for some time, but no birds appeared.

"How long you been in the Navy, Red?" Grainger asked.

"Almost 10 years," he replied. "Should be a lieutenant commander any day now. Heard I already got it, but the paperwork is hung up somewhere. Typical."

"Been in underwater demolition long?" Grainger asked.

"Yeah, right after getting commissioned. During World War II, we had 32 teams. Used to be about 100 men to a team. Now it's cut to five teams — seven officers and 45 men each. A lot of the guys had to transfer to other jobs. Not many amphibious landing forces left that need us to go in and clear the way. Inchon was a breeze, almost no obstacles. That damn tide would discourage anyone."

"What do you guys do for a mission, then?" Grainger asked.

"Good question," Red replied. "Not too much lately. We wish we had more missions."

"Army engineers do our demolition stuff," Grainger said.

"Yeah," Red said. "But they don't do any behind-the-lines jobs, you know, unconventional operations. Lately, we've been training a bunch of Koreans for Colonel Kim. He wants his own Korean UDT unit."

"Really," Grainger said. "How did that happen?"

"Well, we got the request from your headquarters in Tokyo. You're with the 8240th Group in Tokyo, right?"

Grainger nodded.

"Actually, I've got the detachment in Sasebo," he said.

"Yeah," Red said. "Well we got the official go-ahead to train them. And we did. I understand they put the training to good use. They dropped a freighter that was carrying a load of weapons to Shanghai. I guess it was kinda touchy. They had a PT boat that took 'em to a Japanese port, Nagasaki, I heard. We could've had political problems with that one, a Japanese port. We wouldn't have touched that with a 10-foot pole."

A pheasant flew up directly to Grainger's front. He was staring straight ahead, but apparently didn't see it.

"Take the shot," Red hollered.

The bird veered to the left. Red raised his shotgun and dropped the bird easily. He looked at Grainger.

"Wow, you blew that one, Ken. Geez, you look shook up. Don't worry, it could happen to anybody. That's two to one. I'm comin' after ya.

"Well, anyway, we'll probably be going back to Coronado for training in a couple of months. I love that place. Either there or San Clemente Island. Tough duty."

Grainger took a moment to compose himself.

"That ship in Nagasaki," he asked, "you wouldn't happen to know the name by any chance?"

"Nah," Red said. "I dunno. I think I heard it, but I forgot. Maru something, I forget. The Koreans got all excited about it. I know the feeling. They did just what we told 'em, three charges, one under each hold. The way they described it that thing was a sittin' duck. Kinda like that pheasant you just missed."

He smiled.

"Yeah," Grainger said. "Y'know, I heard about a ship that went down in Nagasaki recently. It was the *Kochi Maru*."

"Yeah, you know I think that's it. I think that was the one," Red said. "Yeah, *Kochi, Kochi Maru*. I mean, it had to be. Hell, how many ships go down like that? I can check it with one of the guys, if you want."

"No," Grainger said, "thanks. It's not important."

"Well, you're too good a shot, Ken," Red said later, when they were having a beer. "You started off hot, then you missed the one, too close I guess. Boy, you sure finished strong. Let's see, I got three and you got seven. I guess that means I'm buyin.'"

"You said your outfit's going Stateside in a couple of months," Grainger said. "Have you been here in Korea for a long time?"

"Nope, actually my outfit is UDT 3, Amphibious Group One, in Japan. We're up near Yokuska. It's just a fluke I'm here. I came over on temporary duty to help run some fitness tests for the guys here. It was a chance to see what's going on and maybe pop some pheasants. It worked out okay. We come over here on the courier plane because our guys fly it. They let us know when they got a couple of extra seats on the plane."

"That's the PBY that flies between the Japanese islands?" Grainger asked.

"Yeah, that's the one. The crew's Navy. They give a holler to see if anybody wants to get some first-class kimchee. I love that stuff."

"Any chance of catching a ride back tomorrow?" Grainger asked.

"I don't see why not," Red said. "The pilot's my roommate. I'll have him give you a call when I get back."

Ensign Zane Wenzel, skipper of the PBY, called an hour later and advised Grainger they would be leaving the compound at 2000 hours that same evening.

"We've got room and we'll stop in Sasebo," Wenzel said.

Grainger explained to Colonel Cunningham that he had enough information to work on the SOPs in Sasebo and if there were no objections he would like to complete the job there. There were no objections.

Grainger was sitting on the front porch of the detachment house after an early dinner. Sergeant Henderson joined him with his pipe and a bottle of Lucky Lager beer. A slim man walked by as they were chatting. He was wearing an Australian army hat with one side stapled to the crown.

"There he is," Henderson said. "That's 'Leftenant' Colin Wembly, the Englishman. He's the guy I talked about last night. Said he used to be in the British Commandos. He bunks here, but he's a civilian contract guy with the CIA. He's spooky. Never says much. Couple of times I saw him just sitting in the parlor, staring at the wall."

"What does he do?" Grainger asked.

"That's the problem," Henderson said. After a long pause he said, "He's an interrogation specialist."

"You mean he interrogates POWs?" Grainger asked.

"Yeah, well, I don't know. I'm not sure if they're always POWs," Henderson replied. "For what he does they don't really have a Military Occupational Specialty or MOS number."

He lowered his voice and looked directly at Grainger.

"He questions people … the hard way."

"What do you mean?" Grainger asked.

"I saw him do it once, in the basement," Henderson said.

"In the basement? The basement of this building?" Grainger asked.

"Yeah, I mean yes, sir," Henderson said. "We got a basement downstairs that's soundproofed. One night, me and Sergeant Gladney were sent to bring back a prisoner. The guy looked Caucasian, dressed in civilian clothes. I don't know if he was military or not. They brought him in on a truck and met us at the dock. The guy was in handcuffs and had a blindfold and a gag taped over his mouth. When we got here, we were told to take him down to the basement. The Englishman was there.

"I had never been down there before and I was surprised to see the layout. Some of the rooms had gear stored and boxes of rations. In the back there's this one room that has a heavy-duty chain bolted to the ceiling in the center of this one room. It hangs down to about five feet off the floor. It's right over a small drain in the floor.

"The Englishman points to the chain and we help to raise the guy's arms high up on the chain. The Englishman slips a smaller chain around the links joining the handcuffs and padlocks the whole business to the chain hanging down.

"He then pulls this olive drab hood outta his back pocket and puts it over this guy's head. Then he takes some rope out of his pocket and, quick-like, bends over and ties this guy's legs together just below the knees."

Henderson paused in his narrative, pulled out a pack of Lucky Strike cigarettes, and withdrew one. He lit it, took a deep drag, and looked at Grainger.

"I didn't know if we were supposed to stay or go. The Englishman puts his finger to his lips for us to be quiet and points to the wall. We backed up and just stood there.

"He starts whistling some slow tune; I never heard it before, like funeral music. Then he starts walking around this guy, all the time whistling, low and slow. He walks over to this cloth bag he had sittin' on a chair and takes out some black gloves and puts them on. All the time he's whistling.

"We had no idea what the hell was going on. After a few minutes of this stuff, wham! The Englishman hits this guy a shot to the small of his back. The guy's knees buckled for a second, then he straightened up. I'm wondering, what the hell is this? Is this guy some kind of spy? Did he sabotage something? Did he kill some of our people? What? I couldn't believe this was happenin.'

"There was another minute of circlin' and whistlin,' then a left to the ribs, oooh, even I felt that, then a right. He broke the guy's nose. You could hear it. Then the brown hood turned dark at the bottom and blood started to seep through onto the guy's chest.

"I'm outta here," I said.

"The Englishman quick flashed me a look like he could kill me. I opened the door and we got outta there fast. Gladney and I were upset, so we went to see the colonel. He told me that we shouldn't have stayed there. He said it was none of our business. He didn't like the stuff going on, but there was nothing he could do about it. The Englishman lives here, but he's on the CIA's payroll, he said.

"The colonel said the Englishman's battin' average is 1000. He always gets a name, a place, an address, whatever the hell it is they want.

"I thought I'd seen everything, but I never saw anything like that. The guy must have been a spy. Probably killed some CIA guys. They play rough. But that Englishman, that is one sorry, sick sonofabitch.

"The colonel told me to forget it and just do my job. When I told the first sergeant about it, he knew what I was saying. He said that by the third time the Englishman goes in there and starts whistlin,' the guy on the chain starts pissin' his pants.

Grainger listened in silence. "How'd you get in this outfit?" he asked.

"First sergeant's a buddy of mine from Bragg," Henderson said. "Told me it'd be a good way to get to Korea and not get in a 'leg' outfit. If an outfit ain't Airborne, it ain't shit. At least here I can get my jumps in and collect jump pay. It's easy duty, but they got a lotta weird guys around here.

"How'd you get in the outfit, Captain?" Henderson asked.

"Me," Grainger laughed, "I don't like snow. I was slated to go to Hokkaido with the First Cav and a friend helped me get this job. Right now, to tell you the truth, the snow may not have been that bad." ✦

SEVENTEEN
Nagasaki, Japan

Tsuneo Sakura operated a small diving and salvage company out of a wooden shed near the port of Nagasaki. He learned his trade in the Imperial Japanese Navy during World War II, while stationed at the Sasebo naval base.

Sakura returned to his devastated home town of Nagasaki when the war ended and started a private salvage company. Business was marginal at best, and Sakura was eager to score on any job that would reduce the pressure of barely meeting each monthly payroll while making payments on a floating barge.

Sakura asked port authorities about undertaking salvage operations after the *Kochi Maru* sank. He was told that the location of the derelict posed no immediate problems for the port and that they expected someone, probably the Americans, to assert ownership and claim salvage rights.

Strangely, no one seemed interested. An American Army captain claimed the Korean survivors. He intended to return them to Korea. At least that was the story reported in the newspapers, but, other than that, all inquiries were met with silence.

The chief of police reported that an investigation was now under way. The reporter from the *Nagasaki Nippo* who asked the chief why he had released the Korean merchant marine sailors to an American was told he was in danger of being thrown in jail for obstructing justice. A call from the police chief to the editor-in-chief was enough to squelch any further reportorial interest.

Sakura remained silent and waited. He watched over the stricken ship like a mother hen nesting on eggs. Sakura was ready and eager to move when the waiting period of 72 hours required by maritime law had elapsed. At 0300 of the third day he positioned his diving float directly over the stern area of the sunken ship and claimed salvage rights to the *Kochi Maru*.

"This ship has been abandoned," Sakura shouted to no one in particular.

He planned to go down later, at first light, and conduct a diving survey. His diving mechanic and business partner, Iwao Tomoko, set up the portable, gas-operated air compressor on the deck of the small salvage ship so that the lines extended over to the diving float.

"That ship has been abandoned, and it's ours," Sakura repeated to Tomoko. "I'll go down soon," he said. "This dive is mainly to protect our claim. Get someone from the port to witness it."

"Be sure to check the captain's cabin and chartroom," Tomoko said. "See if they have plans or blueprints."

"I doubt if there are any," Sakura said. "Hirado said it's just an old tramp freighter."

"Hirado?" Tomoko asked. "What does he know about it?"

"He was the pilot who brought it in," Sakura answered. "He said the captain was a crook—a Korean who was always involved with smuggling, stuff like that.

"Actually, she's so shallow we can get a visual on the measurements. At least enough to refloat it. Right now it's more important to get an idea about the cargo and how much is there."

"There'll be some bodies down there," Tomoko said, laughing. "Want me to go along?"

"No," Sakura said. "Besides, it won't be the first time I've had to work my way through corpses."

"Well, I'm glad it's you going down," Tomoko said. "Dead bodies make me nervous, like I'm violating someone's grave."

He shuddered.

"Just keep the compressor going and watch the lines," Sakura said, "and the bubbles. I don't expect any problems, but you never know. Just stay alert."

"You can count on it," Tomoko said.

Sakura, assisted by two members of his diving team, got into his canvas-covered, rubber-lined diving suit. His helpers slid the cumbersome bronze breastplate over his head and bolted it down. They placed a heavy lead belt around his waist and guided his feet into the heavy lead-soled diving boots, laced them up, and pulled the diving suit over the boot tops. They gave the helmet a sharp twist, locking it into place. They coupled the air hose to the helmet, and Sakura turned on the air valve. The suit swelled as it filled with air.

With the weight of the copper and lead suit, the two men had to help Sakura to the edge of the float where a short ladder was positioned. Sakura was totally immersed at the last step. He felt the comforting embrace of the canvas suit as he opened the air valve and adjusted the exhaust valve on the back of his helmet. He wrapped his legs about the descending line and gripped it with one hand. With the other he signaled for Tomoko to lower him.

Three fathoms down, he gave a quick jerk on the line, signaling for a stop. The light was better than he expected, and below him he could see the amidships housing and poop deck. He recognized it as an old pre-World War I freighter with the "Three Island" profile. The plumb bow and counter stern helped make identification easy.

Sakura guessed it was about 10,000 gross tons and wondered at his good fortune that no one had claimed salvage rights as the owner. He approached the deck and counted five cargo holds. He signaled to resume the lowering. This time he continued on until his feet hit the deck.

Sakura jerked twice on the line, signaling for Tomoko to give him some slack.

His lines eased off and he began moving freely about on the deck. He checked his lifeline and air hose.

The visibility was about four to five fathoms. Sakura decided to look below deck before checking the captain's cabin.

He turned carefully and moved cautiously through the water toward the hatch leading to the crew's quarters.

Inside, he noticed two bodies in the early stages of decomposition. They were being gently buffeted by the tidal action. Sakura shuddered. It was eerie seeing bodies that were moving about as if they had life.

Sakura was about to proceed to the captain's cabin directly below the bridge when he spotted a door to a small room adjacent to the sleeping area. He moved slowly across the steel decks and tried to push the door open. Something blocked it. He braced himself and pushed as hard as he could. The door opened just enough for him to push through the opening sideways. The diving helmet barely fitted as he arched his body so he could look inside.

A chill coursed through him. His first impulse was to leave, but he paused. Something he had glimpsed compelled another look.

There were three bodies in the small room. The corpses were beginning to disintegrate. The door was blocked by one of the bodies jammed between the door and a small cabinet next to a double-berth bed. A hand, partially devoid of flesh, was wrapped around a small metal box.

What's so important about that box? Sakura wondered. *Maybe it's money or jewels. This could be the answer to all my problems.*

Even though he realized the box and its contents may be germane to the investigation he knew was under way, the possibility of a financial windfall was too tempting to resist.

Something else attracted his attention and aroused his suspicions. Enough of the man's facial structure was intact to see he had a small round face, not the square-jaw facial structure of a Korean. This man was, almost without a doubt, Chinese. A Chinese crewman on an old Korean freighter? *Very unusual,* he thought.

Sakura didn't want to stay too long on this first dive. Movement was very slow and labored and, from where he was, the cause of the ship's sinking was not apparent. A more thorough investigation could wait until the next dive.

He reached down and pulled the small metal box from the clutching fingers, closing his eyes as he did so. Even in death, access to the box was not given easily. Sakura felt a chill again. He decided to check the captain's cabin and the bridge for plans or diagrams. He found nothing. A half-hour later he grabbed the descending line and signaled to come to the surface. Tomoko answered his signal promptly. The line became taut and he felt his body being lifted through the sea to about three fathoms. There was a minimal need for decompression. Even so, he allowed five minutes for the nitrogen that might form dangerous bubbles in his blood to work itself out. A short time later he signaled on his lifeline. His crew hauled him the rest of the way to the surface. He climbed up the small ladder with assistance from his crew members. Tomoko relieved him of the lead and copper helmet and weighted belt and hoisted him to the float. He was in his office at his desk 30 minutes later in his civilian dungarees and wool sweater. Tomoko was with him as he examined the little metal box with the combination lock.

"One of the crewmen was holding on to this," Sakura said. "He was in a small room off the crew's quarters. Even after 72 hours in the water, he looked more Chinese than Korean. Let's see what was so important in here that it was one of the last things on his mind."

He cut through the oval-shaped metal bar of the lock with a hacksaw. The lid was jammed tightly into place. Sakura selected a crowbar, placed the sharpened edge under the overlapping lid, and with a quick upward movement flipped open the lid, scattering the contents on the floor.

Tomoko and Sakura both bent to retrieve the fallen objects. It was clear that there was no stash of yen or gemstones. There were just some papers folded to envelope size and a few plastic-covered cards.

Sakura picked up one of the cards. He had a limited understanding of English. Even so, it was better than Tomoko's. He mouthed the words slowly as he read "Central Intelligence Agency."

Sakura looked at Tomoko who shrugged his shoulders and said, *"Wakarimasen"* (I don't understand).

The one word Sakura knew for sure was enough to give him an idea of what he discovered. That word was "Intelligence."

Chief Yamamoto of the Nagasaki Police Department nodded his head as the translator he summoned after Sakura's call explained the writing on the four plastic identification cards.

"These men whose pictures are on the cards are some kind of foreign agents," the translator said. "I believe you have found the bodies and credentials of four spies."

"Three spies," Sakura said. "There were only three bodies in that room."

He stopped and bowed as Chief Yamamoto raised his hand indicating he should say nothing further.

"Thank you," the chief said to the translator. "Go back to your office and do not discuss this with anyone. That's an order."

"*Hai*," the translator said, bowing sharply at the waist. He quickly left the office.

Chief Yamamoto told Sakura he could resume his salvage operations provided he delivered all items from the small room in which the agents had been discovered directly to him.

"If you find another body whose face resembles this one," the chief held up the only card that did not, according to Sakura, match a corresponding corpse, "let me know at once. In the meantime, I am ordering you not to discuss your findings with anyone. This is confidential police business. Do you understand?"

"Yes, sir," Sakura said.

He looked at Tomoko who in turn looked at the chief, nodded sharply, and bowed in acknowledgment of the order.

"Good," said the chief. "If no information gets out, you can continue to salvage the other contents. That is all for now. I'll let you know if I want you. Get the other contents of that room over here tomorrow."

Sakura bowed and left the office. Tomoko followed.

Yamamoto dialed the telephone number he had for Colonel Kim and let it ring 15 times.

Kim wouldn't have anything to do with Chinese spies, he thought, *or the Americans. He hates them as much as I do. No. This is the work of that young American captain. He has his own game. He didn't pay me enough to be a traitor.*

Chief Yamamoto pushed a buzzer on the side of his desk, signaling the Watch Commander to enter.

"I want you to contact Mr. Orano, Chief of Security, at the Governor's office. Tell him I must see him immediately to discuss a matter of dead American spies found on the sunken Korean freighter *Kochi Maru*. Tell him the matter is urgent because one of the spies may be wandering around our city."

Fifteen minutes later Chief Yamamoto was on the way to the Governor's office to brief Orano and the Governor on Sakura's surprising discovery.

Governor Jima's approach was not unexpected. He was a small, slender man of 67. Educated as a lawyer, his manner of questioning hadn't changed since his days as a prosecutor. His rapid-fire speech pattern, distinct from the slower pattern in northern Japan, had confused more than one defendant during a long and successful career.

Jima's first question went right to the heart of the matter and had been anticipated by Chief Yamamoto when he reported to Orano on Sakura's finding.

"Why did you release the survivors to the American?" Jima asked.

"They were a sad-looking bunch," Chief Yamamoto said. "I questioned them. They didn't know anything. The ship blew up. It was probably the boiler. They had worked on it in Sasebo and had trouble with it all the way to the port.

"Who knows how long they would have been in the hospital? I don't have the money to pay for that."

"First of all, Chief," Jima interrupted, "the expense would not come out of your budget. Disposition of foreigners is not under your jurisdiction. Now, please answer the question."

Chief Yamamoto blinked. The Governor was no fool, and, despite the disparity in their physical sizes, he knew that Jima was not someone with whom to trifle. Yamamoto sucked in his breath audibly and blinked again.

"Ah, yes, Governor," Yamamoto began, "I believed that it was my problem. The American had credentials saying he was from Tokyo, Far East Command. I wrote that down. He said the crew worked for the American government, and he wanted to be sure they got good medical care at home."

Jima crossed his arms, looked about, then shook his head. He gave Yamamoto a withering look of disgust.

"What is the American's name? Who in the Far East Command does he work for? How do we find him? How did he get here so fast from Tokyo? I understand the ship exploded, the American showed up, you released the survivors, he put them on an American boat, and now he's gone. How did you know his credentials were genuine? Now we have the bodies of American spies along with their credentials turning up in my Prefecture. Are you really this stupid?"

This dressing-down was not only rare by Japanese standards, it was something Yamamoto had never heard before. He flared momentarily at the word "stupid," but quickly assumed a contrite attitude when he saw he was facing a truly outraged Governor.

The Governor turned to Orano.

"You better get to the bottom of this damn fast. I do not like being embarrassed by the Americans. This Prefecture will not be the laughingstock of Japan. I expect you to be on this matter full time."

"Yes, sir," Orano said. "What do we do about the *Nippo*? They have been calling my office asking questions about the salvage company doing the diving. The salvage people wouldn't tell the reporter anything, not even the name of the ship."

Governor Jima studied his fingernails for a moment.

"Tell them," he said finally, "that we have a mystery ship lying on the bottom of our harbor. We found bodies and credentials for what appear to be American agents on a Korean freighter. We have no idea what's going on, but we are investigating the matter. We are checking to see if there are any violations of international law. That's all we know. You will handle all press relations. Is that clear?"

"Yes, sir," Orano replied. He bowed quickly.

The Governor turned to Chief Yamamoto.

"I intend to find out about this mystery," Jima said. "From this point, you say nothing about this matter to anyone except Orano. Do you understand me?"

The chief rose quickly to his feet.

"I understand, sir," he said, bowing low and holding it for three seconds to emphasize his surrender to authority.

"Good," the Governor said. "I expect nothing less than the full and complete cooperation of you and your entire department. You can begin by going back to your office and writing a full report on everything you know about this sordid affair. Leave nothing out. I want your report on Orano's desk today. Is that clear?"

"Yes, sir," Yamamoto said, bowing again and being sure to hold it another three seconds.

Governor Jima scratched his head and looked at the four credentials.

Four American credentials, he thought, *and three Chinese bodies. Where's the other Chinese body? Yamamoto is sure only Koreans were taken to the boats. Only Korean bodies were in the morgue. This was more than a one-man job. Was the missing one working with the ones who blew up the boat? Too many questions.* ✦

EIGHTEEN
Moscow, Russia

"General," Proloff said excitedly as he entered General Petrovsky's office, "important news. I knew you would want it immediately."

"What the hell, Proloff?" Petrovsky said. "You charge in here like a stud in heat."

"It's the *Kochi Maru*," Proloff said, "that ship in Nagasaki that was sunk, the one Svetlana put us on to ..."

"I know," Petrovsky said. "The CIA operation with the Army fellow."

"Yes, General," Proloff said. "Well, listen to this, Andropov just sent it over. This is a translation from the *Nagasaki Nippo*. The headline says `Mystery Ship.' The story on the front page starts off with this question: `Is America using Japan as a base to place secret agents into China?'"

Petrovsky pushed back from his desk and snatched the article from Proloff's hand.

"Well, well," he said, reading. "'A metal box with a combination lock was found by a Japanese diver. It was found next to the body of a Chinese seaman and contained American Central Intelligence Agency credentials. In the same room they found pistols, money, and maps.' Oh, this is great!

"'There were three Chinese seamen in the little room where the metal box was found.'"

"Seamen, my ass," Petrovsky roared. "They're agents. They got caught with their pants down. I love it. Those pious American bastards. Always accusing us of trying to steal their precious secrets. Always pretending that they don't have as big a spy network as we do—because they've got God on their side."

Petrovsky stood up, still reading from the paper:

"'Is this a violation of international law?'" he read.

"Absolutely," he answered.

"'Is this a betrayal of our trust in America?'"

"Hell, yes," he answered again.

"'Will this create problems for the U.S. with China?'"

"I damn well hope so. Mark the calendar," Petrovsky chortled. "This is the day the Americans stepped right on their privates in front of the whole world. Tonight we will have a party and celebrate."

"Think they'll deny it?" Proloff asked.

"Of course they'll deny it," Petrovsky said. "They'll scream denials from the mountaintops. They have about as much chance of being believed as a one-legged man in an ass-kicking contest.

"You know, Vassily," he said, "the Chinese will have a field day. This will help Mao. He was smart when he kicked all the Americans out, especially their missionaries. He knew they were just going to be spies. This one little covert caper will help him silence his critics. We don't have to worry about the Americans and Chinese getting together in our lifetime.

"Okay," he said, pulling his chair up to his desk, "time to go to work. Prepare a report for Marshal Shapnikov. I want to take it over there personally. He'll be delighted. We'll be filing an official protest about the wanton killing of innocent seamen. Contact Andropov in Nagasaki. Tell him to have Larissa keep after her policeman and pay her the bonus. Her friend will know things about the investigation that won't be in the newspaper.

"Tell Andropov I want to keep the heat on the Americans. They are putting the Japanese at risk in their dealings with the Chinese. This is just another kind of bomb.

"Have someone contact the reporter who wrote this story. Give him lots of encouragement. We don't get that many chances to really embarrass those arrogant bastards. Prepare press releases for *Pravda* expressing our shock, dismay, horror, revulsion, you know, at the duplicity and arrogance of the American government. Pile it on about how they're so big they don't respect another nation's sovereignty. Make sure that *Tass* gets it, too.

"Start sniping at the Japanese government's decision to go democratic. They're going to regret it. They're facing changes they've never thought of. With democracy comes problems.

"You know, Vassily, at one time, only the man in Japan could get a divorce. If he got tired of a woman, he just went to the police station and drew a line through his name on the police blotter. Simple. Now, with their new democracy, women have the same right. I heard that in Fukuoka, on the first day of the new change, there was a line of women around the police station six blocks long."

Petrovsky looked down at his notepad.

"What did you find out about that American captain in Nagasaki?"

"He's a Port Liaison Officer in Sasebo," Proloff said. "His name is Grainger, Ken Grainger. He's a combat soldier. He had a good war record in Korea."

"Colonel Proloff, who is it we have in Sasebo? Oh, I remember. I thought I told you to get rid of him. That American is no more a port officer than I am. What's a port officer doing in Nagasaki hours after some old Korean freighter full of Koreans blows up? He's working for the American CIA.

"If Andropov wasn't busy in Nagasaki, I'd send him. We need another Svetlana."

"Speaking of Svetlana," Proloff said, "her new lieutenant boyfriend says that the people in Tokyo are unhappy with the captain in Sasebo. Apparently, he's new on the job. The lieutenant says this Grainger fellow isn't too smart."

"Hrummp," Petrovsky snickered, "he was smart enough to get the chief of police to help him get the survivors out of the hospital and out of Nagasaki. It may be that our captain isn't too smart, but he got that job done. So, he works for Army Intelligence and cleans up after CIA messes. Interesting. He got the survivors loaded on a boat back to Korea. Where in Korea?"

"Pusan," Proloff said.

Petrovsky looked pensive.

"What about those survivors? Don't we have someone there who can get to them?"

"No," Proloff said. "They were taken over to the island off southern Pusan where they train those partisans."

"Well then, they're dead," Petrovsky said. "The Korean CIA is on that island. They've got one guy, a colonel, I first heard of when he was just a captain. Ruthless sonofabitch. Killed his own mother after raping her. She fell in love with a Japanese officer during the occupation.

"We have a file on that guy. He likes to torture people before he kills them, brags about using acid. We have some pictures of his handiwork on women. There's a difference between torturing people to get information to win a war and doing it because you like to see people suffer. You can forget about those survivors."

General Petrovsky pulled a blue file folder out of his bottom drawer.

"Here it is," he said. "I started this file, and a few others, when I got this job three years ago. This one goes back to when we were going through Korea after the Americans dropped the second bomb. This fellow was on a short list our Order of Battle people said should be exterminated without hesitation. Name's Sukow Kim. We just have this old picture taken ..."

Petrovsky stopped and looked at Proloff.

Proloff had suddenly turned pale. His hand was covering his mouth and his eyes were wide open.

"What's the matter?" Petrovsky asked in surprise.

Proloff swallowed, struggling to find his voice.

"Oh, General," he said. "We have a problem."

"What?" Petrovsky asked.

"One of our radio messages from Nagasaki talked about a Colonel Kim being involved with the chief of police there. And then the report from Svetlana. You remember we were talking about having her dump that moron lieutenant and move up in the world—a colonel or something higher, we said?"

"Go on," Petrovsky said quietly, staring intently.

"Well," Proloff said, "in her last message, she said that the lieutenant was bragging to a Korean colonel about this fantastic, rich American woman who couldn't get enough. The colonel said he didn't believe him, he would have to prove it. So, the lieutenant took the colonel to her place for dinner.

"Svetlana said the colonel slipped something into the lieutenant's drink and he passed out. She said that she and the colonel screwed like minks. She wants to dump the idiot lieutenant and have the colonel move in with her.

"She says he's in the Korean Central Intelligence Agency. His name is Sukow Kim."

"Get her out of there!" Petrovsky shouted. "Now! Before you do one other thing, get her out of there! Order her home, say we have an emergency, drop everything, come home."

Proloff hurried from the office. Petrovsky stared out the window. Winter was in the air. The fall colors that had been so brilliant when they dappled the surrounding landscape were now a mottled brown. He remembered that October two years ago when he first saw Svetlana. She was standing in a group outside a bungalow they used as a classroom. It was on the camp grounds, the site selected to train the illegals. Her sweater mirrored the colors of the surrounding woodlands — orange, amber, red, and brown. She had been laughing with her head thrown back, blonde hair tousled. She seemed to sense someone looking at her, and she turned. For him, the chemistry was immediate.

One week later, they had lunch at a restaurant on the outskirts of Moscow. She spoke candidly.

"Comrade General," she said, "I'm so honored to have this lunch with you. Why do I deserve to have you all to myself? I get the feeling I'm going to be the dessert."

He smiled and nodded.

"We pick only the smartest for our illegals training," Petrovsky said dryly.

"Ah," she said, "I understand that all generals have an apartment they use when they are too busy to get home."

She squeezed his hand.

"Comrade General, you will be my first general. I hope there is much you can teach me. It should be a delightful lesson."

"I also understand," he said, "that many teachers say they learn more from their students than they expect."

She smiled and shrugged her shoulders.

"Who knows?"

Inside his car, she threw her arms around him and kissed him.

It was a kiss that started slowly, grew in intensity, and ended with Petrovsky gasping for air.

They both laughed when they looked up and noticed the windows had fogged over.

That evening, after he had taken her back to the school, he kept seeing her as she walked toward him. She had moved slowly and watched as he devoured her with his eyes.

211

If I don't get this stupid smile off my face, he had thought, *Anna will know how I spent my afternoon.*

Now, in his office, his mind drifted back to their many liaisons. Would he ever see her again?

Oh, Svetlana, my little pussy cat, he thought, *I taught you too well. I said you should always go for the higher ranks, colonel and above. What have I gotten you into?*

He smiled to himself as he remembered his frequent offers to get a divorce so they could marry. Each time she became angry.

"If your career doesn't mean anything to you, it certainly does to me," she said, raising her voice. "Remember your lovely wife with the body of a cow is the daughter of your boss. There's probably an outpost in Siberia just made for former generals who do stupid things."

"As a matter of fact, there is," he said, smiling.

"And, darling," she said, smiling, "I do not intend to live in Siberia. I hate the cold. That's why I'm in your school."

Now, Petrovsky sat in a darkened office filled with sadness.

Be careful, little one, he thought. *Be very careful.*

The seaplane touched down at dusk and bounced to a stop near the harbor entrance in Sasebo. Grainger had purposely not asked CPO Michaels to meet him, so he rode ashore on the port launch.

He went to his office, picked up his jeep, and drove to the apartment he shared with Julie. She jumped up and down when she saw him come through the door. Then she stopped.

"What's the matter, Ken?" she asked. "You do not look good. Do you have trouble?"

She came into his arms and they embraced.

I can't involve Julie, Ken thought. *This has nothing to do with her. All this could do is put her in a dangerous situation. I need to talk to somebody about Perkins and his bullshit story. Why did he lie and say the Korean captain sank his own ship? I've got to talk to Salencio, and fast; this thing is way over my head.*

He held Julie's face in his hands and kissed her.

"It's all right," he said, "don't worry. I'll work it out. I just need to go over and talk to Major Salencio."

"It's too late now," she said. "First we go to bed. Then I give you a massage and you sleep a little. I will fix you some food. Tomorrow morning early you go see Major."

Later that evening, as she was leaning over his back giving him a massage, she glanced down at the tattoo on the back of his right hand.

"Ken," she said, reaching over and touching the blue triangle, "why do you have this? What does this mean?"

He shifted to a sitting position with his back against the headboard. Julie straddled him and ran her fingers over his chest.

"When I was a boy," he said, "my father was an alcoholic. He beat my mother and he beat me."

He reached out, took her hand, and placed it on the top of his head. Her fingers could feel a long indentation.

She frowned.

"One night," Grainger continued, "he threw a metal disc at me. I ducked and it split my head open. He did worse. He knocked all of my mother's teeth out. The beatings he gave her eventually killed her."

Grainger closed his eyes for a few moments.

"He skipped town, he ran away, afraid of going to jail. I was 11 years old and wound up in an orphanage. Years later I heard he got married again and lived in Binghamton, New York.

"I began boxing at the YMCA. My plan was to learn how to fight so that someday I could find him and do to him what he did to my mother. My boxing coach was an old black man named Manley Johnson. He used to laugh at how awkward I was, but he said he liked my spirit. Every time I got knocked down, I bounced right up again.

"I know I won a lot of fights. I don't remember how many. Then one day Manley and a friend of his said they thought I needed a tattoo because that's what warriors had. It was supposed to be a mark that linked a man with the gods. I really felt it was a special honor to get invited to have one.

"Manley said, 'Your defense still needs a lot of improvement, but when you hit someone with that left hook, ouch, man, that's like dy-no-mite.'

"What about the letter, 'D,'" I suggested.

"'Pretty good,'" he said with a smile. "'But maybe we can even improve on that.'"

"That night I went to his house. It was a small house, but very warm. His wife was a good cook like my mom. The smell of food made me hungry. I had ham hocks and turnip greens for the first time in my life. He showed me a card with the triangle symbol. 'This is the African symbol for the letter "D,"' he said. 'When you look at it, think: Take charge; do it; do it now; and hit very hard with dy-no-mite. Never be afraid to win.'"

"He had a laugh that boomed all over the house. He was more like a father to me than any man I'd ever known.

"I won 16 fights in a row, I remember that, and won the State Light Heavyweight Championship. A drunk driver hit and killed him as he was crossing a street. I was in a daze. For a while I lost track of time and just wandered around. It was shortly after that that I joined the Army. This tattoo reminds me of him and the need to keep fighting no matter what."

He looked up and saw tears streaming down Julie's cheeks. She leaned forward and kissed him. He could taste the salt from her tears and could not stop the flow of his own.

His voice was low and husky with emotion as he whispered, "I have never told anyone what really happened. I just tell them my parents are dead."

"Is your father dead, too?" Julie asked.

"Yes," Grainger said. "He died while I was in Korea. I didn't go to the funeral. I've also got two sisters living some-

214

where in Wisconsin that I have to look up when I go home. It's time for me to find them and get reacquainted."

It was midnight in Tokyo. Arthur Church was preparing a coded message for transmission to the Director of Central Intelligence at Langley. He pounded his fist on his desk.

"How the hell do I say it?" he said, speaking to his deputy chief, Walter Dole.

Dole threw up his hands trying to stifle a yawn. He had been sleeping when Church called with his emergency summons.

"Right now, I don't know," he said. "Let's work on it. Something will come to us."

"This is an unbelievable disaster," Church said. "My mistake was in trusting that moron, Perkins, to help with this operation. He and that psycho, Sukow Kim, have screwed this operation royally. They've elevated 'fuck up' to an art form."

Dole stifled another yawn.

"Now that we know Chen was a double," Church said, "it's too late to do anything. He's flown the coop. Bastard really set us up. There's no way we could be tied to this thing without those credentials. I don't understand, Walter, why didn't you collect their credentials?"

Dole put his fingers to his forehead and rubbed the perspiration.

"Art, I told Chen to collect all the credentials and keep them in a safe place. He was the head of the team. I just expected that he would automatically give them to me. It was for his protection. If he's picked up, and they find credentials, he's dead. Everyone on his team is dead. Frankly, I screwed up. I can't believe it, but the last time I saw him in Sasebo I forgot to ask for them. I thought of everything but that. I don't have a good excuse. Hell, I don't have any excuse."

"Dammit, Walter," Church railed, "if I had known that, I could have claimed salvage rights for the damn ship. None of this would have come to light.

"Kim's the bastard who caused the problem. If he hadn't gone nuts and sunk that ship, we would have confirmed that Chen was a double and grabbed him. We could then abort the whole mission like I wanted to do. Forty-eight hours, that's all Kim had to wait. Perkins swears that he had no idea what Kim was up to. He said he got a call after the ship was sunk. Frankly, I don't believe him. I've got someone checking with the UDT people to find out who gave the clearance for them to train Kim's people."

Dole's head was down and he continued to shake it side to side.

"Now," Church said, "the whole world knows about the mission. The story in the paper about us using Japan as a base to plant agents in China. Shit! Chen probably intended to give those credentials to the Chinese. He probably figured we couldn't deny trying to ship agents out of Japan since he had their official credentials. Why didn't he take them with him?

"I went there personally to advise the Governor of Nagasaki that the credentials were forgeries, put there to embarrass our government. He laughed in my face, the bastard. He did say that in the interest of good relations with our government, he would officially accept my explanation. He also expects a huge payoff for Japan. We'll pay it even though it's blackmail. General Clark's only comment when he was briefed was to make it go away and damn fast.

"I always suspected that working with Koreans was going to be my downfall. Someday I hope I get something on that sonofabitch, Kim. He's screwed up the best operation we ever planned. It was foolproof. Perkins is finished, too. He was always a lightweight. He gets his jollies playing with the big boys. Well, he better stick to beating up on his subordinates. That's all he's good for."

216

He hesitated and took a sip of coffee.

"C'mon, Walter, how the hell are we going to explain this to Langley?"

"We could always try the truth."

"Yeah, sure," Church said. "I'll just tell them I've been working with a certified nut case who got a wild hair up his ass and blew up the ship. You know, they just may buy it. But when I get to why we didn't pick up their credentials ..."

Grainger arrived at his office the following morning and found a message from Shelvoski tacked to his office door.

"Major Perkins from your Tokyo office called and said you are to call him immediately on your return. He said do not talk to *anyone* at the Camp Sasebo HQ or anywhere else, before you talk to him."

Grainger opened the door and was walking to his desk when the telephone rang. He looked at his watch and noted the time, 0801.

That's probably Perkins, he thought.

"This is Lieutenant Colonel Skinner, S-2 of Camp Sasebo," the voice said. "Are you Captain Grainger of the Far East Command Liaison Group?"

"Yes, sir," Grainger said.

"Captain," Skinner began, "were you in Nagasaki recently, within the past week?"

"Sir," Grainger said, "may I ask why you are asking this?"

"Normally, no," Skinner said, "but in this case I'm going to make an exception. A ship was blown up in Nagasaki at about 0300 on the 10th of October. A policeman in Nagasaki called and informed us that your jeep bumper markings were spotted in Nagasaki on the morning of the 10th. Three days later, Japanese divers went down to claim salvage rights on the ship and in the process found something they shouldn't have."

"Sir?" Grainger said.

"They found the bodies of some alleged CIA agents and, incredibly, their credentials. Actually, four sets of credentials were found. The headline of the *Nagasaki Nippo*, their main newspaper, reads: `Mystery Ship.' We got an English translation. Let me read just the first sentence in that article: `Is America using Japan as a base to place secret agents into China?'

"Now, Captain, we need some answers. The Governor of the Nagasaki Prefecture has called Colonel Beardsley to find out if the American Army captain seen around the Port Headquarters on the 10th is under his command. The colonel assured him that the officer is not. He also told the Governor that he would conduct an investigation to learn who the officer was and who he worked for."

"Sir," Grainger said, "I respectfully request that you call my boss in Tokyo, Major Perkins, or Colonel Beane at AFFE G-2."

"What is that? Some kind of Fifth Amendment, Captain," Skinner asked. "I asked you a simple question. Were you there on the 10th? What I suggest is that you make the call and I think you should make it very soon. In the meantime, and you can take this as a direct order; if you have any information such as documents, or a file, or if you were there as alleged, you are hereby directed to report to the Commanding Officer, Colonel Beardsley, at his office at 1500 today. Do you understand the order?"

"Yes, sir," Grainger replied. "Sir, am I allowed a question?"

"Against my better judgment, what is it?" Skinner said.

"Sir," Grainger said, "if I don't have any information such as a file or other documentation, do you still want me to see Colonel Beardsley at 1500?"

"Yes," Skinner said. "And I will tell you, Captain, if you're not here, I will have the MPs provide free transportation. Now you do whatever you have to do. Somehow, I have to think that responsibility for a snafu of this size just has to be a few notches above your pay grade. In your case, I hope that's true."

Perkins answered the phone.

"Major, this is Grainger in Sasebo."

"Has anyone down there talked to you about Nagasaki?" Perkins asked.

"Yes, sir," Grainger said, "the minute I walked into my office the phone rang. Thinking it was you, I answered it. It was a call from Lieutenant Colonel Skinner, S-2 of Camp Sasebo. He called and asked about a headline and story in a Nagasaki newspaper. He said the CO down here, Colonel Beardsley, received a phone call from the Governor's office at the Nagasaki Prefecture. They have the bumper markings from my jeep.

"I didn't directly acknowledge anything, but they know it's me. Colonel Skinner directed that I bring any documents or files I have on hand and report to Colonel Beardsley at 1500 this afternoon. I did change my bumper markings, but the post has the old markings on file. I asked Colonel Skinner to call you directly, but he declined. I'm sure they expect a phone call from you or someone in Tokyo."

"Didn't my note say that you were not to talk to anyone at Camp Sasebo?" Perkins asked.

"Sir," Grainger said, "I didn't have a choice. He called here, and judging from his comments if I had refused to talk to him, he would have sent the MPs down here to pick me up. I'm sitting here between the Devil and the Deep Blue Sea. People in Nagasaki can identify me. I responded in the most noncommittal way I could. Just tell me what to do about the 1500 meeting."

Perkins was silent for a moment.

"You have no documents, right?" Perkins then asked.

"That's correct, Major," Grainger said. "I do not have any documents and I have never had any documents that have anything to do with that ship in Nagasaki or what I did when I was there. I would still like to get the abstract you promised."

"We're past that," Perkins said. "There will be no abstract or anything else. You have no need to know. Your part of the job is done. Finished. I will see that you get your transfer."

I'd love to let him know I found out he lied to me about who sunk that ship, Grainger thought. *I need to talk to Salencio first, and maybe a lawyer after that.*

"I'm disappointed, Major," Grainger said. "It's tough to think you're part of a team and then not be told what's really going on. I want that letter you promised me detailing those verbal directives."

"The planning of this operation predated your mistaken assignment," Perkins rasped. "If you want to help the team, keep your mouth shut. As far as any letter is concerned, I'll think about it."

"What do I do about the meeting at Post Headquarters at 1500 today?" Grainger asked.

"Be there," Perkins said. "I'll see that things are taken care of. You just show up and don't say anything. Is that clear?"

Grainger called Salencio.

"Morning, Ken," Salencio said. "I understand you may want us to get together?"

Grainger laughed.

"That's an understatement."

"Yeah, I guess so," Salencio said. "Actually, there are some Counter-Intelligence aspects to the Nagasaki incident that I've been asked to look into and report on ASAP. I don't think there's much for us there, but I've got some people on it."

"Well, the first thing you need to know," Grainger said, "is that what will become the 'official version' is not what happened."

"Ken, I've got a little situation that will take me out of the office for a while; can't be helped. And, I understand you have a 'command performance' at the headquarters this afternoon. How about we get together at my office at 1700?"

"Word gets out fast," Grainger said. "Yeah, 1700 will work just fine."

Grippa knocked on Perkins' door.

"Sir," he said. "Colonel Kim is on the telephone for you. When I asked him who was calling he wouldn't give me his name; he just said, 'Tell him he has a call,' but I know it's him."

"Shut the door," Perkins said.

"Perkins," he said.

"I'm not sure it was such a good idea to send your young crusader over to Pusan," Kim said.

"I heard," Perkins said. "Well, he'll be gone as soon as Colonel Beane gets back from the Pentagon."

"I was hoping he would stay over here for a few days. I had a couple of friends who were hoping he would visit some of our Pusan sights. A nice discussion would do wonders for his attitude."

"I don't know what spooked him," Perkins said. "Cunningham said he had no problem with him working in Sasebo, and after your little confrontation, he felt it might be better not to have him at the island. There was no way I could really object. In any event, his status here is only temporary."

"You're right," Kim said, laughing. "His status is definitely temporary."

"What do you mean?" Perkins asked.

"Nothing that need concern you," Kim said. "I am planning a little party for the rash captain. He needs a lesson in showing respect for senior officers."

"For God's sake, be careful," Perkins said, lowering his voice.

"Oh, don't worry," Kim said, crowing like a bantam rooster, "I won't be within miles."

Grainger walked into Colonel Beardsley's secretary's office five minutes before his appointment.

The door to Colonel Beardsley's office was ajar. His voice was loud, and Grainger could tell from his manner of speaking that he was on the telephone. His voice boomed, but the tone was clearly deferential.

The secretary held her finger to her lips and pointed to a chair.

"He's on the telephone," she whispered.

She rose and closed the office door.

For the next five minutes the part of the telephone conversation that Grainger heard through the walls was, "Yes, sir. No, sir. Yes, General. No, General."

As the sweep second-hand on the wall clock reached 1500, Grainger could hear the Colonel say, "General Lowry, I understand your position completely and I will let you handle all further communication with the Governor. Yes, sir. We're out of it. Yes, sir, I understand."

Grainger knew from a conversation with Doutter that Major General Harold Lowry was Colonel Beane's boss and the Intelligence chief, G-2, for the Armed Forces Far East.

There was a long silence after the telephone conversation ended.

"Is Captain Grainger out there?" Beardsley roared on the intercom.

"Yes, sir," his secretary answered.

"Send him in," the colonel said.

The first thing Grainger saw as he walked rapidly into the office was a red-faced man with a decidedly angry countenance. He came to a halt three steps in front of the colonel's desk, stood at attention, rendered a very crisp salute and waited for the return salute.

It never came. When it was obvious that the colonel was not going to return his salute, he lowered his arm.

"Captain," Beardsley began, "I don't know what you're doing here in Sasebo. I don't know what you were doing in Nagasaki, either. Furthermore, I don't give a damn. Actually, I don't give a damn what you or any of your damn spook friends do, or when, or how you do it. I just want you to get your ass out of my office and outta my sight, and I hope, no, I pray, I never see or hear anything about you for the rest of my tour. Have I made myself clear?"

"Yes, sir," Grainger said.

The colonel nodded.

"Get out!"

Grainger was now as red-faced as the colonel. He saluted smartly, not waiting for a return, did an about-face and left.

Grainger was more upset than at any time since he joined the Army. His hands were shaking as he turned on the ignition switch in his jeep.

I've got to do something.

He sat for a moment staring through the windshield of the jeep, oblivious to the passersby who looked at him and wondered why he looked so sad.

Back at his office he began jotting down a chronology of events from the time of his initial arrival in Sasebo to the just concluded meeting with Colonel Beardsley. His writing was very specific, starting with Perkins' phone call telling him of the ship going down, to his confrontation with Colonel Kim and what Lieutenant Shaw had told him during the pheasant hunt. He kept gritting his teeth during the entire process.

He entered Major Salencio's office at 1700.

Salencio smiled.

"You've been busy," he said, as he looked at the sheaf of papers Grainger was carrying.

Grainger smiled sheepishly.

"Today was not one of my better days," he said. "I finally met Colonel Beardsley."

Salencio smiled and nodded.

"That's what I heard," he said. "You know, he's really a good man. He's old Army and would never make it in the spy business. He's from the school that thinks it's rude to read the other guy's mail."

Salencio stood and motioned to a room next to his office.

"Let's go in the conference room. We won't be bothered there. I've asked Dave Levy to come over after he gets off work. Dave's a lawyer, but I will vouch for him 100 percent. He can be trusted. He was also a very good friend of Doutter. I expect that Jerry even mentioned his name."

Grainger nodded.

"The way things are going right now, you may be needing a good lawyer."

Salencio brought in some lined pads and pencils and placed them on the table.

"You know," he said, "translations of the *Nagasaki Nippo* have been circulating all over this post. Everyone is becoming expert on what you do for a living. If we were back home, I'd suggest you run for mayor. You have great name identification. Hell, even the Japanese civilians know who you are."

Grainger sat back, hands on his lap, and audibly expelled a lungful of air.

"I feel bad about the meeting with Colonel Beardsley. He's caught in the middle and I don't blame him for being pissed off. That was probably the shortest and best ass-chewing I ever got."

He smiled ruefully.

"I just wish I could have told him that I'm pissed off, too."

Grainger took out the notes he made at his office.

"I wrote a chronology of pretty much everything that's happened here since my arrival. I was very specific about my telephone conversation with Perkins after the ship went down, and what I learned during my short trip to Pusan. This thing is really over my head. I need some guidance and help. Everyone seems to think I'm going to need a lawyer. They may be right."

A light knock sounded on the conference room door and Colonel Dave Levy entered.

He was slightly built, probably in his mid-40s, with a widow's hump. His thinning gray hair shaded his scalp. He looked more like a librarian than the tough trial attorney he was rumored to be. The feature that belied his appearance was his penetrating dark-brown eyes that bore directly through you and seemed to miss nothing. He wore only his rank and no decorations on a tropical-worsted uniform, wrinkled and a bit tight in the midsection. His Judge Advocate Branch insignia was pinned on sideways, far from regulation.

"Well, you're right on cue, counselor," Salencio said.

Levy looked at Grainger and extended his hand.

"Dave Levy," he said. "Nice to meet you at last, especially since I've heard nothing but your name all day at Headquarters."

Grainger's smile was sheepish.

"Nice to meet you, Colonel," Grainger said. "Both Roberto and Jerry spoke highly of you. Thank you for being here. I'm in some trouble right now and really need the help of some people I can trust."

"I've spent my entire career being a defendant's lawyer," Levy said. "It's a little late for me to try to change. Besides, I like working for the underdog."

"I guess that's me," Grainger said, smiling. "Thanks."

"I doubt the staff at Camp Sasebo will be spending much time on this matter," Levy said. "I heard about the one-sided conversation Colonel Beardsley had with Major General Lowry, AFFE-G2. The issue has been moved upstairs and will probably be resolved there. That's where it really belongs, not here in Sasebo. Sometimes politics can be a wonderful balm."

Grainger began relating some of the points he had written in his chronology. He told of Colonel Cunningham's belief about the eight survivors being assassinated and his confrontation with Colonel Kim and his boasting reference to the problem being handled.

"This thing is really convoluted," he said. "One of the Navy chiefs who runs one of my PT boats is apparently not a great friend of Major Perkins. He told me that Navy records will show that Perkins signed the letter for Colonel Beane clearing the way for U.S. Navy UDT people to train the Koreans. It was an official request for the Far East Command Liaison Group. The chief also showed me his log where he transported the Korean demolition team from Pusan to Nagasaki and back to Pusan.

"When I went to Nagasaki to get the survivors out of the hospital and ship them back to Korea per his instructions, Perkins told me the Korean ship captain had double-crossed him and sabotaged his own ship. He said the captain was afraid that if the agents were picked up in Shanghai, he would be named as a spy.

"The reason he wanted the survivors back in Pusan was to avoid any problems with Japanese immigration people. That was also a bald-faced lie. When I was in Nagasaki, I bribed the chief of police, gave him $5,000 worth of yen to release the survivors to my custody."

At this point it was Salencio who audibly exhaled a gust of air.

Levy's eyes hooded over and he wore a deadpan expression that seemed more like a trance than someone engrossed in listening to a story.

"My argument with Colonel Kim over the survivors was not pleasant. And I did go further than I should have. But I remembered how helpless and afraid they looked clutching their bathrobes as they got on board the PT boats.

"Lieutenant Shaw, the Navy UDT guy, told me they had trained the Koreans because they were informed officially that the ship had a cargo of contraband weapons that was bound for China. At this point I don't believe that either Major Perkins or Colonel Kim are aware that I know who really sank the ship and that their cover story is BS."

"I think we can conclude that your biggest problems are not with Post Headquarters," Salencio said. "Colonel Kim's methods are well documented. He is a very scary and dangerous person. His own people can't control him. He believes he's destined to head the Korean CIA and one day run the country. Fortunately, I haven't heard of too many people who agree with his thinking. But you need to stay on high alert."

"You're aware," Levy asked, "that officially you're being set up as the sacrificial lamb?"

"Yes, sir," Grainger said. "For at least part of it. They may try to stick with the idea of being double-crossed by the Korean captain, but Navy documentation will blow that out of the water. I guess I could have refused to get the survivors out of the hospital, but other than being in shock, none of them looked wounded. I could never imagine that they would be assassinated. I suppose I did take part in breaking some of Japan's immigration laws. I don't know if that's enough to get me bounced out of the Army, but it could give me an OER that will accomplish the same thing."

Levy nodded.

"That's a possibility," he said. "It depends on how hard they want to push it." He paused. "And how hard we may want to push back. We can, and should, subpoena the Navy records. See if you can get a copy of the PT boat's log. If you can't take a picture of it, get a certified true copy made at the

Post Headquarters. My secretary can help you with that. Do you have the name of the Navy UDT lieutenant and his unit?"

"Yes, sir," Grainger said.

"Call me Dave," he said. "I'm more comfortable with that."

Grainger nodded.

"Do you have any idea why you were told this lie about the ship's captain?" Levy asked.

"No, sir, uh, Dave." Grainger smiled. "I have no idea," he said. "I would have done exactly the same thing to retrieve the survivors if Perkins had said nothing about who sank the ship. I never would have expected them to sink their own ship. The problem with me in this assignment is that Perkins never trusted me with anything."

"Telling you that story means they never intended to tell you the truth about the operation," Levy said. "Now, they are in hot water because four sets of Intelligence credentials were found, and Japan is in a good position to embarrass the United States internationally. That's really something, considering that Japan has only recently been accorded its sovereignty."

He stopped to make some notes on a yellow pad.

"Of course, the protests from the Chinese and Russians can and will easily be dismissed as propaganda," Levy continued. "We're at war with China, and everyone expects the Russians to take any side that would embarrass us. As I said, it will be resolved politically. I'm sure our ambassador in Tokyo is working right now to mute the concerns of the Japanese government. That would leave only one other major problem."

Levy stopped and looked at Grainger. He rubbed his chin thoughtfully.

"You know what that is of course?" Levy asked.

Grainger hesitated, then bit his lower lip.

"Me?" he asked.

"Ah, yes," Levy said. "As old Jerry, may he rest in peace, would say, 'Bingo.'"

"I think that's what Doutter was concerned about," Salencio said. "And that really is our major concern, but there are other things. According to my sources there were three Chinese bodies and four credentials. As a Counter-Intelligence specialist, I'd like to find the fourth guy, if he's still in Japan. I imagine that Frank Church in Tokyo is focused on discovering what the hell happened to the missing agent."

"I can't help but wonder," Grainger said, "why they didn't claim salvage rights to the ship?"

"Ah, double bingo," Levy said. "That has to be a classic case of bad judgment on someone's part. It's just axiomatic that they claim salvage rights. They must have thought they had covered their tracks pretty well. How could they not know the agents had their CIA credentials on board? That's a mystery we may never solve."

"Another question," Salencio said, "is why they just didn't sail directly from Sasebo to Shanghai. Why did they have to go to Nagasaki? Do you suppose someone on the inside was trying to prevent this mission from being carried out?"

Levy scratched his head and frowned.

"Since this Colonel Kim is such a loose cannon," Levy asked Salencio, "isn't there something we can do to divert his attention away from Ken?"

"Nothing legal, of course," Salencio said. "There are ways to set people up, but it takes a lot of planning. In the short term, I think Ken's going to have to be ready to fight fire with fire and really stay on guard."

"I think we should focus on this Kim fellow," Levy said. "He's a hothead. He has total freedom of movement and ample resources. I see him having no qualms about trying to kill Ken, who then becomes the perfect scapegoat. Kim's apparently already stepped on a lot of toes, and I doubt his actions would draw favorable comment from the Korean government, or maybe even the Korean CIA. There has to be a way we can use that to our advantage."

"I agree," Salencio said. "Maybe we could at least neutralize him by going after Perkins. Here's a guy who signs a request to the Navy to have our UDT guys train Koreans to sink a ship that Perkins says is loaded with weapons. It wasn't in the *Nippo* that those divers found any guns on the ship. If weapons were found on a ship destined for Shanghai, which the Port Headquarters said was its destination, that bit of news would have been in the story."

"One of the things that Jerry emphasized," Grainger said, "was that if I write a report it will really piss Perkins off. He hates written reports because there are always copies floating around. I can write a report and send it to more than one person."

"That sounds like a good idea, Ken," Levy said. "You certainly appear to have nothing to lose with Perkins. He's already your enemy. In addition to Colonel Beane, I can make a list of the people to whom the report can be sent, including the Inspector General and the press. Are you prepared to sign such a report?"

"Not right at this moment," Grainger said. "First I want to send a letter to Colonel Beane outlining what we've been discussing. I honestly don't know if he was aware of this operation. He may not even be back from Washington. It seems clear that his boss, General Lowry, now knows there was a snafu, but that doesn't prove Colonel Beane knew. I want to send him a copy of my report before I release it to the world. If he refuses to discuss the matter after he gets my letter, then I'll agree to going outside. I feel I owe him that much."

"I appreciate loyalty," Levy said. "But if they're asking you to take one for the team, and that one is your life, you better think again. No matter what happens after this is over, I'm not sure you have much of a career ahead of you in the Army."

"The funny thing is, Dave, anyone can agree on the need to get agents into China. I have no problem with that. And I'll have time to get my side told. At least I think I will."

"It's getting late," Salencio said. "Let's meet for breakfast over here at 0600. I don't think we should be seen together at the club. Ken, you write a draft of your report tonight, and we'll review it and make our recommendations."

19 Oct 1952

Dear Colonel Beane:

On 10 Oct 1952, in the course of my duties as Detachment Commander of the Sasebo Liaison Detachment, I became involved in a damage control operation for an apparently failed covert operation that took place in Nagasaki, Japan. (Appendix 1—a copy of the *Nagasaki Nippo* newspaper with an English translation.)

I was directed to obtain the release of the survivors of the *Kochi Maru*, the ship involved in the operation. Major Perkins advised me that my actions were necessary because "we" were "double-crossed" by the Korean ship captain who sabotaged his own ship for the salvage rights. I subsequently learned this was not true. (Appendix 2—certified true copy of log of PT 143 confirming posting of said boat to Nagasaki for purpose of transporting Korean UDT-trained personnel. Sworn affidavit of Lt. Cdr. Parnell Shaw, USN.)

Subsequent to my sending the survivors back to Pusan, per Major Perkins' direct order, it is my understanding and belief that all eight surviving crew members of the ship were assassinated by Colonel Sukow Kim of the KCIA. (Source: Col. Cunningham, FEC/LD—Pusan and comments by Colonel Kim.)

I have been denied access to any of the operational documents. Moreover, in view of your impending retirement, my request for an appointment with you was denied. In addition, information that I believe to be true indicates that my safety is at risk.

I am hereby requesting the opportunity to discuss these matters in detail with you at your earliest convenience.

Very respectfully,
Capt. Kenneth D. Grainger, USA

✦

NINETEEN

Colonel Kim smoothed back his coal-black hair and adjusted his military tie before ringing the doorbell.

Jane Farnsworth (nee Svetlana) opened the door to her apartment with a barely concealed look of surprise.

"Why, Colonel Kim," she exclaimed, "how nice of you to visit. I'm just packing for a trip. Is there something I can help you with?"

"I was just in the neighborhood," Kim said. "I thought perhaps you could take a few minutes for a drink and help me with a problem."

"Well, I don't know," she said. "I'm really on a tight schedule."

"I'll only be a minute," Kim said, pushing his way past her and into the apartment.

"Yes, of course," she said, looking around the hallway and seeing no one. She closed the door and turned around.

Kim was standing right in front of her. He smiled. He put his hands on her arms, bent over and kissed her on the cheek. She reached up and gripped his arms. His muscles were tense.

"Oh," she said, "have you been working out?"

"Not any more than usual," Kim said. "I just learned that your young friend, Lieutenant Grippa, is going to be detained at his office, so I thought I would come over and see you. By the way, I love your perfume."

"Why, thank you," she said. "I didn't have any plans to see Lieutenant Grippa tonight since I have to go out of town. I'm going to meet my father in Kyoto. Uh, what kind of a problem do you have that I could help you with?"

"Yes," Kim said, "I do need your help on a difficult problem that has me very confused, but first, could you make me a drink?"

"Of course," Jane said. "What would you like to drink?"

"You forgot what I drink? That hurts my feelings. And please call me Sukow."

"Scotch and soda, wasn't it, Sukow?"

He smiled and nodded.

Colonel Kim was studying her paintings intently when she brought the drinks into the living room. He accepted the scotch and soda and toasted her.

"There are definite advantages to having a father in the import-export business," he said.

He gestured toward the paintings and the crystal pieces in the hand-carved Oriental hutch.

"You must have a small fortune in art objects," he said.

"Thank you," Jane said. "I'm glad you like them. I enjoy looking at beautiful things."

"So do I," Kim said smiling broadly.

"Hmmm, thank you again," she said. "Are you posted here in Tokyo, Colonel?"

"No," Kim replied. "I am not stationed here, but I come here as frequently as I can. I love this city."

"So do I," Jane agreed. "What kind of job do you have that lets you travel so much? I'm surprised you're not assigned here."

"Actually," Kim laughed, "I'm a fireman. I put out fires."

"Sorry," Jane said, "I don't understand."

"I really shouldn't be so mysterious," Kim said. "I'm with the Korean CIA."

"Oh," replied Jane. "I didn't even know that Korea had a CIA."

She's really good, Kim thought.

To anyone but a trained operative, the brief change in Jane's demeanor would have been imperceptible. But Kim was looking for the very reaction he observed.

"How did you meet Lieutenant Grippa?" Kim asked.

"Oh," she replied, "it was all very innocent. He was kind enough to help me fix a flat tire on my car. In the process, he soiled his uniform, and I felt sort of responsible. When he got here, one thing led to another—oh well, you know how things go."

"Oh, yes," Kim said. "But please excuse me, it's none of my business. I was just curious how a woman as beautiful as you got connected with the young lieutenant."

"Well, thank you for the compliment, Sukow. That's very nice. I don't intend to build a long relationship over a flat tire. He was nice, I appreciated it, and now I'll have to tell him I intend to see other people, that I have other plans and interests."

"I hope those other plans include a certain colonel," Kim said.

"I wouldn't be a bit surprised," Jane said. "Would you like another drink?"

"That would be very kind," Kim said.

As she poured the second drink, Colonel Kim joined her at the small wet bar. With a circular motion, he caressed her buttocks. She moaned in apparent appreciation and finished pouring the drink. Then she turned to face him.

"I like older men," she said. "They know when to hurry and when to go slow."

Kim stepped forward and caressed her in his arms. They kissed and he waited until she closed her eyes. He rocked her slowly back and forth and as he leaned to the right emptied an envelope of white powder into her drink.

She regained consciousness 30 minutes after she had drained her glass. She was stripped and seated on a kitchen chair placed in the center of the living room, hands tied behind her back with a heavy cord. Her legs were slightly separated, feet and calves bound to the front chair legs. A dishtowel served as a gag. Kim knew that the heavy doors of the living room, along with Mozart, played at full volume, would block out the sounds he expected to follow.

As the fog cleared, Jane saw Colonel Kim sitting on her leather-covered wingback chair smoking a cigarette and smiling at her. She attempted to stifle a shudder as she looked into his eyes.

"Ah, my dear Jane," Colonel Kim said, "you're back with us. Good. We need to have a little talk. As we can both see, you have an absolutely fantastic body, an apartment that cost a small fortune to decorate, and a new Jaguar automobile. You also have a story that doesn't check out.

"No Alexander Farnsworth in or out of the import-export business has ever presented a passport at Japanese immigration. I must say, the biggest mistake you ever made, in addition to dazzling me the other night with a variety of exotic sensual maneuvers, was the attempt to persuade anyone with an IQ over 10 that you were truly enamored with that boy imbecile who fetches coffee for his boss."

He continued in a menacing tone.

"So, who are you? Who do you work for? What are your instructions regarding the Liaison Group about which you have manifested such a profound curiosity, and to whom do you report in Japan?"

He stood up and walked toward her.

"If you like, we can take the questions one at a time. But I assure you, that before I leave, you will answer those and any other questions I have. From the look in your eyes I sense a defiant attitude. Good, I hate it when things are too easy."

He took the cigarette from his mouth and blew the ash away, leaving a red-hot tip exposed. He leaned forward and pressed the flaming ember against her right breast just above the nipple. The smell of her burning flesh filled the room.

"We must be symmetrical," he said, repeating the process on her left breast.

She writhed in pain, her lips twisted in agony and hate.

Kim's voice was very slow and deliberate. "Now that we know I am serious about what I said, I am going to remove your gag. You know that no one can hear you if you call out. You chose this apartment very well for its privacy. I appreciate that."

With that, he removed the cloth towel from her mouth.

"You rotten sonofabitch," she snarled.

That was as far as she got. He immediately replaced the gag.

The tears flowed involuntarily. At times she would shake vigorously as he continued to apply the burning cigarette to sensitive parts of her body. It was as if she were trying to shrug off the pain. It was no use, but even so, she continued to glare at him.

"Too bad," he said. "I see you're not ready yet to confide in me."

He picked up a kitchen broom he had found in the utility closet, snapped off the metal housing holding the corn bristles, and swung the stick handle like a baseball bat across her breasts. He then proceeded to hit her on her thighs, shins, and stomach.

Colonel Kim began to perspire from his efforts. He paused to watch her twist and turn in pain, and, as if for good measure, he applied vicious blows to each of her arms.

"Now," he said, his breathing labored, "we're going to try once more. I advise you to think about adopting a more cooperative attitude."

He removed the gag. Once again she shrieked a long, continuous stream of invectives. There was one difference in these words, however, that caused Colonel Kim to listen in attentive silence instead of immediately replacing the gag.

Jane now recognized that, no matter what, her time on earth was about over. She screamed her hate-filled and vituperative adjectives in flawless Russian.

The next day Jane did not answer Lieutenant Grippa's insistent knock. Seeing her car parked in the underground garage, Grippa persuaded the concierge to open her door.

They found her still tied to the kitchen chair. The horrified concierge stood aghast, both hands at his mouth. Lieutenant Grippa took one look, turned, and vomited all over the carpet.

His late lover's nearly decapitated head was hanging over the back of the chair. Black and blue abrasions covered the rest of her body. Shattered teeth were visible through bruised and swollen lips. A broken broomstick protruded from between her bound legs.

There was no doubting the horror of her death.

Tokyo radio accounts of the brutal murder of the American socialite, Jane Farnsworth, were far less gruesome than the pictures taken at the morgue. They were not shown on the *Tokyo Evening News*.

Those interviewed in the American community were shocked, but the reporter was unable to find anyone outside of Lieutenant Grippa who knew her. Her father, Lieutenant Grippa advised, was traveling and expected back any day.

The Soviet attaché knew Jane Farnsworth's true identity and notified Colonel Proloff who informed General Petrovsky.

Petrovsky called his home and told his wife that one of his agents had been found murdered and that he wanted to review the files at his office to see if he could discover a link to the guilty party.

"Don't expect me home tonight," he said, "but if there is an emergency you can call the duty officer and he will let me know."

He dismissed his staff, took out a bottle of cognac and set it on the desk, then placed a record on the phonograph. It was Tchaikovsky's *Romeo and Juliet*, Svetlana's favorite. He played it late into the night and consumed almost the entire bottle of cognac as the haunting melody washed over him. He cursed and wept and cursed again. And he swore revenge. ✦

TWENTY

Grainger nodded to the smiling Japanese women in the large file room of Shelvoski's warehouse operation. Julie had asked him to visit so that she could show him how she was progressing. She also wanted the chance to show off her handsome boyfriend. Shelvoski came over to her desk and shook hands with Grainger.

"She's really learning faster than most beginners," he said. "In fact, I've been using her to help me explain things to the other girls."

Julie's hand crept toward Grainger's as she tried to touch him without everyone seeing.

"I have to go," Grainger said. "I'll see you at dinner time."

At the doorway, she looked up at him, beaming.

"I am very happy," she said. "I have a good job and a good man to love me."

Grainger started to hug her.

"Oh, no," she said. "Other girls will see. Am not supposed to have business and pleasure together."

"Mix business with pleasure," Grainger said, correcting her.

"Yes, thank you, Ken," she said. "I cannot 'mix' business and pleasure."

"I've got to go out and check on some boats," Grainger said.

"Tonight I will cook your favorite dinner," Julie said.

Grainger went down the stairs, and slipped the wire loop through the hasp. Since Perkins' "no-notice" inspection he felt it was not necessary to get a new padlock since there was nothing in the office to safeguard. He heard Butch growl as he was getting into his jeep. He turned on the ignition switch and leaned out of the jeep to pet the dog.

"What's the matter, big fella?"

At that instant, the windshield of his jeep exploded. He froze momentarily; then his combat reflexes took over, and he dove to the concrete floor just before a second bullet shattered the wooden steering wheel. He crawled on his belly around the back of his jeep to his office. He slammed his shoulder into the door, easily snapping the wire, and pushed the door open.

Moving on all fours, he snaked over to the safe with its door ajar, took out the .38 Smith and Wesson and checked to make sure it was loaded. It was. He reached in and got the box of ammunition. He could hear other shots being fired outside.

Grainger crawled back to the doorway and from a kneeling position tried to look out the open door. A husky young Asian man ran into the warehouse brandishing a pistol. He looked wildly around the warehouse, first at the empty jeep, then to the right, searching for a human target. He aimed his pistol back at the jeep and then at Grainger's office, not seeing him crouched behind the front of the jeep. But Grainger had a good look at the man and hesitated just for a moment.

That's one of the Koreans who ran away from Smuggler's Gulch. What the hell is this?

The Korean started toward the office door just as Butch, coming around the corner of Grainger's office, charged toward him. He swung his weapon toward Butch.

Grainger stood, raised his pistol and fired. His first shot hit the man in the chest. The hand with the pistol flew back over his head. He staggered backward still focused on Butch, and tried to control his wavering arm. Grainger's second shot hit him in the left temple. The right side of his head exploded and he spun to the right into a stack of cardboard boxes.

Grainger's pulse pounded as his eyes darted in all directions to locate any additional threats. He heard Julie scream and call his name, but he knew that Shelvoski would keep everyone upstairs. He didn't want to take any chances.

"Keep everyone up there, Pete," he hollered. "Call the MPs."

His adrenaline pumped furiously as he turned one way, then the other, eyes wide, trying to broaden his field of vision.

The sound of sporadic small arms fire came from the main port guardpost to Grainger's right. He quickly checked the inert body of the gunman and looked cautiously into the street, surveying the roofline across the street. No one was there. When he looked up to the guardpost, he saw two men standing with their arms raised. Another was lying on the blacktop roadway. Six Japanese security guards surrounded the two men, rifles at the ready. The brief firefight appeared to be over.

Grainger checked the area, including, once again, the tops of the surrounding buildings, then stepped carefully out into the street.

"There's one down here," he called to the guards, placing his pistol in his waistband.

The senior guard looked Grainger up and down as he ran past and went into the warehouse. He glanced down at the lifeless body and came out.

"Do you know him?" he asked Grainger.

"No," Grainger said, "do you?"

The guard shook his head and looked at him.

"Never see," he said. "I am officer. My men just say they ask for you."

"Well I've never seen him before," Grainger said. "I don't know him."

"Please come with me, Captain," the guard lieutenant said.

Army military police and Japanese police quickly gathered at the scene.

When Grainger approached, the two men with their hands raised glowered at him with undisguised hatred.

"Where my brother?" the older of the two Korean men asked in badly accented English.

"Do you know these men, Captain?" an MP lieutenant asked.

"No, I do not," Grainger answered. "I don't know what any of this is about."

One of the Japanese policemen spoke to the older Korean and then turned to Grainger.

"He say his brother on *Kochi Maru*, sunk in Nagasaki. You get brother from hospital. He say Colonel Kim tell Korean families in Osaka that you kill his brother."

"I did not kill anyone from any ship, and I do not know what the hell he is talking about."

"He say Colonel Kim say, 'Captain Grainger know about your brother,'" the policeman repeated.

"Then I suggest you talk to Colonel Kim," Grainger said. "He obviously knows more about this than I do.

"Lieutenant," Grainger said to the MP officer, gesturing toward his warehouse, "There's a dead Korean down there. You'll find he was armed. He was pointing a gun and looking for a place to use it. I fired first. Check the windshield on my jeep and the steering wheel. My office is in the warehouse. I'm billeted at the Field Grade BOQ. I don't know what this is about. It's some kind of mistake, and it has scared the crap out of me. I don't like getting shot at. If you don't need me for anything, I'd like to go."

"Yes, sir," the lieutenant said. "We'll work with the Japanese police on this. If they need you for a statement or anything, we'll let you know. We can contact you here or at the BOQ."

"Where my brother?" the older Korean shouted at Grainger.

The Japanese policeman shouted at the Korean and struck him on the back with his club. He quickly lowered his eyes to the ground.

All eyes were on Grainger as he walked away.

Grainger went upstairs and comforted Julie and the others. He explained to Shelvoski that it was a case of mistaken identity. Excusing himself, he called Perkins to report the incident.

"I can't believe Colonel Kim told anybody anything," Perkins said.

"Well, they kept using his name and they sure as hell knew my name," Grainger said. "If I hadn't leaned out of the jeep when I did, someone else would be filing this report. There's a bullet hole in the upper center of the driver's seat. I've got my rear end exposed down here, and I don't care for it. I think your friend Colonel Kim has gone stark raving mad."

"Well, it's over now," Perkins said. "We'll make sure the Japanese police hold those guys until your transfer comes through. I don't think you have anything to worry about."

"You think this is over?" Grainger shouted. "What makes you think this is over? Do you know something I don't know? Major, I just killed a guy with a gun six feet outside my office door. How do you know there aren't other family members of those guys that Kim killed just waiting around the corner?"

"There's no proof Kim killed those survivors," Perkins said.

"Then you need to talk to Colonel Cunningham," Grainger said. "And if you think this is over, I'm sure you won't mind if I go outside and tell those Korean goons that they should see you up in Tokyo and you can tell them about their relatives?"

"That's gross insubordination, Grainger," Perkins said.

"Then you better file the charges," Grainger said. "This is not supposed to be a war zone. I know now to be on the lookout for Colonel Kim, or someone he may send. I'll be sending a written report on this incident and this conversation to Colonel Beane tonight."

"Don't bother," Perkins said. "I'll prepare a record of this telephone conversation."

"It's no bother, Major," Grainger said. "I'm also sure the Post Headquarters will be sending a report to General Clark at AFFE, the Far East Headquarters."

"My report to Colonel Beane," Perkins said, "will also include your paranoid comment about looking for Colonel Kim. You have no proof he sent anyone. You should have stayed with the Infantry."

"You and I agree on that, Major, but for different reasons."

Perkins hung up.

Grainger knew he had to make another call and he did.

Word of the shooting incident at the port spread like wildfire across Camp Sasebo. It was the first incident of its type that had taken place in the jurisdiction of the small Army post. The most surprising reaction came from the Executive Officer of Camp Sasebo, Colonel Robert Ulysses Murphy, AKA "Colonel Rum."

"Sir," Murphy said to Colonel Beardsley, "I know how you feel about spooks in the military. I feel the same way. But we have to deal with this situation. The way everyone at AFFE seems to be running away from that *Kochi Maru* thing tells me that Grainger really had damn little to do with it. If he were really responsible, they would have hauled him out of here right after it happened. He hasn't been here long enough to set this up. I think he was sent to clean up someone else's mess. Sir, I would recommend and request that we have an MP posted down at his office and at the BOQ."

"You may be right, Bob," Beardsley said. "I was pretty tough on him when he came up here. I know about his combat record. It's hard to believe that someone who can keep things together so well in combat could screw up so badly in handling the duties of a detachment. Go ahead and do it. Frankly, I appreciate your thinking of it."

When Grainger went to the BOQ for his laundry, he found a note on the door from Chief Michaels requesting that he contact him. He drove down to the PT boat dock.

"While you were involved in that shootout we heard about," Michaels said, "I got a radio message from Tokyo. Five people, four Koreans and a sergeant, are coming over to pick up that Japanese fishing boat anchored out at Smuggler's Gulch. They're coming over on the Red Ball. I checked with the port and they said the ship was late getting out of Pusan because of engine trouble, so they won't be arriving until late tonight. Do you want me to meet them?"

"That's okay," Grainger said. "I'll meet them, but we're going to do things a little differently this time. When the ship docks, I'm going to bring them over here. The weather's warm so they can sleep on the deck of your boat. Any problem berthing five guys for the night?"

"No, sir," Michaels said. "I'll just move my boat out into the harbor. That oughta slow down any possible AWOL problem. I'll send an engineer over with them to make sure there are no delays in them getting under way."

"Thanks, Chief," Grainger said. "I'll come and get them

in the morning. By the way, who sent you the radio message from Tokyo?"

"Grippa called me, but it was from Major Perkins. It's the first time he's done that."

I wonder why Grippa didn't call me? Grainger thought.

He then called Julie and reassured her that he was all right.

"I have to get together with Colonel Levy and draft another letter to Colonel Beane, then I'm going to meet a boat. This is going to take a while. I'm sorry about dinner tonight. I'll have something when I get home."

"Please be careful, Ken," she said. "I am so afraid. I don't know what is going on. Why would those Koreans want to hurt you?"

"That's over now," he said. "Please don't worry about it. I'm glad that Butch is with you at the apartment. I don't feel you're in any danger, but Butch is a good watchdog. If you hear any strange noises or get worried, go down and stay with the apartment manager."

"Sometimes, Butch is too good a guard dog," Julie said. "He moves around a lot and his tail knocks things over."

"It'll take him a little time to get used to things," Grainger said. "If he's a problem, just put him in the bathroom until I get there. K-9 dogs don't spend too much time in a house, but he does respond well to orders."

"I love you," she said.

Grainger met the *USNS Sergeant Muller* at midnight.

At the same time, Colonel Kim was trying to pick the lock on the door of Grainger's apartment. Earlier, Perkins called Kim and told him that Grainger had survived an attack by some Koreans. Kim expressed amazement and surprise and told Perkins he would investigate and find out exactly what had happened. What Perkins had not told Kim was that the ship Grainger was to meet was delayed, and he would not be at home until quite late.

The noise at the front door caused Julie to jump. Thinking it was Grainger, she rushed to greet him. When she opened the door, she was surprised to see a Korean man pushing his way into the apartment and looking anxiously over her shoulder.

"This is not your apartment," she said, standing in his way. He sneered at her, then she saw the pistol in his hand.

"Where is your Captain Grainger?" he asked.

"He's not here," she said. "Who are you?"

"I am a friend of his. Perhaps he mentioned my name, Colonel Kim?"

"No," she said. "He does not talk about his work."

"Liar!" Kim shouted.

Julie screamed and Butch, locked in the bathroom, started barking and pawing at the door. She moved backward, trying to flee, but Kim was too fast.

He moved rapidly to her and smashed the side of his pistol against her cheek. Blood spurted from the ruptured skin as she fell to the floor.

Butch growled ferociously and pawed at the door with both front feet.

"You think I didn't know about your little love nest?" Kim taunted. "I knew the day you moved in. You and that sniveling Grainger—bothered by a few worthless Korean seamen. We'll just wait for him."

Julie rose to one elbow, fear masking her face.

"He's a good man, better ..."

Kim kicked her in the face. She rolled on her back, and he brought his heel down sharply, first on her forehead, then on her throat.

Butch, now raging, clawed furiously at the door.

"He's weak," Kim shouted, "too weak to live. Most Americans are weak. They don't understand that you have to grind your enemies into the dirt, make them suffer. When you do, they fear you and will be happy if you don't punish them.

"Your stupid captain was lucky to get away from the families of the survivors. I told them what he did, shooting their people. Well, he won't be lucky tonight."

Blood spewed from Julie's lips as she tried to speak. She stirred slowly and looked at Kim with glazed eyes. "He will kill you," she choked, struggling to breathe.

"Ha," Kim said, "don't make me laugh. He'll have time to see you here. When I get finished smashing your pretty face, he'll have to look hard to be sure it's you. I'll be waiting in the corner. When he starts to scream in rage, I'll step out, tell him you died slowly, and then he will die. He has been a problem too long."

He bent over and slammed his pistol again and again into her face. Tissue and bones splattered his uniform.

Butch leaped again at the flimsy door and it gave way. He came roaring into the living room and headed straight for Kim.

Momentarily startled, Kim only had time to raise his left arm to defend himself. Butch sank his teeth into his wrist. The dog began to jerk his head left and right, his teeth sinking deeper with each movement.

Kim screamed in pain and began to hit Butch with his pistol as the dog's teeth dug deeper. He continued to yank his head from side to side, oblivious to the pain, as Kim beat him on the head. Kim began to feel faint from the excruciating pain. He raised his pistol and began firing into Butch's body. The third bullet found Butch's heart. He released his grip, but with a final lunge Butch clamped his jaws on Kim's right hand, forcing him to let go of the pistol. It was flung across the room. Butch collapsed next to Julie's body.

Shouts from outside panicked Kim. He grabbed a towel, wrapped it around his badly torn wrist. He looked around the floor for his pistol, couldn't find it and fled.

When Grainger turned into the street leading to his apartment, he saw the revolving blue light of a police vehicle.

Oh no! he thought, and sped up to the parked police car.

Neighbors pointed to him and spoke rapidly to the police. A gray-haired man in a rumpled jacket held up his hand. "Captain," he said, "I am Detective Uzio, Sasebo police. I work in what you Americans call homicide. Please listen to me. This is bad."

Grainger pushed past the detective, rushing to get to his apartment. Uzio tugged at Grainger's arm in an unsuccessful effort to slow him down.

"Is Julie all right?" Grainger asked, half dragging the detective up the stairs.

"Captain, please, please stop," Uzio said, finally giving up on his effort to keep Grainger from the apartment.

At the door, he tried one last time, jumping ahead and momentarily blocking Grainger's way long enough to blurt, "Young lady … I am sorry, she is dead. So is dog."

"Nooooo," Grainger wailed, picking up the little detective and thrusting him aside.

Uzio slumped against the door, holding up his hand to prevent other officers from intervening.

"Please," he said, shaking his head, "don't go, she is not pretty."

Grainger forced his way past two other policemen standing inside and frantically looked for Julie.

She was on the floor face up, eyes swollen, but still open. Her cheeks and lips were torn and split as if hit with some kind of wooden bat. Butch was lying next to her, blood pooled around his chest. His snout and mouth were still wet with Kim's blood.

"Oh my god, Julie … Julie … Julie," Grainger cried.

Tears flooded from his eyes. He pulled away from the policeman who was holding his arm and knelt on the floor beside her, stroking her long black hair. The tips of his fingers gently caressed her torn lips and swollen eyes. He couldn't swallow and began having problems breathing.

"I should have been here," he choked. "I should have been here." He sobbed uncontrollably.

Detective Uzio motioned the policeman away.

"He shot dog," Uzio said. "That is how we knew he was here. Neighbors hear gun, they call. Where were you? Why you no here?"

"At the port," Grainger said. "I was at the goddamn port."

"You work at port?" Uzio asked.

"Yes," Grainger said. "I had to meet some people coming in on the *Sergeant Muller.* I took them over to one of my PT boats so they could sleep there tonight. It's berthed in the harbor."

Uzio wrote down the information.

"Do you know who would do this?" Uzio asked.

"I have an idea," Grainger said. "There's only one ruthless sonofabitch this vicious. I didn't think he would do something like this, not to Julie. I underestimated how cruel he could be. What about you? Do you have any witnesses? Did anyone see anything?"

"There is one thing," Uzio said, ignoring Grainger's questions. "Do you have a pistol?"

Grainger wiped away the tears streaming down his cheeks.

"Yes," he said, "I have a .38, four-inch barrel, and I have military authorization for it."

He lifted his jacket and showed that it was tucked into his waistband.

Uzio nodded.

"I think," he said, "whoever beat your girlfriend was attacked by the dog. He had to shoot the dog to protect himself. See, the dog has blood on the outside of his mouth, but was shot three times in the chest. Dog must have bit man after he shot. We found this .45 automatic under chair."

Uzio held the pistol by the barrel, between his thumb and forefinger, and Grainger saw the wooden pistol grip carved in the shape of a rattlesnake about to strike.

"I know exactly who the sonofabitch is that owns that pistol," Grainger said. "I saw him with it in Pusan. His name is Sukow Kim. He's a colonel in the Korean CIA. He works on projects with my boss in Tokyo, Major Templeton Perkins at the Far East Command Liaison Group. They know how to reach him."

Uzio exhaled loudly.

"I cannot write so fast," he said. "You must come to police station so we can write information. We will call your major in Tokyo and find where Korean colonel is."

"He's here in Sasebo," Grainger shouted. "The goddam pistol tells you that. What kind of a detective are you?"

Grainger turned away and kneeled again at Julie's side and stroked her hair and groaned softly. "I'm sorry, honey. I should have been here."

"Does Colonel Kim have address here?" Detective Uzio asked.

"I don't know," Grainger said. "He may, but knowing that bastard, he's either hiding or on his way back to Korea. If I find him first, you won't have to worry about any interrogation."

"I'm sorry," Uzio said, "but that cannot happen. He will be arrested and charged with murder of a Japanese citizen. My advice, Captain, do not interfere with our investigation or it will go badly for you. This is my job, not yours."

"Then you better find the sonofabitch first," Grainger said.

He brushed a few loose bloody strands of hair away from Julie's face, removed his jacket and laid it gently over her head and chest. Bending over her, his face contorted in grief, he tried to embrace her. His shoulders rocked back and forth as he was overwhelmed with rage and pain.

"I'm sorry, Julie," he sobbed. "I'm so sorry. I got you into this. I should have been here. I'm so sorry, honey."

Grainger's eyes were still puffy and red-rimmed when he met with Salencio and Levy.

"Ken, I'm really sorry about Julie," Salencio said. "I'll help you find that bastard."

"I'm terribly sorry," Levy said. "I can't imagine how a person could be so vicious. The man is totally evil."

Grainger nodded, sat back in his chair at the conference table with his arms crossed, stared at the table, and fought back tears.

"Let's talk about the only thing that matters at this moment," Salencio said. "I expect that Kim is going to get back to Korea as fast as he can. The question is, how can we get to him?"

"You know," Levy said, "we've been going about this the wrong way. There isn't anything we can do to draw Kim into a fight on our terms. I think I told you I was thinking about another approach. While we've been talking, I've been trying to think of ways to shoot down my own idea. The more I think of it, the better I like it.

"Here it is. We've been told that Kim isn't loved by some people high up in the government in Seoul. His bosses can't really control him. That means they'd probably believe the worst about him, provided it came from a credible source. How about forging a letter from someone, someone high up—say a general—to the effect that Kim is interested in assassinating Syngman Rhee? Hell, the KCIA will turn on him like a pack of wolves."

"I see what you mean," Salencio said. "Use the Dreyfus approach. Frame the bastard. I like that. Go for the jugular."

"That won't work," Grainger said. "Someone will just ask the general if he wrote the letter and he'll say 'No.' End of plot. And Kim gets stronger because someone is trying to frame him."

"What if it's a general they can't talk to?" Levy asked.

"You mean a general who's dead?" Grainger asked. "One who left behind a document among his private papers?"

"That might work," Salencio said. "But what about a general they can't reach, like a Russian general? Someone who would love to throw a monkey wrench into the South Korean Intelligence community. One who writes and tells Kim what a great guy he is, thanks him for all the favors? Did you get the cash? Someone they couldn't or wouldn't ask for confirmation?"

The three men looked at each other.

"It should be an Intelligence general," Salencio said.

"He'd be writing a personal letter to Kim as if responding to a query of some kind or a proposal from Kim to assassinate Rhee," Levy said. "Accepting the terms and conditions of the contract, telling Kim they've got a deal. The basic offer-and-acceptance manifestation of a contractual intent, and all that."

"The letter gets waylaid. We take it off a courier," Salencio said.

"Ken's fingerprints can't be anywhere remotely on this," Levy said. "That would be the kiss of death. Any hint that Grainger's in the picture, and guys like Perkins will come rushing to Kim's defense."

"Too bad we can't indict Perkins with the same letter," Salencio said. "We know there are couriers coming through here all the time. We'll pick one up, identify him, and hold him until the bait is taken and Kim is dealt with."

"If it were Kim, he'd kill the courier and not worry about a comeback," Grainger said. Then he paused. "I know, that's why we're here, we're not Kim. Frankly, I want to do it myself."

"I know you do, Ken," Salencio said. "You got plenty of reasons, but you have too many disabilities. For one thing you're not Asian. Let's stay with this idea a little longer.

"I could get the forged letter to Art Church in Tokyo," Salencio said. "He's the CIA Station Chief. I'd swear I took it off a courier who escaped, that we're not sure where he is.

I'll tell him this is outside my jurisdiction, I'm just trying to cooperate, and ask him if he wants the letter."

"I'm sure he'll be very happy to receive it," Levy said. "Have you ever cooperated in this way before?"

"No," Salencio said, "but we really haven't had a chance. Besides, there's always a first for everything. This would be one of those once-in-a-lifetime situations."

"Would Art Church expect you to know the name of the courier?" Grainger asked. "And would he know if the name was a real courier?"

"Good questions," Salencio said. "In both cases, the answer is a definite 'maybe.' Part of our mission in Counter-Intelligence is to track these guys. If we have the guy in custody, it wouldn't make any difference if he knew him or not."

"How can we kidnap a courier?" Grainger asked.

"A special kind of courier," Salencio said. "It has to be one who moves between Russia and Japan."

"This isn't going to be easy," Levy said.

"No, it's not," Salencio said, "but it's doable."

"Too bad we don't know any Russian agents in Sasebo," Levy said. "I'll bet if we asked the right guy he could find us a general in Moscow who'd like to write a 'dear brother Kim' letter, maybe even love it. Don't you know any Communists, Roberto? Is there someone like a resident Soviet agent?"

Salencio nodded.

"As a matter of fact," he said, "I may have the ideal point of contact. I don't know if the same guy is still there. His name is Fyodor. He runs a unique house—it's the only one I've ever heard of in Sasebo. They specialize in oral sex, no dipping the wick. They have a bouncer who can be downright mean if you don't abide by house rules. It has a limited but very loyal clientele.

"One of my agents went there once and considered the oral part as foreplay. He had to crawl across the floor to get his .38 to keep the resident gorilla off him. He said they screamed at him all the way down the stairs and into the street.

"We had Fyodor in here once," Salencio continued. "Kept insisting he was White Russian, hated the Reds. He said his family was of the nobility, aristocrats. If that guy's an aristocrat, I'm Little Orphan Annie. We had a Nisei agent one time, camped outside his place for a month, with instructions to note every place he went. He went to a few bars. Didn't talk to anyone or leave any messages. He rarely strays from his house. I think he's more interested in making money than anything else."

"Let's contact him," Levy said, "and tell him if he helps us, we won't let his boss in Moscow know how much he's really making. Roberto, you're the obvious one to make the contact."

The business establishment had no identifying markings. Japanese men all knew it from word of mouth. Similarly, new American "clients" arrived because of a referral.

Salencio arrived shortly before 1700. He asked for Fyodor and showed his credentials printed in Japanese to the gray-haired mama-san. A few seconds later a seemingly bewildered Fyodor presented himself in the reception area.

Salencio almost didn't recognize him. He had added 50 pounds since their last meeting. The weave pattern of his suit coat clashed with his trousers in both texture and color. Any effort to button the coat would miss by a wide margin. His hair was brushed straight back with a hairline two inches above his brow. The growth of a dark beard marked Fyodor as someone required to shave twice daily if his job included meeting the public. His lips were pouty, and his eyes flicked at Salencio then darted away like a nervous fly aware that a predator was near.

"Good evening, Major," Fyodor said. "This is a surprise. Can I help you?"

"I believe you can and hope you will for your sake," Salencio said.

"What have I done?" Fyodor said. "I'm just a businessman, a poor refugee from the Communist dictators who took my family's possessions and my country."

Salencio smiled broadly.

"Cut the crap, Fyodor. You make more money here in a month than your family ever saw. I'm not interested in either your heritage or what lies you tell your boss in Moscow. I just want you to get a message to him from me."

Fyodor gave Salencio a hard look, then smiled. Dropping the whining tone he said, "Maybe you should come back to my office, Major."

Fyodor's office was a 10-foot x 10-foot cubicle. It had one desk that sat on a worn carpet, two chairs, and a decrepit three-drawer wooden file cabinet. The walls were absolutely bare. He sat down behind the desk and motioned for Salencio to sit across from him.

"Assuming I could help," he said, "what's the message?"

Fyodor listened intently as Salencio described in detail what he wanted.

"If you do this," Salencio concluded, "and continue to restrict your movements to the local bars, I will do nothing to interfere with your little popsicle stand."

Fyodor shrugged.

"I'll do what I can," Fyodor said. "There's never any guarantee." ✦

TWENTY-ONE
Kalinin, Russia

General Petrovsky's dacha was located on the Volga River nearly 100 miles northwest of Moscow. After learning of the death of Svetlana, Petrovsky decided to spend a few days alone at his rustic four-room cabin, constructed of logs from the nearby forest and centered in a rectangular-shaped clearing. Almost a quarter-mile from the main gravel roadway, it had a boat dock that housed Petrovsky's pride and joy, a 40-foot mahogany sloop. Sailing on the Volga was the one place he knew he had absolute privacy.

One of the four rooms was an office-study. It was here he allowed the only telephone in the cabin. Petrovsky had bookshelves built along two walls. His reading tastes, in addition to an ample collection of party literature, ran to biographies and history. His copy of *Plutarch's Lives* was dog-eared from frequent readings.

"I need to get away from this shit," he told Proloff. "I'll be gone a few days. Unless it's extremely important, don't bother me."

That evening, Vasily Proloff called his general.

"What the hell do you want?" Petrovsky slurred.

"We have a request from the Americans in Japan," Proloff began. "It seems that a certain Colonel Sukow Kim has walked all over some American toes, and they want to castrate him, at the throat."

There was a long silence as it took time for the fog bank to clear. Memories of a smiling Svetlana kneeling over him in bed, massaging him, flitted across Petrovsky's mind. He flashed to the newspaper accounts of her murder and her reports describing a liaison with Colonel Kim.

"Proloff, you old bastard," Petrovsky rasped, "you know we may have been wrong all these years. Maybe there is a God!" He coughed violently. "How did you find out?"

"You remember, General, you told me to get rid of Kozlov in Nagasaki and Fyodor in Sasebo? Well, I got rid of Kozlov right away. He stayed so drunk he thinks he's still there. But Fyodor wasn't that easy to replace. I'm still working on it. You know, we do get enough from his little sideline to help with other expenses.

"Fyodor was contacted by a Counter-Intelligence major who had an unusual request. He asked for a letter from you."

"What kind of a letter?" Petrovsky demanded.

"They want a letter implying a long-term relationship between you and Kim and some comment about a large, regular stipend. They also want it to appear that Kim has initiated a plot to assassinate President Rhee."

Petrovsky whistled.

"What are they going to do with the letter, if I write it? Which of course I will, with the greatest of pleasure."

"I don't know," Proloff said. "They must have some plan for getting the letter to Rhee. They sent a draft of what they want."

"Why the hell don't they just forge my signature?" Petrovsky asked. "What do you think of their letter?"

"It's perfect for the job," Proloff said. "But it doesn't sound like you. It's a little too sweet."

"You have no idea how sweet I can be," Petrovsky said, "when I'm talking to someone who is willing to betray his country and join our cause. You have to make a traitor think you love him. It compensates for his guilt feelings."

"Yes, General," Proloff said, "I apologize for my remark."

"Then don't drag it in my face," Petrovsky said brusquely. "If you don't like it, you write one, too. Get them both to me damn fast."

Petrovsky's eyes narrowed and he cleared his throat.

"You think this might be some kind of trap?"

"No, I don't," Proloff said. "Judging from the source and Fyodor's comment about a shooting involving that Army captain from Nagasaki, I'd say it was 99 percent legitimate. Someone wants Kim badly and they're in a hurry. I'd bet the dacha it's genuine."

"Don't be so generous with my dacha, Proloff," Petrovsky said. "If it turns into a disaster, remember what happens to the messenger."

"Considering what that bastard did to Svetlana," Proloff said, "and that we just missed getting her out in time, I'd take this gamble 10 times out of 10. Besides, Fyodor said he knows this Counter-Intelligence major and says he does not play games."

"Any way to stop Kim is fine with me," Petrovsky said. "Frankly, I was hoping we could kidnap that bastard and bring him to Moscow.

"Prepare a draft letter for me, on my fancy stationery. Bring it up here so I can review it, sign it, and get it back to Fyodor. As a reward for being involved with the Kim solution, give Fyodor six months before you start looking again for a replacement. Also, tell the American Counter-Intelligence specialist I will expect a quid pro quo. I don't do things like this for nothing."

Roberto Salencio owned three German shorthaired pointers, two males and a bitch. He had trained them to sit with their rumps on the living room couch and their forelegs on the floor. He would pace about in the living room and address them individually and collectively. On cue they would look at the ceiling, then left and right or nod their heads as if in approval. Their names were Hotrod, Ramrod, and No-Rod. It was common knowledge in the American community that when Salencio was not at home, no visitors would dare go to his home unless they first called his wife to make sure the dogs were locked in the tool shed.

Three days after Proloff's phone call, there was a knock on the front door of Salencio's residence. All three dogs exploded at the door. A stern command had them all retreat and sitting at attention warily eyeing the door.

When Salencio opened the door, the foreign smell was too much for No-Rod. She broke ranks, lunging toward Fyodor, who stood there in an old overcoat and beat-up fedora. He recoiled and slipped off the porch, landing on his knees.

Salencio's sharp command brought the bitch to a stop. She stood with her head low. A menacing growl rumbled in her throat.

Fyodor recovered his balance and looked down to examine his knee where his trousers were torn. He exhaled loudly and extended his arm to Salencio.

"This came for you today in the diplomatic pouch delivered in Tokyo," Fyodor said to Salencio, eyeing the dog crouched at his side. "I made a special trip to pick it up. I've been told it meets your requirements. Oh yes, I am instructed to tell you the general expects that one day you will give him a quid pro quo."

"Thank you," Salencio said. "If I can return the favor to the general without compromising my oath to my country, I'll be glad to be of service."

Fyodor turned and walked quickly to his 1940 Chevrolet parked in the driveway with the motor running.

Salencio went into the kitchen, sat down at the table where the light was good, and slowly and carefully opened the package. Inside, in a 5 x 8 official general officer's envelope, was a sheet of heavy-gauge linen stationery with the general's emblem of rank embossed at the top. The letter read:

To My Loyal and Faithful Friend Colonel Sukow Kim:

Dear Sukow:

You will be happy to note that I have arranged to have this and all future correspondence translated to English for you. I am sorry our Russian language is so difficult. Of course we will continue to avoid any correspondence in Korean.

In answer to your inquiry, your semi-annual payment was made, as always, to the Zurich bank, but a faulty transmission delayed posting for six (6) days.

Your new proposal was most interesting, but I fear, potentially very dangerous for you. If you can cause it to be done, and replace him with someone who would be more favorable to us, it would be well worth the significant amount you mentioned in your transmission. We have heard that your target is in failing health and may go to the West to see a specialist. Maybe his illness will take care of our problem and then we could simply send you a list of potential replacements who would be acceptable.

Please note that I will use our most trusted and reliable courier in all matters of correspondence. Only personal deliveries will be made for security reasons.

Best personal regards as always,
Arkady Petrovsky

P.S. Svetlana sends her warmest regards. She can
hardly wait for you to join her in the hotter climes.
She is thinking about converting to Christianity.
What a waste.

Salencio smiled and slid the letter back into the envelope and then into his attaché case.
Now, he thought, *all we need is the messenger.*

Progress in the hunt for an agent-courier moved gla-
cially.
"You know," Salencio quipped, "you can never find a
foreign agent when you need one."
"What about that nervous guy you once told me
about?" Grainger asked.
"Krueger," Salencio said. "Yeah, his ship hasn't stopped
here in a long time. To tell you the truth, all the couriers
we've had under surveillance are a little squirrelly."
"Couldn't the Navy help us?" Levy asked. "Don't they
monitor ship traffic?"
"Yes, and no," Salencio said. "I asked them once. They
said they're aware of what's happening generally with the
regular traffic, and they may follow a tramp if it gets in the
wrong area, but there's too much traffic to keep close tabs
on all of them."
"What about the Japanese maritime office?" Levy asked.
"I suppose so," Salencio said, "but I don't want to ask
them. They'd want to know why I was interested in a civilian merchant ship. But that does give me an idea."
"What's the name of this guy's ship?" Grainger asked.
"The last time Krueger was here he was on the *Matson*,"
Salencio said. "I'll have my secretary call the maritime of-

fice, tell them her boyfriend is on the ship, and ask them when it's expected in port."

Salencio picked up his phone and spoke briefly.

Fifteen minutes later, his phone rang.

"Great," he said. "That was easy. The *Matson* will be here in five days. They're scheduled to lay over for two days."

Hans Krueger was enlisted as a Soviet courier in the classic manner. He was the Ichabod Crane of his high school class. Tall and gawky with a long skinny neck and prominent Adam's apple, he wore hand-me-down clothes that were frequently the subject of sneering comments by his classmates.

As Krueger grew up in a small town in southern Illinois, his father, who failed in every business venture he attempted, blamed his frequent setbacks on the unfair competitive practices of a capitalistic system that rewarded the "haves" and passed laws making success impossible for the "have-nots." He had no time for his son, who looked to his mother for understanding and support. Unfortunately, she felt imprisoned in a loveless marriage and powerless to extricate herself from the suffocating poverty that was their lot. She did not understand her son's desperate need for affection and conveyed a sense of hopelessness when he attempted to communicate his anxiety about the future.

Krueger left home after graduation from high school. He hitchhiked to southern California and worked as a janitor in a warehouse complex in Long Beach. With his earnings, he enrolled in night school, and while there made friends with a homely girl named Elsa in his economics class.

One night she accepted his invitation for coffee after a class session and listened with rapt attention as he poured out his heart to the first person who ever seemed to care about him as a human being.

She appeared lethargic in the classroom environment, which is what gave him the courage to ask her for a date. But he soon found that in sharing her enthusiasm for the goals of the Communist Party, USA, she became animated and voluble. He liked the way she wrinkled her nose whenever she smiled, and it did not register that the only time she smiled was when she discussed the Party. She invited him to attend a Party meeting the following Saturday evening.

The speaker reminded Krueger of his father, especially in his railing against the capitalistic system. At the urging of his new friend, Krueger agreed to sign a membership form, pay the two-dollar initiation fee, and attend meetings on a regular basis. His acceptance into the group gave him his first feeling of ever belonging to anything. He willingly carried out assigned tasks such as handing out leaflets and bringing prospective members to the meetings. The insults and taunts he received from passersby on the street, such as "Red scum" and "Commie rat," only drew him closer to the point of commitment.

He graduated from the local community college and was able to complete the requirements for a "degree" in electrical engineering from a vocational school of little renown. He actually received only a certificate of completion, but to the untutored eye the diploma appeared to be a bona fide degree from an accredited institution.

Krueger, through his contacts in the Party, was able to get a job in the Merchant Marine as an able-bodied seaman. He gradually worked his way up in the deck department to earn a license as a Third Mate. Unlike most of his highly mobile shipmates, Krueger shunned the opportunity to move from ship to ship and cast his fortunes with the merchant freighter named *SS Matson*.

Elsa moved into Krueger's apartment as his common-law wife and bore him a young daughter, Princess, who was the only person to whom Krueger could convey genuine affection. He always brought home something for Princess when he traveled. He loved the way she would squeal with delight as she rummaged through his sea bag until she found her gift ornately wrapped and always with a tag reading: "Princess."

He frequently provided a payback on these voyages for his employment assistance and Party membership by serving as a courier during his regular stopovers at ports of call. He never knew the content of the messages he carried and didn't want to. He accepted that there was some element of danger to his extracurricular duties, but he swore he would never do anything to jeopardize his ability to return home to Princess.

He developed his own style of making sure the Counter-Intelligence specialists or the "enemy agents" he feared, could not observe him performing his duties. He deduced from furtive glances and quickly averted eyes that he was being followed. He placed the item that would go to a contact in the bottom of his sea bag and, once on shore, would frequent a number of bars before going to the delivery point. He would order a beer at each of the bars, take a sip, and then systematically study the face of each patron. When he was sure he could recall each face, he moved quickly to the next bar. He kept repeating this process because he had learned that each local Intelligence office only had four or five agents. He would abort the delivery whenever he saw a face he recalled from an earlier stop, return to his ship, and try again the following day.

There were times when he was not able to find the peace of mind he required. He would simply return the letter or item to his contact person explaining that the risks were too great. His control generally expressed great disappointment at his failure and urged him to take additional risks. Krueger would always promise to try harder next time. However, he had no intention of being arrested as a spy. Going to jail meant being denied the opportunity of seeing his Princess grow to womanhood.

He was carrying a packet of letters when he arrived at Sasebo. His instructions were that they must be delivered at all costs. Since the *Matson* would only be in port two days, Krueger was anxious to complete his task the first evening if possible.

He moved quickly and easily from one small bar to another. The first three bars had no Caucasians to arouse particular attention.

Maybe they are catching on to my procedure, he thought, *and won't send anyone to the first few bars.*

At the fourth bar he eyed six men with military haircuts. He ordered a glass of beer, studied their faces, and left. His beer was untouched.

By the time Krueger reached the ninth bar, he couldn't be sure, but he felt he recognized a face. However, the bright red windbreaker was not familiar. He had not seen that earlier. He wondered if he was simply nervous and perhaps unduly cautious. He remembered the admonition from his control who said simply, "Hans, I don't want these back. Do you understand? You *must* make delivery."

Krueger had promised to get the job done. However, after the 12th bar he couldn't escape the signals his antennae were receiving. He had just about decided to abort the mission for the evening when he spotted the Blue Heaven, an establishment he previously frequented where ladies in the world's oldest profession plied their trade.

Maybe a quickie will help me relax, he thought.

He entered the house.

The living room had three divans, a few upholstered chairs, and game tables where patrons sat drinking beer or stronger refreshments before going upstairs.

The madam approached him. Her toothy smile reflected an investment in gold.

"Ah, good evening," she said, "not all girls busy. Can go now, please."

She beckoned toward a slim, young, moon-faced girl, whose hairstyle copied the Veronica Lake peek-a-boo look of the 1940s.

Krueger glanced at the tables where young men were drinking beer and engaged in casual conversation.

The mama-san smiled.

"They already go, wait for friend," she said.

At that moment, the door opened and a husky-looking young man entered. Despite the summer weather, he wore a dark-green military-style windbreaker. He glanced at the madam and nodded, then at Krueger, and finally at the men at the tables. He took a seat.

For some unknown reason, Krueger's inner alarm went off, but instead of leaving, he motioned to the madam that he was now ready. She signaled for the young moon-faced girl, who forced a smile as she took his hand and led him upstairs. Five minutes later the relative quiet of the room he had entered was shattered by the cry, "*Pisutoru, pisutoru!*"

Pistol, the word registered.

Krueger pushed the surprised girl kneeling in front of him, pulled up his trousers, and quickly rezipped his fly. He grabbed his sea bag, yanked the door open, and sprinted down the hall opposite the stairway leading downstairs.

At the end of the hall a wooden-framed window faced a large oak tree. He reached down and lifted the window open. Looking out, he decided to use the tree as a kind of fire escape. He leaped out, grabbing for the nearest branch.

For a moment he thought he made it. He was wrong.

The branch gave way and he landed, feet apart, with a jolt, severely spraining his left ankle.

Still in a panic, Krueger clutched his sea bag to his chest and lurched away from the grassy area under the tree. He was limping badly as he attempted to cross the street opposite the Blue Heaven.

This was a final error in judgment. In his panic he failed to look to his right. With his second step he walked directly into the headlights of a speeding beer truck. The impact lifted Krueger out of both of his shoes. The driver jammed on the brakes, but by the time his truck screeched to a halt, Krueger was dead.

The first person to reach Krueger's prostrate form was Major Roberto Salencio. He looked up at Grainger, who was wearing a red windbreaker, and shook his head.

Agent Nixon, whose pistol tucked in his waistband had alarmed the young lady attempting to undress him, stood at the second-floor window and looked down at the gathering crowd.

"What the hell happened?" he asked. ✦

TWENTY-TWO

Colonel Beane paced his office like a caged animal, then stopped at his desk and flicked on the intercom.

"Edna, for the third and final time, I want Major Perkins in my office now. Do we have to send for the MPs?"

"The major just arrived," Edna said.

Perkins knocked once and entered the colonel's office.

"Don't bother to sit down," Beane said.

Perkins stood in front of Beane's desk, feet apart and his hands locked behind his back.

Beane waved Grainger's letter at him.

"I believe you've had this letter for some time," he shouted. "It's from our Detachment Commander in Sasebo, Captain Grainger. Now, would you mind telling me just what in the hell is going on? This is the damnedest thing I've read in over 30 years in the Army. I still can't believe it's real."

Colonel Beane slammed the letter on his desk.

"You can start by telling me how long you've had it," he demanded. "It's dated October 19th. It's addressed to me, came by special courier and I received it today, at the end of the month. Where the hell has it been?"

"Sir," Perkins began, "may I ask how you got a copy of that letter?"

Beane's face flushed as he slapped the palm of his hand on his desk.

"Do not ask any more questions. Simply answer what I ask you. Can I possibly make that any clearer?"

"Yes, sir," Perkins replied. "I mean, no, sir. Uh, what you said is clear, sir."

"Well?" Beane said.

"Sir," Perkins began, "there is an explanation. Yes, I did receive the letter earlier. I'm not sure of the exact date. I wanted to investigate some of the allegations, uh, points in the letter before I brought it to you. I knew you would be upset with the letter and would want to get some answers."

"Investigate what?" Beane stormed. "For God's sake, Major, the letter is addressed to me, and the documented charges are all about things that you are doing or causing to be done in my name, without my knowledge or consent."

"Sir," Perkins said, "the officer who wrote the letter doesn't understand the way things are done in military Intelligence. He's naïve."

"Naïve, my ass," Beane interrupted. "He's listed a series of events that have been conducted under the auspices of my command. Things I allegedly approved. Some of them appear to be criminal, and, if they are not criminal they would sure as hell embarrass the Army and the government of the United States. Again, things of which I had no knowledge."

"Uh, well, sir, yes and no. I believe I have briefed you about some of the things, not all. That's my mistake, sir. Grainger has puts things down as fact, sir, and he doesn't know what the facts are."

"He seems to have ample supporting documents attesting to what you say he doesn't know. Please explain how he manages that. This is your only chance to tell me where he lied and what the true facts are."

"Yes, sir," Perkins said. "I appreciate that, sir."

Perkins coughed and cleared his throat.

"You're aware of the mission, sir. I reported on it. I told you it was Art Church's idea for getting agents into China. You knew I was going with him to the Office of Policy Coordination meeting at Atsugi."

"I remember I told you the idea seemed to have a lot of unanswered questions. On the Atsugi meeting I specifically told you to go as an observer and take no part, whatsoever, in the proceedings. Is that correct or not?"

"Yes, sir," Perkins whined, "it is correct. OPC approved the funds and unfortunately there was a small operational disconnect."

"Operational disconnect! Good God, Major, it was a friggin' disaster. I told you some of the things that I thought could go wrong and apparently most of them did. I also distinctly remember telling you that if any glitch came up, no matter how small, I wanted you to abort our participation in the operation immediately and bring it to my attention. I directed you to pull the plug at the first sign of trouble. You, and any of our people, were not to have anything to do with damage control. I was most clear on that point. Is that correct?"

"Sir, yes," Perkins replied. "That is correct. It's just that when things went bad everything moved too fast. We had to act very fast."

"I remember when Art Church called, I tried to reach you, and Lieutenant Grippa informed me that you were over seeing Art Church because a problem developed with the boat plan. I was here," Beane said. "You came back and didn't say a word. I assumed you remembered my directive and were taking steps to immediately end our involvement. It was beyond my imagination that you would involve Grainger in a damage control operation."

"Sir," Perkins said, "you may recall that General Clark has been asking for Intelligence information on Chinese capabilities. Art Church said the DCI has been railing at Joe Fellinger to stop giving excuses and get some people placed there. Sir, you told me that General Lowry has ordered us to do everything possible to cooperate. That's what I was trying to do. At the 11th hour we found there was a mole on the ship."

"First of all," Beane said, "when my boss, General Lowry, spoke to me, he did not sign a blank check. He expected me to exercise my best judgment, which I thought I had. When I was in Washington you called General Lowry and intimated that I knew what was going on and had him call the post commander down in Sasebo.

"I have since advised General Lowry that you acted without my knowledge and consent and that you completely disobeyed my specific directive. I could care less about Art Church's mole. That was his problem, and we should have been out of it. The sinking of that goddamned ship was apparently the work of a lunatic. And what makes it worse, the lunatic's people were trained by us because you signed the authorization for the Group."

"Sir," Perkins said, "no one believed that Colonel Kim would blow up the ship. It was his idea. He acted alone."

"Oh, dear God," Beane said. "And you said Grainger was naïve. Where are your brains? Why do you suppose he wanted the UDT training for his Koreans? The enemy doesn't have any ships in Korea or Japan. You expect me to believe that the Agency would send four trained agents into China if they weren't sure of their loyalty? That's bullshit. Art Church knows it's bullshit. Furthermore, if I had known you were even talking to that maniac, Kim, I would have fired you immediately.

"I have to go over and see General Lowry in a little bit. I know what he's going to say and part of it will be 'I don't mind you helping the Agency, but good God, man, I don't expect you to wipe their ass when they crap all over themselves.'"

"Sir," Perkins said, "Art told me we had to be sure Chen was a double agent. Before Art got the final report, Kim sank the ship. Art said that if we aborted the mission too soon we would expose people the Agency has in deep cover."

"And you believed that bullshit?" Beane said. "Did Art tell you how that could happen to agents in 'deep cover'? Did you think to ask him?"

"I took his word for it, sir," Perkins said.

"And not once did you ever send me a memo or call and ask to discuss any problems with the operation," Beane said. "Perkins, I've had enough of this horseshit. What about the other points in Grainger's letter?"

"I don't have a copy of it with me, sir," Perkins said.

Beane shook his head.

"Selecting you," Beane said, "was not one of my glowing achievements. You have exceeded your authority more than I thought was possible for an Army officer."

Perkins lowered his head. His face, damp with perspiration, had a scarlet hue.

"I heard about the credentials foul-up," Beane said. "Unbelievable. Church has sent a memo placing the responsibility on his deputy, Walter Dole, who has been allowed to take an early retirement.

"This is really a nightmare without end. A member of the KCIA assassinates ship survivors. Makes an attempt to assassinate an American Army officer, Grainger. He murders Grainger's girlfriend in their apartment. This is the officer I asked you to help and you did nothing but pile abuse on him from the first day of his employment."

Beane looked at Perkins and slowly shook his head.

"This won't take much longer," Beane said. "There's a maniac around, who is supposed to be one of our allies. He makes two attempts on Grainger's life, and you don't throw him a lifeline and get him the hell out of Sasebo. Unbelievable. Do you happen to know where this maniac is at the present time?"

"Sir," Perkins said, "I understand he injured his wrist in a fall. He's recuperating now at the Korean compound in Pusan."

"Do you understand, Perkins, that when you authorized an American UDT to train Kim's people you became directly involved in the sinking of that ship? You took care of the capability Kim lacked."

Beane again shook his head.

"You betrayed my trust. You put me in a position where I have failed in my duties as Commanding Officer of this Group. Have you thought about the impact of your actions at a time when we are still in a state of war?"

Perkins paled and swallowed hard.

"Sir," Perkins said, "I believe I am loyal to my country."

"You may really believe that," Beane said. "I'm not impressed. If you'd like a lesson in real loyalty, you might start with Grainger. He could press court-martial charges against you and this Group. We could be reading his letter in the *Stars and Stripes*. Those people are still reporters first and love a sensational headline. Maybe you'd prefer a follow-up story in the *Nagasaki Nippo*. The 'Mystery Ship' headline made the whole country aware of your stupidity. Not to mention giving our enemies ammunition to fire at us, putting us on the defensive.

"I'm not sure how all of this is going to play out, but if I have my way, you'll be spending time in Fort Leavenworth.

"There is one thing in Grainger's information that bothers me enormously and makes no sense whatsoever. It's the coincidence in timing and the fact that I tend not to believe in coincidences. Is there any connection, to your knowledge, between this operation and the untimely death of Jerry Doutter?"

"Colonel," Perkins said, "if Colonel Kim was involved with Doutter's death, I know nothing about it. I never liked him, but would never do anything to hurt him once he got out."

Beane shook his head.

"I'll meet with Grainger. I'm pretty certain he's going to leave the Army. That's too bad. He could have gone a long way and served with distinction. I will try to make him understand that people like Colonel Kim are beyond our power to control. I'm ashamed to think about his impression of Intelligence people. Like other branches we've got some pretty stupid people. I may be the biggest idiot of them all for not stopping the *Kochi Maru* business the first day I heard of it."

"Perkins, I'm weary of this affair. I'm tired of looking at you, and there's nothing else for me to say except that you're fired! I want your credentials, NOW. You're confined to quarters pending the filing of court-martial proceedings against you. I don't want you in this building or your office ever again."

Beane flicked the intercom lever.

"Edna," he said, "send in those MPs who have been waiting to escort Major Perkins to his quarters. I want one of them to remain on guard outside his door until I can pursue his status a bit further. Call that lieutenant in Perkins' office and tell him to place all of Major Perkins' files under lock. I especially want all files, classified or not, that have anything to do with the *Kochi Maru*. We'll use the little office across from you. Bring in the documentation on my order confining Major Perkins to his quarters and give him a copy.

"Call General Lowry's office and get me an appointment ASAP. Tell the General's aide that the subject is *Kochi Maru* and that I'm formulating a white paper on the incident. You can tell the aide to let the general know this is not a good-news meeting."

When Beane looked up at Perkins, he saw that two MPs had placed handcuffs on his wrists.

"I'll do my best to get General Lowry to convene a general court-martial for you," Beane said to Perkins. "People like you scare the hell out of me. You're ambitious, well trained, and dangerous. What's most frightening is that you've got the morality of a slug. I saw your type in Europe, a young hotshot wearing a swastika. I shot that sonofabitch. Because this is so sensitive you may get lucky and avoid a trial, but your career with the Army is over. Regardless of what you believe, let me tell you that your concept of duty and loyalty is an aberration."

Perkins' once-starched khaki uniform, now soaked with perspiration, draped on him like a wet towel. His eyes were wet with tears.

Colonel Beane stood, ramrod straight, his lips pressed tightly together. He motioned, with a wave of his hand, for the MPs to take Perkins away.

When Perkins left, Beane sat down heavily and looked at the file on his desk. He reread the letter from Grainger to Edna:

30 Oct. 1952

Dear Mrs. Rasmussen:

I am sending you a copy of a letter I sent by courier to Colonel Beane on 19 Oct. 1952. To date I have received no response. I can only assume that Major Perkins has somehow intercepted it. I do not believe he will stop your mail. That's why I put no return mail address on the envelope. Please see that Colonel Beane gets my letter.

Initially, I planned to request a transfer, but I've been doing a lot of thinking lately. Accordingly, I will be resigning my commission in the very near future.

Someone needs to look into the issues raised in my letter. I would prefer that Colonel Beane directs the investigation rather than the Inspector General.

Respectfully,
Ken Grainger ✦

Twenty-Three

Tokyo

The phone in Art Church's office rang at 0900.

"This is Major Salencio, 516th Counter-Intelligence Detachment in Sasebo. May I speak to Mr. Church? It's about an urgent matter."

The secretary pressed the intercom button to Church's office.

"Mr. Church, there's a CIC Major Salencio calling from Sasebo, says it's very important."

"I'll take it," he answered. "Stay on the line and take notes."

"Hi, Major, this is Art Church. What can I do for you?"

"I'm not sure," Salencio said. "We had a situation early this morning about 0200 that we're trying to unravel and something came up that's a little out of my jurisdiction. I wanted to run it by you to see if you have any interest."

"Okay, go ahead," Church said.

"We were doing surveillance on a Hans Krueger. He's an electrical engineer on the *Matson*, a Merchant Marine freighter out of San Francisco. Krueger is a card-carrying courier for our friends in Moscow."

"I think I've seen his name in some spot reports," Church said. "A real 'Nervous Nellie,' usually low-level stuff, but definitely Red."

"That's the one," Salencio said. "What we call a `runner,' only this time what he's into isn't that low level. Do you know a Russian general named Arkady Petrovsky?"

Church sat up immediately. His voice betrayed heightened interest.

"Yes," he said. "Is Krueger doing something for Petrovsky?"

"Was doing something," Salencio answered. "We knew his ship was coming into Sasebo. I had a guy keeping an eye on it and sure enough Krueger came down the gangplank shortly before midnight. We decided to follow him. He went into his usual evasive routine and was starting to settle down when he went into a whorehouse. One of our guys followed him in and went upstairs after him with one of the girls.

"Our guy was in the next room trying to get his girl to slow down when she was undressing him. She saw his pistol in his shoulder holster and started yelling, 'Pistol, pistol.'"

"Krueger panicked, jumped out of a second-floor window, tried to shinny down a tree, slipped and apparently sprained his ankle. He limped out into the street without checking the traffic and got clobbered by a beer truck. He never knew what hit him. We scraped him up and called for an ambulance.

"In the process we frisked him. Among his papers was a sealed letter to Colonel Sukow Kim, one of your Korean counterparts, I believe."

"I know Kim," Church said.

"I figured you did," Salencio responded. "Well, I opened the letter and it's from Petrovsky to Kim. Petrovsky tells Kim he's very interested in his proposal to help with a change in the government. He never mentioned any name, but he said that the target was getting some medical attention in the West. The only major Korean political figure that I know getting medical treatments in the United States, which I assume is the 'West,' is President Syngman Rhee. It was in the *Stars and Stripes* about a couple of weeks ago.

"Petrovsky says he will personally guarantee all of Kim's terms and suggests it's a big number. The letter also references earlier payments."

"Terms? Payments?" Church asked, his voice bordering between skepticism and outright doubt. "Does it say which terms he'll guarantee?"

"No," Salencio replied. "It just talks about some significant amount."

"Significant amount," Church repeated. "Is the letter dated?"

"Ten days ago," said Salencio.

"Do you know where Krueger's ship was then?" Church asked.

"We checked with the skipper," Salencio said. "Ten days ago the *SS Matson* was in Vladivostok, Russia."

"Very interesting," Church said.

"I thought so, too," said Salencio. "Look, the KCIA is not part of our jurisdiction. Frankly, we're not really equipped to get into a full-scale operation to defend against an attempt to assassinate any Korean leader, Rhee or anybody else."

"It could get to be expensive," Church agreed. "How do you know the letter's not a phony?" he asked.

"I don't," Salencio said. "The stationery appears to be legit, but I haven't seen anything with Petrovsky's signature."

"I think we have something on file. In fact, I'm sure of it," Church said. "Do you want me to handle it?"

"I'd appreciate it," Salencio said. "I was going to buck this over to G-2 in Tokyo, but I got to thinkin' that if someone in the KCIA turns out to be a rotten apple, it might affect something you're doing. You've probably worked with them."

"As a matter of fact, I believe we have," Church said. "I don't mind telling you, Colonel Kim's the last guy I would have suspected of turning."

"Isn't that always the case," Salencio agreed. "It's always the smart ones, the ones whose promotions don't keep up with their ambitions. They feel their genius is not appreciated or recognized. I don't know much about him, myself."

"Tell you what," Church said, "I'll have someone stop by this morning to pick up the letter. We'll check it out. I appreciate this, Major. By the way, could we also get a copy of Krueger's autopsy and any pictures of the corpse?"

"Sure," Salencio said. "No problem. I've heard that Rhee's security people shoot first and ask questions later, but it's different if a senior member of the palace guard is out to nail him."

"Exactly," Church said, "and I think I know how to handle this," his voice now buttery and conspiratorial.

I'll bet you'll handle it personally, Salencio thought.

"That's good," Salencio said. "Sometimes Army channels get a little bogged down, and this appears to require quick action."

"I appreciate your confidence, Major," Church said. "If something comes up, and you need my help, don't hesitate to call."

"I'll expect your agent this morning?" Salencio asked.

"Within the hour," Church said.

When Salencio hung up, Church said, "Did you get that, Mary Ann?"

"Yes, sir," she said. "Every word."

"Good. Call Schilling in Sasebo; tell him to pick up that letter now and get it to me fast, top priority. Type up a record of the telephone conversation. When it's ready, get me the deputy director. I think the good major just dropped a bonanza in our laps."

Seoul is the largest city in Korea. Its political, psychological, and sociological importance far outdistance any military value. It is difficult to imagine any other city that evokes the emotional and mystical obsession evinced by South Koreans for their capitol.

Art Church's plane landed at Kimpo Airport in Seoul. He had received instructions from CIA Headquarters to personally deliver his documents to the President himself.

A motorcycle escort convoyed Church's limousine from Kimpo to the Government House in the eastern part of the city. He was met by a personal representative of the President who spoke flawless English and was accompanied by General Suung Park, head of the Korean CIA.

Steve Hammersmith, the CIA liaison officer in Seoul, handled the brief introductions. Dressed in a dark suit and sunglasses, Hammersmith assured Church that no one, other than himself, knew the nature of his business.

"Sir," Church began, addressing the President's representative, "I have been directed by General Bedell Smith, acting with the full knowledge of President Truman, to deliver these documents to President Rhee.

"The first document is the original letter I received that was removed from the body of a known Communist courier. Another is a letter from General Smith advising that our analysts confirm the authenticity of General Petrovsky's signature. The third document is a portion of a field report from one of our agents, confirming that General Petrovsky was heard to speak glowingly of Colonel Sukow Kim and refer to him as my 'Korean Watchdog.' Finally, I have included the autopsy report of the dead courier and pictures taken by the medical examiner."

The president's representative reached out and took the package from Church. The representative glanced briefly at General Park, who nodded. Park did an about-face and left the group without saying a word. The representative addressed Church.

"Please express to your president and to General Smith the deep appreciation of President Rhee and the Korean people for these documents. I am sure President Rhee will want to express his thanks personally to your President, also, but let him know immediately of our gratitude."

"I will, sir, and ..."

The representative smiled and extended his hand, interrupting Church's comments.

"Thank you, Mr. Church," he said. "You will be escorted back to Kimpo. I hope you have a safe journey back to Tokyo."

Without another word, the representative turned and left the office. A smiling aide to the representative kept bowing and pointing to the door.

"I guess the meeting's over," Church said to Hammersmith. "Let's go."

Colonel Kim's two-room bungalow on the island of Yong Do was located at the rear of the KCIA compound, 50 yards from any other structure. Normally, Colonel Kim, a notoriously light sleeper, would hear anyone approaching the cabin, but on this night he was not sleeping. He was entertaining a female friend, who surprised him by calling and saying she absolutely needed him that evening. She was studying to be an opera singer and loved to sing to her lovers, but throughout the Korean compound she was known as "the screamer."

Kim's first awareness of other visitors came when the doors to his bungalow and his bedroom door were kicked off their hinges.

Kim had only time to say three words: "What the hell ...?"

His attackers dragged the colonel out of bed, naked and protesting. His female companion heeded the finger-to-the-mouth gesture of the Englishman, who was accompanied by six Korean men. She tried to stuff as much of the sheet as possible into her mouth to stifle any sound.

Kim screamed his objections to the outrage. The Englishman slapped a piece of wide tape over his mouth. He then took an olive-drab hood out of his back pocket and placed it over the struggling colonel's head. Moving ahead of the little entourage, he led the party across the dirt road of the compound, into the back door of the 8240th Far East Command Liaison Detachment building, through the kitchen, past an astonished group of Americans playing poker at the dining room table, and down a flight of stairs to the soundproofed room in the basement.

The husky Koreans bound Kim's hands and feet and lifted him easily, securing him to the chain extending from the ceiling. Before they left, the leader of the detail applied a vicious karate chop to Kim's exposed groin. Kim's animal wail could be heard despite the hastily applied tape.

"Don't!" the Englishman cried, pointing at the attacker. "This is my contract," he snarled.

The one who had struck Kim turned and sneered. He rushed at the Englishman, who recoiled and cringed in fear, then watched as the man veered off and ran back toward the totally vulnerable Colonel Kim. He leaped into the air and delivered a resounding flying kick to Kim's stomach. Landing lightly on his feet, he turned and swaggered from the room.

The Englishman listened to the sound of pounding boots echoing in the stairwell, as a deathly silence filled the damp interrogation chamber. He placed a chair in front of the chained form of Colonel Kim who was gasping, trying to get his breath. The Englishman sat down, excited by the challenge he knew would be presented by this prisoner.

He licked his lips, like a child savoring a piece of chocolate. This was one assignment he would have paid the Koreans to give him. Here was no sniveling, frightened, confused, or disoriented subject who would urinate in his pants whenever the Englishman started to whistle his plaintive dirge. This was the famous Colonel Sukow Kim, who disdained even speaking to subordinates, who insisted on choosing the projects he would work on, and who was regarded fearfully, even by Liaison Detachment personnel.

"Well, what do we have here?" the Englishman said. "I believe it's Colonel Kim, the traitor. Colonel Kim, the renegade. Colonel Kim, the whore who sold out his country for an annual retainer from his Russian pimps.

"You know how I work," he said. "You've watched me many times down here in the basement. Usually you hid over there in one of the dark corners, whispering questions you wanted answered. I remember when you intruded yourself into my interrogation and kicked some poor chap in the balls.

"You don't like my body odor," chided the Englishman. "You insulted and embarrassed me in front of the Americans, saying I was afraid of water and have never followed basic hygienic practices. That shit smelled better than my breath. All of these things I remember, Colonel Kim. My fantasy was having you in the exact position you now occupy. Lucky me. My fantasy has come true."

The Englishman partially lifted the cloth hood and tore the tape from Kim's mouth. The flimsy hood slipped back into place. The Englishman could almost feel Kim's legendary glare through the cloth mesh.

"Well, Colonel," the Englishman said, standing directly in front of Kim, face to face. "How does my breath smell now? Any better? Better than that rotten, stinking kimchee you love to eat? Hmmm? Speak up. They caught you with your grubby hands in a Russian cookie jar. Shame, shame.

"Did you notice that I've changed the rules in your honor? Usually there is no talking. I'm not going to waste my time preparing you to talk. You should know better than most that you will tell me all about it. So, how's it going to be? The easy way, or the other? I need your answer right away, as you can appreciate, so please don't disappoint me."

Kim had recovered from the punishment administered earlier. As the pain subsided, his arrogance returned.

"I will tell you this," he spat venomously, "you are a foul-smelling piece of shit. My superiors will soon know I am here. When they order my release, no power on earth will stop me from putting you where I am."

"My, oh my," the Englishman said with a sneering tone, "aren't you vicious. Let me assure you, Colonel, there is no mistake. I heard all about General Petrovsky's letter. No one will show up to save you from our time together. I will remember your hostile attitude as you progress from your old defiant self to a new, more compliant piece of dung, begging for mercy. I'll give you every measure of mercy that you would give me."

The Englishman looked at Kim's bandaged left wrist.

"What do we have here?" he asked, ripping off the bandage. "Oh my, that looks nasty. What happened? Did you try to eat a dog before it was dead?"

He wrapped his gloved hand around the torn wrist and twisted it back and forth, shearing off some loose flesh.

Kim sucked in his breath, but could not stifle a grunt of pain.

"That's the least of your problems," the Englishman said.

With that, he slammed his boot into the colonel's exposed genitals. Kim groaned as he tried to cope with the exquisite pain.

"Oh, please, you can do better than that, Colonel," the Englishman said, as he delivered a vicious blow to Kim's kidney with the fist covered by a bloody, black leather glove.

Kim gasped in shock as the blow temporarily paralyzed him.

"You're not trying," the Englishman said.

He turned and walked to a small wooden table, whistling as he selected a thick, leather belt. It had a large bronze buckle with the figure of a tiger molded on its face. On the reverse side where the leather strap was folded over a small metal bar holding the buckle to the belt, a series of heavy thread stitches made removal of the buckle from the belt virtually impossible. The Englishman had found that the single snap in the belt's initial construction gave way too easily whenever the belt struck an object. For the Englishman, that object was usually a secured victim's body.

The Englishman wrapped the strap around his hand with the buckle hanging free and proceeded to swing his arm in a wide circle, gradually gaining speed.

Then the Englishman changed the pitch of this arc and smashed the heavy buckle into Kim's face. He repeated this maneuver again and again, striking Kim's ribs, arms, shins and back. The floor began to pool with Colonel Kim's blood from countless small puncture wounds.

The Englishman's grunts from his physical exertion almost drowned out Kim's moans and groans of pain. Kim was now past caring about keeping silent to mask his agony.

Finally, the Englishman stopped. He stared at Colonel Kim's inert form. He knew that Kim would eventually break.

"You'll talk, Kim," he said. "They all do, every last one. We want the names of your conspirators. Who is in this with you?"

Kim, in dumb defiance, said nothing. Soon, he kept telling himself, his superiors would learn of the monstrous error and he would have his turn. That thought was all that kept him sane and alive.

The Englishman left the basement for some breakfast and a brief nap.

Kim remained alone with his thoughts.

It was the head of the Korean CIA, General Park, who decided the Englishman should have the honor of interrogating Colonel Kim.

General Park knew that the Korean brand of questioning brought death much too quickly and would not allow time for coherent answers to questions that needed to be answered. The general was also impressed by Colonel Cunningham's recital of the Englishman's record—100 percent of the time, a name; 100 percent of the time, a place where the person could be located.

For four days, the Englishman alternated between whistling, walking, and attacking every part of Colonel Kim's body. For the hundreds of repeated questions there was one response: Silence. It was apparent to the men of the detachment during mealtime that the Englishman was becoming increasingly frustrated. That frustration was reflected in the daily negative reports he dispatched to General Park.

The only sustenance forced past the bruised and torn lips of Colonel Kim was an occasional drink of water from a metal canteen cup. He swayed unsteadily, not able to stand and not able to kneel, more unconscious than not, now ready for death.

On the evening of the fourth day, with the concerned General Park in attendance, the Englishman lowered Kim to the floor of the room. It was still damp from the daily hosing to rid the room of blood, excrement, and urine. Even in the dim light, it was apparent the urine contained blood.

The Englishman pulled the hood from Kim's head.

Even in his stupor, Kim's eyes blazed with hatred.

General Park looked at the Englishman.

"No name?" he demanded.

The Englishman shook his head.

"No name?" Park repeated.

"No, nothing," the Englishman said, almost in a whisper, lowering his head.

General Park looked at the prostrate form on the floor. He drew his right leg back and let go with a brutal kick to Kim's head as he demanded in Korean, "Who is with you in this plot?"

When the kick was delivered, the Englishman screamed, "No!"

He brushed by the general and knelt by Kim's side. The colonel's body began to twitch violently. Kim looked up at the Englishman and through broken and bloody teeth he forced a smile. Then, with a sudden tensing, he arched his back, groaned, and collapsed.

He was dead.

The Englishman, inconsolable, ran from the room shrieking, "No, no, no!"

General Park looked down at the inert form and smiled.

"Dead men don't talk," he said, laughing.

He turned and left the basement. ✦

TWENTY-FOUR

Mainichi Building
TOKYO, JAPAN

Edna Rasmussen telephoned Grainger in Sasebo.

"Captain Grainger," she said, "Colonel Beane would appreciate it if you would stop by his office during your out-processing."

"Sure," Grainger said.

"You know," she said, "I've been with the colonel a long time. I don't believe anything has upset him more than the situation that caused you to resign your commission."

"Thank you," Grainger said. "I think it's the best thing to do."

Colonel Beane rose and greeted Grainger when he entered his office.

"This mess was my responsibility," he said to Grainger. "I failed to exercise proper supervision on a mission that I recognized had the potential for disaster."

Grainger shifted uncomfortably.

Beane drank from a water tumbler and looked directly at Grainger.

"I can only offer my sincere condolences for the loss of your girlfriend, Julie. I understand you were contemplating marriage."

Grainger nodded.

"Many other lives were unnecessarily lost," Beane continued. "Our Army and our country have been put in a precarious position. Thanks to the efforts of some skilled people in our State Department, I expect this sordid affair will not receive the spotlight of attention it so richly deserves."

Beane sat back and sighed. He shook his head, then pinched the bridge of his nose.

"Major Perkins is gone," he said. "His resignation was authorized by someone in a pay grade higher than my own. Knowing he will never wear a uniform again is not enough for me, but it wasn't my call. I felt you had a right to know this."

Colonel Beane took a deep breath.

"There is one other point I need to cover," Beane continued. "I'm recommending that your letters and report be classified for the maximum period of time. Scholars will read about it in the year 2003. I fully recognize this is well beyond the period needed to protect any operational secrets, but this has been a dismal chapter in our history and right now closure is important. Maybe future generations can benefit from these lessons."

"Do you have anything you want to say, Captain?" Beane said.

"Yes, sir," Grainger said, "only one thing really. A long time ago, in a different life, I was told to be a good boy, do what I was told, and keep my mouth shut. I have learned that there are times when silence is not the right course of action. People can take silence as some kind of assent or agreement. I don't intend to be silent any more." ✦

EPILOGUE

Early on a November evening the first snow of the season came early and covered the ground of the Washington Heights compound in Tokyo where Arthur Church lived. Traffic was sparse and it moved slowly.

The streetlights came on as Church turned into Patton Court and he looked down the street toward his home. Just before reaching his driveway, a man stepped from behind the neighbor's hedge and tried to run across the street. He collided with the side of Church's car and fell down. Church was seized with panic. *My God*, he thought, *that idiot ran right into my car. He must be drunk. I hope someone saw him run into the street. Oh, shit.*

He got out of his car. Looking around, he didn't see anyone except the person on the ground. In the distance he could hear the sound of Christmas carols coming from a nearby home.

He stood over the body.

"Hello," he said, "are you all right? Gee, you ran right into my car. Can you hear me?"

There was only a muffled groan.

I better go in and call the MPs, he thought. *First, I'll drag this fellow off the road.*

He bent over and turned the person on his back and found himself staring into the muzzle of a .22 pistol equipped with a silencer.

"Hi, Art," the man said. "Long time no see."

The man grabbed Church's coat lapels, keeping him bent at the waist as the gun was pointed in his face. There was very little light, but enough for Church to make an instant identification.

"Oh, my God," he said. "Chen. I thought you were dead."

"I would have been, Art," he said, "if you had your way. The last time I talked to Walter, early on the night before I left, I noticed he avoided looking directly into my eyes. I figured you knew something. I decided I'd better leave, so I went for a swim."

Holding onto Church, the man got to his feet.

"There, that's better. Let's see, yeah, I went for a swim. I made it to that little promontory in the harbor, you know, the one Puccini made famous. Did you like my little gift of the credentials? I left them in the metal box on the bunk. It was my way of resigning. Who would have figured that you guys would sink the ship? Boy, was that stupid. But you made my taking-off look brilliant to my boss."

He looked around at the homes with lighted Christmas trees in the front windows.

"I hope you appreciate I had to get special permission to come back from Shanghai and give you this early Christmas present."

He fired twice in rapid succession—one bullet in each eye. As Church was reeling backwards, Chen shoved him into the shrubs along the gutter. Turning, he got into Church's Buick and drove away.

Soviet authorities claimed Svetlana's body, declaring that she was a Soviet citizen brutally murdered while on holiday in Tokyo. There was an initial problem with the Japanese government about the release of her remains, but Major Salencio's quid pro quo was enough to cut through the red tape and expedite General Petrovsky's request. She was buried in Moscow with high honors.

On a wet and cold December day in Hartford, Connecticut, a brown delivery van with a high profile stopped in front of a blue and white split-level home on a street lined with shade trees. The driver rang the bell and left a package at the front door. It was addressed to Ken Grainger.

Inside the box was a squad of painted lead soldiers, U.S. Infantry Squad, handmade in Ireland by PAM in 1904, and a note: "Dear Ken, I've thought of you often and appreciated your kind letter about Jerry. I understand you are out of the Army. I also heard you were responsible for forcing Perkins to retire. That was a good job.

"Jerry had a huge collection of lead soldiers, enough to field a division, I believe. Of all the soldiers in his collection, his pride and joy was this squad of Infantry soldiers. I know he would want you to have them. Thanks, Elizabeth Doutter." ✦

About the Author

Dan Helix retired from the U.S. Army as a major general in 1989, after 41 years of active and reserve duty. A combat veteran of the Korean War, he served as a platoon leader and the commander of a rifle company. Helix was awarded the Combat Infantry Badge, Army Distinguished Service Medal, Silver Star, Legion of Merit, Bronze Star with "V" device for valor, Purple Heart with one oak leaf cluster, among others. He earned Parachutist Wings at the age of 50, and in 1981 he was inducted into the U.S. Army Hall of Fame at Fort Benning, Georgia.

In the Army Helix served in a number of positions of increasing responsibility. He commanded the 351st Civil Affairs Command, served in the Deputy Chief of Staff for Operations Directorate at the Department of the Army (Pentagon), was the Commanding General of the 63rd Army Reserve Command, and retired as Deputy Commanding General of the Sixth U.S. Army at the Presidio of San Francisco. He is authorized to wear the Department of Defense Identification Badge.

Dan and his wife, Mary Lou, live in Concord, California, where he served eight years on the Concord City Council, two of those as mayor. He also served three years as a director of the Bay Area Rapid Transit District representing Contra Costa County. Dan and Mary Lou have a son and a daughter, and six grandchildren.

Helix has a Bachelor of Arts degree in history from the University of California at Berkeley, and a Master of Arts degree in political science from San Francisco State University, both degrees with honors. He has published short stories in military journals but this is his first novel. ✦